THE COCAINE PRINCESS

Lock Down Publications and Ca$h
Presents

The Cocaine Princess
A Novel by *King Rio*

Lock Down Publications
P.O. Box 944
Stockbridge, Ga 30281
www.lockdownpublications.com

Lock Down Publications
Like our page on Facebook: Lock Down Publications @
www.facebook.com/lockdownpublications.ldp
Book interior design by: **Shawn Walker**

Stay Connected with Us!

Text **LOCKDOWN** to 22828 to stay up-to-date with new releases, sneak peaks, contests and more…

Thank you!

Submission Guideline.

Submit the first three chapters of your completed manuscript to ldpsubmissions@gmail.com, subject line: Your book's title. The manuscript must be in a .doc file and sent as an attachment. Document should be in Times New Roman, double spaced and in size 12 font. Also, provide your synopsis and full contact information. If sending multiple submissions, they must each be in a separate email.

Have a story but no way to send it electronically? You can still submit to LDP/Ca$h Presents. Send in the first three chapters, written or typed, of your completed manuscript to:

LDP: Submissions Dept
P.O. Box 944
Stockbridge, Ga 30281

DO NOT send original manuscript. Must be a duplicate.

Provide your synopsis and a cover letter containing your full contact information.

Thanks for considering LDP and Ca$h Presents.

Acknowledgments

I acknowledge and give thanks to the Creator, first and foremost. Thanks for blessing me with this gift. I won't let you down.

Secondly, I want to thank all the thousands of readers who pushed The Cocaine Princess to #1 on the Amazon's African American bestsellers list and #1 on the African American Urban Fiction bestsellers list. I sincerely appreciate the support, and I promise to keep hitting y'all with that heat until I'm old and gray. Don't forget to post your honest reviews on Amazon (to let others know what you thought of this saga so far) and tell everyone you know to cop these bangers if you love them.

Shout out to the conglomerate of urban authors doing their thing in the writing game. May God continue to bless you all with ideas to wow the masses.

To my family and friends, I love y'all. Thanks for the support!

Okay, enough of the chit-chat, lets get to it!

Undying love,

Rio

Dedication

This series is dedicated to the memory of Angela Raboutte, the stunning cover model of the original The Cocaine Princess novels.

King Rio

Prologue
Brownsville, TX October 2010

"There were seven hundred kilos in the back of our eighteen-wheeler when my sister had it delivered to your men in San Antonio. I'm not understanding how two hundred of them suddenly disappeared," said Juan "Papi" Costilla.

He lit a Cuban cigar and scowled at his captive, who he knew only as Salvador. The bloody-faced man was tied to a ladder-back chair in the garage of Papi's five hundred thousand dollar Spanish-style villa. Flanking Papi were his two younger siblings, Flake and Jenny, and Jenny's two sons, Santiago and Savio, were sitting on the trunk of their mother's sleek blue Rolls-Royce Phantom. The car was only a shade darker than the custom tailored Hartmarx suits that all of them were wearing.

"When that semi-trailer made it to us," Salvador said through a mouthful of blood, "those kilos were already missing. You know I wouldn't steal from you, Papi. Do you honestly believe I'd steal from the fucking Costilla cartel? I'd try ripping off the Sinaloas AND the Zetas before I'd steal from the Costillas. I've sold thousands of kilos for your family! If it wasn't for me, Santiago would have never rubbed shoulders with that Big Meech guy in Atlanta. He'd have never met Reesie Cup in Chicago or those gangster rappers in—"

Salvador's aching pleas ceased abruptly, and he gasped as Jenny pulled a gold-plated revolver from inside her suit jacket and aimed it at his blood-soaked Gucci shirt. The mask of horror he wore was illuminated by the headlights of Papi's eighteen-year-old daughter's ocean blue Mercedes; she was leaning forward in the driver's seat, her chin resting atop the steering wheel, her dreamy green eyes stretched wide with shock, her dog-eared Nika Michelle novel open and left unattended on the dashboard.

In Spanish, Jenny said, "You fucking roach! Nobody steals from the Costilla cartel!" She squeezed the trigger, and a ribbon of fire blew from the barrel of her .44 Magnum. The bullet tore through Salvador's chest, knocking the chair over backwards.

Papi looked back at his daughter. "Go inside and make sure Rita's still asleep. Don't let her come out here. Tell her I accidentally fired my gun."

Alexus pushed open her door and stepped out of the Benz, looking like Onika Maraj from the waist up and Tahiry Jose from the waist down. She had on a fuchsia-colored Valentino dress that accentuated her enormous derriere, and her diamond-encrusted five-inch heels had been custom designed by Christian Louboutin.

"I'll keep Momma inside", she said, grabbing the Nika Michelle novel off the dash and a Straight Stuntin magazine that had been lying on the passenger seat.

"Let her stay and watch", said Jenny. "Show her how we deal with thieves in Mexico. It's about time she learned the ins and outs of this business."

Papi briefly considered honoring his sister's suggestion, but when he glanced at Alexus, she was already leaving the garage.

He looked at his Audemars Piguet watch: 11:58 pm. "She'll learn", he said, picking up his 24-karat gold-plated machete from the hood of his ex-wife Rita's Porsche SUV. He walked over to where Salvador lay, moving rather swiftly for a man in his early sixties. Salvador was gargling up blood, and his eyes were like saucers-wide, round, and glossy. "Why couldn't you remain loyal?" Papi asked, raising the machete. "You would have lasted, Salv. Loyalty is everything."

He swung the machete in a downward arc, and it's razor-sharp blade sliced through Salvador's neck, instantly separating his head from his shoulders.

"We're moving to Indiana," Rita said as soon as Alexus pushed open her parents' bedroom door. Dark and lovely-faced, Rita was the epitome of "strong black woman." She was sitting up in bed reading the Bible. The dim light from her bedside lamp revealed her troubled expression.

"I take it you heard the gunshot," said Alexus.

"How could I not have heard it? Sounded like a cannon going off."

"Papi accidentally-"

"I don't care, Alexus. I really don't care. I'm getting us out of here. We're leaving Texas for good. Your uncle Dennis and his kids are doing good in Indiana. I'm getting us a house up there. "

"I'm not moving to Indiana, Momma. I'd rather move to Mexico with Granny Costilla. Hell, I'll get my own place. Or I'll stay here with Papi."

"Watch your mouth", Rita said. She set her Bible aside and turned to Alexus. "Your father's family is full of criminals. People are getting killed left and right down there in Matamoros, Mexico, and I'm about ninety- nine percent sure that those mentally unstable Costillas are responsible for most of those murders. God don't like ugly, and neither do I. That's why Papi and I are divorced now..."

Alexus looked down at her impeccably manicured fingernails, tuning her mother out. Papi was to Mexico what Pablo Escobar had been to Colombia, and Alexus wanted to be just like him.

When Rita finished voicing her frustrations, Alexus yawned and said goodnight. Then she headed down the hall to her own bedroom, took a quick shower in the adjoining bathroom, turned on some Trey Songz, climbed into her high priced Baldacchino Supreme bed, and utilized her battery-operated lover to buzz herself to sleep.

Five hours later, she was awakened by the roaring sound of helicopter blades chopping through the air above her parents' home. She vividly remembered shutting her bedroom door last night, but now it was open, as was her bathroom door.

"What the...?" she muttered sleepily as she sat up and wiped her eyes.

"Get in here and help me with these, Alexus!" Papi shouted from inside the bathroom.

Sensing the urgency in his tone, Alexus leapt out of bed, put on a brown fur Louis Vuitton robe, and ran into the bathroom. She found Papi on his knees beside her toilet, dumping a kilo of cocaine into the water. There was another brick of coke on the floor to the left of him.

11

"This is the DEA," a loud voice boomed from somewhere outside. "We know you're in there Juan Costilla. Come out with your hands in the air and we won't bother your family. Don't make us come in. We have you surrounded."

"Oh shit!" Alexus said, flushing the toilet with one hand and pickingup the kilo with the other, wondering what her life would be like withoutPapi.

She was about to find out.

Chapter 1

"Excuse me." Rita Mae Bishop stopped the U-Haul truck beside a boisterous foursome of young Black man who were standing next to a gray Chevy Caprice. "Would you gentlemen be so kind as to help me and my daughter get some of this heavy stuff inside? I'll give you all a few dollars for the help." Her sweet, southern voice was gentle and benevolent, the voice of an older, loving mother.

"Where to?" asked a hideous-faced boy, the Ugly Duckling of the group. He stepped closer to Rita's door and peered past her, studying her beautiful, reddish-brown skinned daughter.

Rita Mae Bishop's new home was three houses down from where the four boys were standing. It was a yellow, three bedroom house that sat on the comer next to a vacant lot on Eighth Street and Willard Avenue.

But the four guys wouldn't have cared if Rita had lived fifteen states away. After getting a look at her eighteen-year-old daughter, they would have lugged every item in back of the U-Haul from Indiana to California.

Rita's daughter was Alexus Costilla, a thickly-proportioned, young woman who was mixed with Mexican and African-American, and was often mistaken for the rap artist Nicki Minaj. Her supersized derriere and meaty thighs had made her the most sought after girl in Brownsville, Texas. But her strict Mexican Father hadn't allowed her to date.

"Wait until you're twenty-one," he once said from his seat at the dining room table, where he had always repackaged the drugs that he had smuggled in, before hitting the streets to sell them.

But Alexus didn't want to wait. So, whenever the opportunity had presented itself, she'd crept around, meeting and seducing and sexing boys *and* girls at her school, then dropping them abruptly and moving onto the next. It had been fun, exploring her sexuality, learning what she'd liked and disliked.

Now things were different, she told herself, because Papi

was away in prison.

Clad in a cherry-colored Fendi jacket--one of the few things the Feds had not seized, over a snug-fitting pair of Apple Bottom jeans and red-and-black Jordan sneakers, with enough layers of MAC lip gloss on hersucculent lips to thoroughly coat ten sets of kissers, Alexus Costilla stoodquietly on the sidewalk in front of the new house, keeping a close watch on the boys as they carried the last of her and Rita's boxes up the concretestairs and through the front door.

Two of the boys had already introduced themselves -a skinny, light- skinned teenaged boy said his name was Young D, and a similar-looking young thug had introduced himself as Lil Mike-but Alexus had only nodded solemnly and turned her head, setting her pretty green eyes on a passing city bus.

A short and chubby, handsome faced boy who had been the recipient ofbrief, clandestine stares from Alexus as he lifted the heaviest boxes withease, walked up to her and said, "You missing some teeth or something?"

"Hell no!" Alexus felt insulted. She looked the fat fool up and down, searching for something to degrade him about. But his black-and-gray Coogi sweater, his baggy black Coogi jeans, and his jet black Timberland boots wereflawless.

"I'm Blake," he said, smiling. "Didn't mean nothing by that teeth comment. I just couldn't understand why you weren't talking." He turnedto glance at his three comrades, who were standing just inside the front door of the house, taking orders from Rita. Then his eyes moved back toAlexus, and for a moment he gazed at her wet lips. "You know who you looklike?" he asked finally.

Alexus crossed her arms. "Who?" She looked at him as if her eyes were daggers and she was ready to stab him directly in the heart.

Raising his hands in surrender, Blake said, "Hold up, baby, I

apologize. You're the last person on Earth I want upset with me. I'm just tryna be nice, welcome you to the neighborhood, get to know you."

"I'd like to meet the person who taught you how to start a conversation," Alexus said snidely.

"Can I get your name?" asked Blake.

"Bad Bitch. Any more questions, officer?"

"Aw yeah?" Blake's thick eyebrows rose, and an ingratiating smile grew on his face. "I like you already."

"I'm sure you do," replied Alexus. She took a thick ponytail holder from her left wrist and pulling her long and curly black hair back, said, "I need some weed, and not just any weed. I'd prefer Kush or Haze."

"Ain't none of that out here. My bruh Streets got some dro, that blueberry shit. I know a nigga in Chicago who sell Kush, though. But that's a forty-five minute drive from here."

"Can you get a few pounds?" Alexus asked.

Blake's eyes went wide. *A few pounds of Kush?* He wondered if she was joking.

"Prob'ly," he said.

"What do you mean *probably*? Call and find out!" Alexus's nasty attitude was out of habit, but her prudent mind was swarming with monetary thoughts, and she knew that she would need thug's assistance to survive in the drug game without her father. Especially in a new area. Hustling was in her blood, and she had a family reputation to uphold and protect.

While Blake was on his cell phone talking, and staring at the crotch of Alexus's tight jeans, Alexus inhaled deeply, loving the scent of his cologne. She looked him up and down and concluded that she liked him, although he was in serious need of a haircut. She figured he was a small time drug dealer, judging from the rust-laden Caprice he and his crew had been crowded around.

Blake ended the call and slipped his Blackberry to the waistline of his jeans. "Forty-five hundred for a pound," he said. "My nigga got seven left."

Nodding thoughtfully, Alexus said, "Okay, I need you to take me to him sometime today." Then out of the blue, she palmed and squeezed the crotch of Blake's jeans.

He froze in complete shock.

"Hmm." Alexus smiled, "Impressive. I might need a taste of that, too." Her hand dropped. "Leave your number in the mailbox. I'll call you in a bit."

She sashayed away from Blake, shaking her thick, round ass harder than usual. She was certain it would hold his attention. No man could resist her biracial features, her unblemished, perfect face, and her perfectly shaped *ghetto booty*, as her schoolmates had called it.

As Alexus started up her front stairs, she took a peek over her shoulder and saw that Blake had his phone aimed at her round backside.

Grinning, Blake recorded video of Alexus's ass until she disappeared inside the yellow house.

Chapter 2

Rita Mae Bishop was a pleasant, and polite Southern woman with deep brown skin and an intransigent sense of morality. Born and raised in Baton Rouge, Louisiana, she had encountered evils of all shapes and sizes and managed somehow to remain a fairly decent human being. For Rita, all who knew her would do anything, because she was the ideal woman. A trustworthy, honest, God-fearing lady who listened to their problems without judgment, and who held a conversation without being a gossip. She graciously shared with man and woman alike and expected nothing in return.

As gratitude, Rita gave the boys who had helped unload the U-Haul a hundred dollars each before sending them on their way. Afterward she searched through the house and found Alexus in an upstairs bedroom. Looking through a box marked "A.C." which looked to be full of expensive designer bags that Juan Costilla had purchased for his only child.

"I thought you lost that," said Rita, referring to the large leather Louis Vuitton shoulder bag that Alexus was lifting from the box. "We looked everywhere for that bag."

"It was at Aunt Jenny's house." Alexus set the bag on the fresh tan carpet and instinctively contemplated calling her aunt Jennifer Costilla. "Papi had left it there by accident. I went over and got it after he and Uncle Flako were arrested. After those punk ass FBI tore our house up."

"Watch your mouth." Rita crossed the room to the window. As she looked out at the neighboring house, images of the raid on the Spanish- style mini-mansion that she had shared with her ex-husband flashed through her mind.

They had seized nearly everything. Juan's silver Bentley coupe. Rita's pearly white Porsche Cayenne. The brand-new Mercedes-Benz E350 that Juan had purchased as Alexus's birthday gift six months ago. Most of their clothes, all of their paintings, jewelry and furniture were gone. A kind-hearted DEA agent named Dewitt Larkson had allowed Rita and Alexus to pack an assortment of clothes and shoes into boxes shortly afterthe raid.

"You're an educated, and strong Black woman," the agent had said. "I don't know how you ended up in a relationship with Costilla, and honestly I don't care to know. Just get away from here and stay away."Larkson had went on to say that Rita's bank account had not been frozen, which meant that RitaMae Bishop had just under ninety thousand dollarsto restart her life with. Eighteen grand had already been spent on the twenty percent down-payment for her new home.

"Why couldn't we stay in Texas?" Alexus inquired. "It's too cold here."

The sound of her daughter's voice shook Rita from her thoughts. She turned and sat on the window sill.

"Your cousins Bookie and Kenya live here," said Rita. "I haven'tspent any time with your uncle Dennis since eighty-nine. He's the onlybrother I have and I miss him."

Alexus knew that hermother wasstill profoundly saddened by theHurricane Katrina disaster. It had claimed the lives of both Rita's parents and her younger sister.

"Is Uncle Dennis coming over?" Alexus asked. She was seated Indian-style on the carpet, poring over the newspaper article that declared her father the "Costilla Cartel leader."

"He'll be here in" Rita pushed the sleeve of her New Orleans Saints sweatshirt and checked her rose gold Cartier watch about three hours. He gets off work at three o'clock."

Planting her hands in the carpet behind her, Alexus leaned back andstared up at Rita.

"The newspaper says federal agents seized over two hundred kilograms of cocaine and seven million dollars in cash from Papi's condo in Houston," Alexus said.

"I know."

"That's a wholelot of money."

"Yes, it is. Papi's been rich for a long time. Avery long time. When I met him at the Mardi gras back in '91, I had just received my master's degree from Harvard. The girls and I were out celebrating on the strip, looking awkward and out-of-place among all those half-naked girls, when your uncle Flako stumbled up to us, in a drunken stupor-"

"A what?"

"He was pissy drunk," Rita said."Oh." Alexus giggled.

"And he began feeling on my butt, making nasty little com-ments,with his breath smelling like sour salami."

Alexus fell over in a fit of laughter.

Struggling to suppress her own laughter, Rita continued:"I showedhim how a real Baton Rouge girl can kick some tail. Didn't even need my girls. I had him on the ground, kickin' his head when your father pushed through the crowd with about ten big Mexican's behind him. OnceI explained to Papi what had happened, he had his goons help Flake toa silver Rolls-Royce that wasparked up the street. Then he asked me to follow him and his 'familia' to the Marriott Hotel."

"Well, did you?" Alexus raised her eyebrows, intrigued."

"Of course I did! I mean, here I was, twenty-eight years old, single and fresh out of college, and I meet this well-dressed forty-year-old Mexican man with a three-car fleet of Rolls Royces-your grandmamma didn't raise any fools." Rita smiled at the memories."He asked me to move in with him about a week later. Bought me an LS400 Lexus and a six-caratengagement ring shortly after that. We married on his parents' ranch in Matamo-ras, Mexico, a year later, right after I had you."

"Is that why you named me Alexus? Because of the car?"

Rita showed a conspiratorial grin as she started toward the bedroom door. "Come on," she said. "We need to find a furniture store. I want to get as much done today as possible."

King Rio

Chapter 3

Blake King and two members of his trigger happy clique, the Dub Life Goons--were all staring attentively at the screen of his cell phone, ogling the new girl's incredible body. They were standing in the trash- littered living room of Blake's crack house, a sparsely furnished dungeon of dilapidation that catered to a smorgasbord of addicts.

On average, Blake's crack house raked in about $1,500-a-day in sales, which meant that he needed at least an ounce of crack-cocaine on hand every day to supply the demand. Currently there was a pocket-flattening cocaine drought all throughout the Midwest and many hustlers found themselves paying upwards of a grand for a single ounce. Blake was one of them, and he hated it. He had four thousand dollars stowed away in a shoe box in the hallway closet of his girlfriend Ashley Joy's apartment, and every dollar of it had come from selling crack rocks.

Blake thought about tricking off every dollar of his savings on the new girl up the block form his crack house. For the umpteenth time Blake restarted the video on his cell phone. *I could watch this all day,* he thought.

"That lil sexy bitch look like Nicki Minaj, don't she?" Young D asked, as he lit the end of a blunt.

"Bitch grabbed my dick and said she wanna taste it," Blake said. He whistled through his teeth, shook his head in disbelief, and kept his eyes on the girl. "She fresh to deaf, too. J's on her feet. Apple Bottom jeans. And that's a Fendi jacket she got on pro'bly cost 'bout three racks."

"And she got a fat nigga fetish." Young-D chuckled and took a few puffs from the blunt.

Jokes made at Blake's expense, particularly when pertaining to his weight, had always had a way of angering him, usually to the point of violence.

This time was no different.

Blake straightened his left hand and chopped it across Young-D's throat. Young-D's blunt plummeted to the multi-stained carpet, and hedoubled over, clutching at his neck with both hands, gagging and chokingand gasping.

"Stop fuckin' playin' with me so much," Blake scolded. He slid his cell phone into its clip-on carrying case on his waist.

Lil Mike picked up the smoldering blunt and smiled. He took his fair share of inhalations before passing it off to Blake. Then Lil Mike was at the back door, ushering a pair of crackheads—an older white couple—into the kitchen.

"One twenty-five," Lil Mike shouted a moment later, indicating that the addicts had $125 to spend.

Blake went to the small gray card table that was in the center of thetiny dining room and seated himself in one of the four matching fold-out chairs that surrounded it. Atop the card table was a circular gray digital scale, thinly veiled with a film of crack-crumbs; a box of sandwich bags; ascattered pile of cash and coins; a bag of crack-cocaine, filled with about twenty grams of the hard yellowish-white substance, and a glass ashtray brimming with cigarillo tobacco, cigarette butts, and blunt roaches.

As Blake King weighed up then bagged 1.8 grams of hard, he observed Young-D-Dante Roscoe-hoist himself up onto the raggedy old sofa with one hand, his other hand still massaging his slender neck. Young-D shot Blake a look full of contempt, but held his tongue. Maybe because it would have pained him to speak, but more likely due to his first-hand knowledge of Blake's violent temper.

Thirty minutes and five drug deals later, things returned to normal. Blake and Lil Mike were sitting on the couch with Young-D, their thumbs hammering away at PlayStation 3 controllers, their eyes stuck to the fifty-inch screen television that Lil Mike and Young-D had stolen from a stripper's house. They were playing "NBA Live 2010. Blake had the Lakers and Lil Mike, who was born and raised in Memphis, Tennessee, had chosen the Grizzlies, who were now busy being victimized by Kobe Bryant's effortless jump shots and indubitably superior ball-handling skills.

In the kitchen, the back door issued a slight, barely audible creak asit was pushed open.

The creak sounded just as the halftime horns of the poignant basketball game blared. So deeply focused on the television screen, Blakeand Michael "LilMike" Lane failedto hear the opening door.

Young-D thought he heard something like the squeak of a shoe on the linoleum kitchen floor, but figured it was probably Alonzo "Blubby" Jones, the Ugly-Duckling of their crew, returning with their Taco Bellorders.

Neither Blake King nor his comrades could have guessed that a team of three doped-up masked men had just entered their trap.

"Face-down, nigga!" Bookie shouted aggressively, as he rushed into the living room carrying a twelve-gauge Mossberg pump-action shotgun in his gloved hands. "Play if you wanna, homie!"

Bookie's thick black lips curled up into a sarcastic grin, behind the black cotton ski-mask. He was juiced off cocaine and ready to shootsome-damn-body. Hell, everybody.

Two of his closest guys—Goldman, who was just as high as he was, and Johnny Lay, a lanky dude—stormed in behind him,. aiming their semi-automaticguns at Blake and hls crew.

"Ain't this a bitch," Blake muttered, as he looked up at the armed robbers.

"Damn, mane," seconded Lil Mike.

Bookie landed a glancing blow across the side of Lil Mike's blue mesh Cubs cap with the butt of the gun, opening a deep laceration that instantly gushed blood down the side of his neck.

Within seconds Blake, Young-D, and Lil Mike were on the floor and K.G. was dropping the money and crack from the card table inside the backpack he[1]d brought with him.

"Take every damn thang," Bookie said. "The PlayStation, too. We need all this shit." He kicked Blake's head and smiled when he heard the painful grown that followed. "Punk ass niggas think y'all ballin', huh?" Bookie's voice was high-pitched.

Johnny crouched over Lil Mike and began searching through

his pants pockets. After retrieving a hefty bankroll and a baggy containing about a half ounce of marijuana, Johnny dropped it all in K.G.'s backpack and went on to search Blake and Young-D.

Bookie and his Eastside crew, who were better known as the Tenth Street Hustlers, left Blake's crack house with over three thousand dollars incash and drugs.

Today was the last day Blake would ever leave home without his forty-caliber Smith and Wesson.

Alexus laughed sarcastically. "Very funny," she said dryly. "You justmay be the next Cedric The Entertainer, fat ass."

"My dick's fat."

"So is your belly."

"You know, I hit a nigga in the throat earlier for one of them fat jokes. Don'tend up like him."

"Boy, please! I wish you would," Alexus said. She was gazing out her window at the Lighthouse Mall as they passed it on the Eighth Street."I'm on my way home now. We're following the furniture trucks."

"You still want meto drive you to the Chi'?"

"I have to help my mom get the house situated first, and I think myuncle Dennis and his kids are coming over for dinner. I'll be readytonight,though. So, make sure your girlfriend doesn't have you on lockdown."

"Ain't no bitch got me locked down," Blake said. He paused for a moment. "I got robbed right after I left from talking to you," he said finally. "Niggas got off with my lastounce of-"

Blake became quiet suddenly, and the background whispers were replaced by metallic clinks. Alexus thought she heard someone say, "I think that's him right there." Seconds later Blake was back on the line.

"My bad, lil mama. But yeah, muhfuckas robbed me," he said. "Cameright in through the back door, laid us down, took everything."

"What was that noise?" asked Alexus, as Rita pulled up in front of the house.

"Don't be nosey like that. Come and see if you wanna know some shit. BadBitch."

24

"You're full of jokes today, huh?"

"I ain't joked about nothin'," Blake said.

Rita climbed out of the U-Haul, leaving Alexus alone. Alexus's voice shifted, oozing with sexiness.

"Don't worry about that little bit of nothing they took, daddy. We'll be fucking in a Lexus by tomorrow, I guarantee it." Just the suggestion of sex made Alexus moist between the thighs. She pushed her legs together in anticipation of what the night might hold. "Can you eat pussy?" she asked, and immediately wished she hadn't. She didn't want to come off like the nymphomaniac she truly was.

"I can do a lot of shit," Blake said.

"What if I wanted to ride your face?" Alexus could not contain herself. "Would you let me do that?"

Blake chuckled. "You's a freaky lil Bad Bitch, ain't you? I thought you was gon' be all stuck-up. 'Specially to a nigga like me."

"I've never been that kind of person. And besides, I like your swag. And you're strong. And handsome. Who wouldn't want to be seen with the epitome of pretty-boy swag?" Alexus was taking in the neighborhood the people who drove by, walked by, and occasionally peeked their heads out of the windows and doors. A group of young boys who were trying without progress, to gain the attention of two girls at the bus stop, and she noted that either this section of the small city was predominantly Black, or the whites were vampires, avoiding the sunshine like characters from the Twilight Saga.

"I ain't no pretty boy," Blake said.

"Yeah, yeah, whatever." Alexus pushed open her door, deciding that she was not going to spend the remainder of her day trapped in her mother's vapid presence. "I'm about to get showered and dressed. Forget what I said a minute ago, I'm not about to be stuck with my mom all day. Be here in an hour."

Alexus ended the call then, feeling remarkably better than she'd felt since the raid a week ago. She missed her Benz, her expensive wardrobe and diamond jewelry, but now that her future seemed promising to say the least, Alexus didn't feel so bad.

She thought of her brown leather Louis Vuitton shoulder bag and the mountain of cash bundles it contained. There were twenty-five bundles, and each one held one hundred bank-new Benjamin Franklins.

Shortly after her brother's arrest, Jennifer Costilla had phoned Alexus and told her about the money.

"Papi dropped it off about a week ago," Jenny had said. "He said to give it to you if anything ever happened to him. I think he knew they were onto him weeks in advance. I saw it in his eyes."

In retrospect, Alexus thought she may have discerned a subtle change in her Father's eyes as well. And he had begun to display a more affectionate side of himself—an idiosyncrasy that had attenuated after the divorce—toward she and her mom. Papi had flown them to Cancun, Mexico, on Alexus's eighteenth birthday, where the three of them enjoyed a splendid week of fun and relaxation that only the affluent could afford. A month after that he'd sent Rita and Alexus to Paris, France, to attend a Dolce and Gabbana swimsuit event. A short vacation to Egypt followed. Then came a lavish trip to China, then Jamaica, then Barbados.

As Alexus showered, she dexterously fondled her clitoris with one hand while squeezing her taut nipples with the other, envisioning her and Blake somewhere overseas, his head between her thighs on a deserted beach, the euphonious sounds of crashing waves and chirruping seagulls in the distance.

The body-writhing orgasm Alexus experienced made her yelp unintentionally and caused a warm stream of juices to gush from her quivering pussy. She collapsed against the wall, panting and spent.

Chapter 4

"You *absolutely* sure it was Bookie?" Blake King's inquisitive brown eyes stared hard at Lil Mike, who was seated beside him in the passenger seat of the Caprice, his lips enwrapping a blunt, his thin brown fingers nervously gripping a nine-millimeter Ruger handgun.

Lil Mike wore blue from his top to his bottom, and the 'C' on his Cubs baseball cap represented Crip. Staring past Blake, who held a fully-automatic AK-47 assault rifle in his hands, at the white house where he'd seen Reggie "Bookie" Nelson. Mike was ready for war.

"I'm *sure*, bruh." Lil Mike's deep tone brought a sense of reality to his certainty. "I know his voice from anywhere. Don't nobody talk like him. That was Bookie."

Blake turned back to the house, hoping that Lil Mike was telling the truth, keeping shit one hundred percent real. *I ain't got time to be shootin' the wrong muhfucka,* Blake thought. But he believed Lil Mike. Blake had known Bookie for a while. And the more he thought about Bookie's high-pitched voice, the more Blake believed that Bookie was indeed the man who had kicked him in the side of his head, took his crack *and* his money.

"Y'all know what time it is then," Blake said, as he looked first at Lil Mike then to the back seat, where Young-D and Tim-Tim... another Dub Life Goon-sat quietly, revolvers on their laps.

And then it happened.

A tall, perilously thin, hawk-faced young man exited the front door of the house Blake and his guys had been watching for close to an hour. Then Bookie appeared behind him, smoking a cigarette, nervously looking back and forth. He was in his hood, on Tenth and Lafayette; the black section of the city where you could find a drug dealer on almost every corner.

There were maybe two dozen people on the block, all immersed in their own conversations, none expecting the hell that was about to be unleashed.

As Blake lowered his tinted window, he and Bookie

27

momentarily lockedeyes.

Then Blake pushed his AK-47's long barrel out the window and opened fire.

The stentorian blasts rocked the street and compelled everyone with amodicum of sense, to haul ass.

A volley of 7.62 millimeter rounds from Blake's AK-47 burned numerous holes in the lanky man, until he fell flat on his back, bleeding profusely, unmoving; while his friend Bookie pulled a handgun and started shooting in the general direction of Blake's car while sprinting back into the house.

When the door behind Blake swung open, he assumed Tim-Tim was about to chase down Bookie. But Tim-Tim began running west up Tenth Street, dropping his pistol as he went.

Lil Mike and Young-D had emptied their weapons over the '92 Caprice's roof As they slid back into the car, Young-D asked "What the fuck Tim on?"

"Close his door! Blake demanded.

The tires on Blake's Caprice burned and smoked and emitted an ear-piercing screech as he sped away.

Chapter 5

They sure do have a bunch of cops out here, Alexus mused. She was standing at the comer of Eighth and Willard Avenue, staring in wonderment at the swarming Michigan City Police Department vehicles that were zipping up and down the streets, eyeing every non-cop they passed as though he or she were Taliban operatives.

Alexus had been waiting outside for Blake for going on twenty minutes, and she was getting angrier and colder by the second. She had on a too tight magenta Versace dress with nothing under it, a pair of black Versace stiletto boots, and a very expensive black Russian Sable fur coat, which came with the matching purse, that she had stocked full of cash-she'd felt the need to bring along two $10,000 bundles, a roll of Magnum condoms, and her personal belongings.

She had originally planned to give Blake a taste of pussy, and maybe ten grand. Now, she thought about strangling him.

Her thoughts strayed as a glistening-clean white Chevy Suburban, raised up high above the street by a suspension kit and a refulgent chrome set of thirty-inch rims, coasted to a halt at the curb beside her.

"Damn, lil mama. Who you know over here?"

Alexus recognized the dark and braided man's face as he stuck his head out the passenger's window of the SUV, twisting his expression into what Alexus surmised was his 'handsome' look.

"You're my cousin, Bookie," said Alexus.

"Auntie Rita's daughter?" Bookie looked confused, then lowered his hand out the window until his open palm hovered about three feet over the street."I ain't seen you since we was this big," he smiled.

But his eyes were sad and sullen, and Alexus noticed, that they were filled with a pain that wouldn't go away.

"That's me," Alexus said, approaching the Suburban with a smile. She hadn't laid eyes on Bookie since the '97 Bishop family reunion in Baton Rouge.

The Suburban's driver-a narrowed faced, brown skinned man with a mouthful of white-diamond flooded gold teeth and a left-cantingNew Era Bulls fitted cap, leaned forward in his seat and examined Alexus.

"I'm LilCraig," he said, suavely. "I know you gotta be cold out there. Get in the back and ride wit' a nigga."

Alexus looked back at her house first, checking to see if Rita's seemingly omnipresent eyes were stalking from a window or something. Then Alexus said to hell with it and climbed in back of the Suburban.

The sweet scent of fresh leather invaded Alexus's nostrils as she climbedonto the smooth back seat and shut the door.

"Nice, really nice." Alexus ran her hands over the white leather seat,

looking around at the many televisions that were methodically placed throughout the Suburban. Craig gazed overtly at her reflection in the rearview mirror, and Alexus boldly returned his stare.

"Mmm, mmm, mmm," Craig groaned. Bookie punched Craig's arm. Craig laughed and stepped on the gas pedal, propelling his massive carriage forward.

"Shit," Alexus said, "you must have paid a grip for this, huh?"

"Hell yeah," Craig boasted. "'Bout a hundred racks altogether. Got the fiberglass door panels full of speakers, seven-inch t.v.'s in the headrests and visors, heated hardwood floors, and an Xbox 360 built in into the dash. This 'Burban is my mistress."

Craig gave Alexus that look again, cracking a subtle grin to show off his glittering diamonds.

"I like it," Alexus concluded. "Reminds me of my Benz. And it smells good, too."

"I'm at the car wash faithfully every morning," Craig said.

Bookie concurred with a nod. "That nigga'll kill somebody 'bout this truck." He shifted nervously in his seat and glanced alternately from his left to his right.

Several uniformed officers were harassing a group of teen-aged boyson the street.

"Who wouldn't?" Alexus asked.

Craig turned the Suburban around and upped the volume on his booming sound system. Gucci Mane's *Makin' Love to the Money* filled the air, and Alexus swayed her head to the beat while absorbing the drab scenery.

"So," Craig asked, "you got a Benz?"

"Had a benz." Alexus scowled. "The DEA and FBI agents who seized everything are probably driving around in it now, dirty bastards." She reached in her furry black purse, took out the cash and fanned through it. "I'm getting a Lexus now, since that's my name. Might get me some big ass rims like you."

Both Craig and Bookie's eyes grew wide when they saw the stacks of cash.

"Damn, cuz!" Bookie exclaimed. "Lemme get a couple hun'ed!

Damn! Alexus tossed one of the bundles to Bookie.

"That's ten racks, family." Alexus laughed arrogantly. "I gotsomethin' else for you later this weekend."

Bookie looked over to Craig with a beaming smile. "Told you herdaddy had that *bread!"* he screeched.

"The Mexican who got popped off in Texas last week? The one whowas on CNN?" Craig asked.

Alexus nodded. "Juan Costilla is my father."

Then, as he was pulling into the drive-thru of a Rally's restaurant, Craig asked the question that Alexus had been waiting for.

"You got a 'caine connect? 'Cause I'll get you *rich.* Especially right now. Niggas in Chicago payin' outrageous prices for them bricks, so you*know* it's a drought."

"Outrageous? Outrageous like what? Twenty thousand?"

"Try thirty," Craig said. He crept forward until the chrome grille ofhis Suburban was close up on the bumper of a red Ford pickup before continuing his spiel. "Shiiit, if a muhfucka had them whole thangs for twenty apiece," he shook his head at the mere thought and whistled through his teeth, "they wouldn't last a day. A hundred of 'em wouldn'tlast a week."

Alexus pondered Craig's claims while she and him placed

their orders. Bookie seemed to be makin love to the money; he had yet tostop counting it.

As Alexus was finishing off her first spicy chicken sandwich, Craigsaid, "You know, you look just like Nicki Minaj in that *Right Thru Me* video."

"Thanks, sweetie," Alexus said. She chewed and swallowed a bite ofher sandwich. "Back to the money, though. You sure about those figures?"

"One hundred percent." Craig sipped from the straw in his Styrofoam cup. "I know a nigga in Chicago who got a quarter million for ten bricks. 'Nother nigga outta Detroit might want some of 'em. I can getoff five or six bricks here."

Nodding thoughtfully, Alexus said. "So, what if someone laid tenkilos on you? How long would it take you to sell them? I mean, when would the money come?"

"Either the same day or the next day. I can more than likely grab like three by myself. That's up frontmoney."

"Hmm." Alexus gazed down at her pink-painted fingernails. Then,she put the thick stack of bills in her purse and checked her iPhone to seeif Blake had called yet. He had, three times. *Fuck him,* Alexus thought to herself. *Nigga shouldn't have beenlate.*

Raising her eyes to Craig, she admired the white leather Pelle Pelle jacket that was scrunched down around his lower back, and his crisp white t-shirt, and the gold watch with the diamond studded face on his gaunt wrist.

"How does fifteen a key sound?" Alexus asked.

Screeching to a halt at a stop sign, Craig snapped his head around tolook Alexus in the eyes. "I'll buy four today."

Bookie turned to her, also. "Shit, I'll give you this ten back for a brickof soft and—"

"Hush, Bookie," said Alexus. ul got you, family. You and Kenya and Uncle Dennis, I got y'all.'' He:r eyes shifted back to Craig. Bookie will be calling you within a few days. He'll have ten kilos of the best-quality cokeyou've ever run across. I want that sixty grand up front as you promised, and the other ninety thousand dollars-''

"Next day," Craig interjected. "I guarantee it."

32

"We'll see about that." Alexus was scrutinizing the jam-packed street they were coming up on..

A quick glance at a sign told Alexus what street she was on: Tenth and Lafayette. There were tear-streaked faces everywhere Alexus looked, the majority of them staring at a bullet-riddled white house that was blocked off by a long strip of "Crime Scene" ribbon. There were about twenty police officers present, but their mannerisms were not as threatening as the cops Alexus had seen near her new Westside home; these officers showed gentle, friendly gestures, and they weren't patting people down, either.

"My God," Alexus gasped. "What in the world happened out here?"

"Niggas came through sprayin'," Bookie informed her, and when he turned to her this time he had tears in his eyes. "Killed my nigga wit' some bullets that was ·meant for me. I saw who did it, though... And I'ma blow his thoughts out when I catch him."

King Rio

Chapter 6

The tension was palpable. Standing amid the gun-toting young hustlers on East Tenth Street, Alexus could feel the tension on her skin. Every car that drove past was angrily stared down. Bookie and Craig were a few feet away from Alexus on the sidewalk, chillin' with their associates, smoking overstuffed blunts.

After enduring the unbearable wind for half an hour Alexus decided enough was enough and asked Craig to take her to a car dealership where she could purchase her own vehicle, because she sure in the hell wasn't about to freeze to death over someone *else's* death. Nuh-uh, not Alexus Costilla.

Bookie was far too distraught to even notice Craig and Alexus climb into the big SUV and drive away.

"Why not just deal with me directly?" Craig asked as he turned onto Michigan Boulevard, a four-lane strip lined with a smorgasbord of small businesses.

Alexus shrugged. "To keep my hands clean, I guess. Turn on the heat in here. I'm freezing."

Craig pressed some buttons and the heat kicked on powerfully. "I understand that," he said, "but Bookie ain't go'n do shit but snort all that dope up. I know him better than anybody."

"No, he won't. Besides, if he uses, I'll make sure he has enough to supply his habit."

"You could still deal with me. You can look at me and *see* money. Why not fuck with me?"

Looking over to Craig, Alexus smiled. "Well, aren't you the persistent one," she intoned, giggling jubilantly. "Let's talk about something else, sexy face. Tell me about this city. Where are the hot spots, the clubs?"

"Something else, huh? A'ight, let's talk about Juan Costilla. The other day, Anderson Cooper's show on CNN said that your dad and his cartel was moving a hundred kilos every month. That true?"

"No." Alexus slipped out of her fur coat and laid it and her purse on the seat behind her. "Those people didn't know a thing about my father's operation. And please don't ask questions about him. He wouldn't like it. In fact, you'd probably end up committing suicide by leaping from an eighth-story window the next day. It always happens that way."

Craig chuckled but said nothing. His expression was indecipherable, Alexus noticed. He had on his poker-face.

"I'm from Chicago, originally," he said finally. "CVL from the Southside. Been out here for some years, though. Only time I go back home is to make some money."

"What's a CVL?" Alexus asked. "Conservative Vice Lord," Craig replied.

"Oh. I think I saw them on an episode of Gangland."

Looking at Alexus with lust-filled eyes, Craig said, "I can't believe this shit." He dropped his head back and laughed. "Never in my lifetime."

"

"You can't believe what?"

"How sexy you- damn-you's a bad chick, lil mama. Pro'bly the finest girl I ever seen up close. *Definitely* the baddest I done met."

Alexus was thinking of a response to Craig's compliment, when a candy orange bubble Caprice, with rims that were just as chrome and almost as large as the Suburban's, veered in front of them suddenly and slowed to a crawl, forcing Craig to do the same.

Craig reached beneath his seat, and when his hand reappeared it was clamped around the handle of chrome-plated nine-millimeter Sig Sauer pistol with an extended magazine hanging from its bottom like a taut chrome tail.

"Duck down," Craig said, calmly.

But before Alexus could even slide down in her seat, an MCPD patrol car pulled up alongside them and ended the tense and possibly deadly situation. The orange Caprice turned right and started up a side street, and the cop car followed.

"Niggas gon' make me shoot the shit out of 'em," Craig said, as he continued up the boulevard, eyes fluctuating rapidly from the rearview mirror to the busy road ahead.

"What was that all about?" Alexus said.

"Them niggas in that Chevy," he replaced the gun under his seat, "was Dub Life, same clique who killed Johnny. I guess we at war now." He gave a sarcastic chuckle. "Like they know what war means. This city's too small for a war. I'm from Chicago. I *know* what war really is."

Alexus's heart was pounding in her chest from the potential danger of riding with Craig-yet at the same time, her pussy began to moisten and throb at the thought of how brave Craig was, and how quick he'd grabbed his strap.

"Lean your seat back," Alexus said. And when he did, she unzipped his baggy Girbaud jeans and carefully tugged his flaccid penis out.

She sucked him fervently, increasing her pace until her head was like a jackhammer in his lap. Deep pockets formed in her cheeks from the power of her suction. Alexus considered herself somewhat of an expert giving head, and she knew that Craig would surely say the same. He grunted just minutes after she'd begun pleasuring him, pushing a trembling hand down on the nape of her neck, and clogged her throat with a load of warm semen.

Raising her hand from his lap, Alexus showed a creamy smile. "Feel better now?" She asked, swallowing his cum.

"Damn," was all Craig could say.

***

Five thousand dollars in cash took care of the down payment for Alexus' brand new silver 2011 Lincoln MKX. She utilized its navigation controls to find her way home, learning the use of every button inside the spacious SUV as she traversed the streets of Michigan City, Indiana.

When Alexus made it home it was going on five-thirty and Rita was in the kitchen with Dennis, toiling over a stove covered with pots and pans.

Alexus felt her stomach rumble at the scent of frying chicken as it wafted through the air, and she wondered what else her mother was whipping up for dinner.

"My beautiful niece!" Uncle Dennis, said excitedly.

Uncle Dennis waddled his short self over to Alexus and hugged her as she entered the kitchen. He looked like a retired pimp, with a straw hat and a cheap pair of dark sunglasses that hid the top half of his face completely.

"Hey, Uncle Dennis." Alexus smiled at him, trying to keep a straight face and an open nose; Uncle Dennis' breath was ratchet. Smelled like he had just tongued a cow's asshole.

"Go on upstairs and help your cousin Kenya and her friend put that bed frame together," said Rita. "They've been up there trying since you called from the car dealership. And where'd you get money for a car, anyway? It sure didn't come from me."

"I, uh, well ... I plead the fifth." Alexus laughed and turned to leave "Love you, Momma," she said quickly and was halfway up the stairs when Rita shouted back.

"God don't like ugly!"

Kenya, a short, dark-skinned twenty-year-old who had just been voted MVP of Michigan State's women's basketball team, was hanging a set of tan-colored curtains over Alexus' window when Alexus walked into the bedroom. Kenya's loose-fitting blue Michigan State sweatpants and hooded sweatshirt spoke volumes about her lack of femininity, but she was a pretty young woman, just like her light skinned friend, whom Kenya introduced as Cereniti Stingley, her college roommate.

"Just call me Tee-Tee," Cereniti said. She had on a sweat suit that was identical to Kenya's, only difference being that Cereniti's was two sizes too small. "I've heard a lot about you, yo. Heard you got mad cake, B. Wordup."

"She's from New York," Kenya explained. "Don't mind her. I've always had a hard time understanding her."

Holding up a curtain rod with one hand, Cereniti flipped Kenya the bird with the other. "Hi, hater."

Alexus shook her head, and laughed as she took off her coat and laid it across the center of her bed which, contrary to her mother's belief, was perfectly assembled.

"We were just talking about those trapped miners in Chile," Kenya said. "I would have gone half-crazy by now, I swear.

Trapped down in the dark like that. No Facebook, no My space, no basketball. Don't know how they did it."

"Because they *had* to, Kenya." Cereniti's tone was laced with sarcasm. She backed up from the properly hung curtains and examined them, then turned to Alexus. "Your cousin has got to be the smartest dummy on the planet, yo. I'm serious. Straight up. The broad's fried up here." She tapped a fingertip against her temple.

Alexus shook her head again, finding humor in Cereniti's East-coast dialect.

The three of them sat and started talking about everything from the B.P. oil spill to the major role First Lady Michelle Obama played in the White House to Juan Costilla's arrest and its effect on the lifestyle Alexus was accustomed to living.

"This entire bedroom isn't even as big as my old closet," Alexus complained, and she was not lying. She was used to luxury, to first-class flights to foreign countries; the new little house didn't quite fit her tastes.

"You plan on going to college?" Cereniti asked Alexus.

"I just finished high school," Alexus answered. "I'm thinking about becoming a licensed real estate agent like my cousins Savio and Santiago. They flip houses for a living. You can't fail in real estate. I mean, like, you spend a hundred grand on a house, spend another hundred on renovations, and sell for four hundred thousand. It's sweet as Hershey's."

"Apparently you haven't heard," Kenya said, "but the country is going through a recession as we speak. Home sales have declined drastically. It's almost impossible to sell a house now."

"Almost," Alexus replied, and she left it at that as Rita let them know that dinner was ready.

Kenya stopped Alexus at the bedroom door as they were leaving out. "Put on a bra, at least," Kenya advised. "And brush your teeth. You got dick breath."

At the new dining room table, Rita Mae Bishop took her place as matriarch at the table's end. A Louisiana native, she was a culinary geniusof Southern dishes. Lined up along the table's center were dishes of fried chicken, macaroni and cheese, cornbread, delectably seasoned collard greens, and a host of palate-pleasing baked cookies.

Rita told everyone to hold hands and bow their heads. Then she launched into a lengthy prayer. Begging God for protection and guidanceand blessings and every other thing she could possibly think of at the moment. She prayed for Juan Costilla's safety and freedom. She prayed for her daughter's future, for her brother's health, and she even took time to pray for Flake Costilla's well-being, though she couldn't stand him.

By the time Rita muttered "Amen," Alexus was hungrier than ever.

She filled her plate and began eating.

Uncle Dennis had obviously never learned to chew with his mouthclosed. "Niggas triedto kill my son today," he said with his mouth full.

"Who, Bookie?" Alexus asked curiously.

Uncle Dennis gave a confirming nod. "Only son I got. They say theshooters were aiming for my boy but ended up killing his friend Johnny."

"That's what happened," Kenya concurred. She bit into a crispy, hot sauce-drenched drumstick. "I went to Elston High with Johnny. He was anice kid. Real quiet. Hard to believe he's gone at such a young."

"Your auntie got *mad* skills with the bird game, yo. *Mad* skills."Cereniti interrupted, chewing her chicken.

Cereniti gave Rita two thumbs up and went back to her meal. Rita-like Alexus, Kenya, and Dennis-laughed heartily at Cereniti's well-meantcomment.

"Tee-Tee ain't got it all, Aunt Rita." Kenya looked embarrassed.

"I was just riding around with Bookie and one of his guys," Alexus said. "They took me over there where the shooting took place. It looks bad, whole bunch of bullet holes, shatteredwindows."

Rita said, "Where did you find Reggie?" She never used

Bookie's nickname.

"He found me," Alexus said. "I was standing outside when they drove up and stopped."

"Payback," Uncle Dennis grumbled. "It's why they was over here. Can't twist my nuts and tell me different."

Alexus choked on her cornbread as she started to laugh. *These folks are crazy,* she thought to herself.

But it was deeply comforting to be in the company of family, no matter how unfamiliar Alexus was with them. This was her maternal family-except for the hilarious little New York chick, who Alexus thought looked remarkably similar to Alicia Keys, and Alexus welcomed the experience. She was used to being around her father's Mexican family.

After dinner Kenya and Cereniti accompanied Alexus to Blockbuster Video for a movie rental. Alexus selected two Denzel Washington movies-American Gangster and Man on Fire -because he was Rita's favorite actor. Then the three girls were back at the house on the living room sofa with Rita and Dennis, who dozed off before the movie previews had even ended on American Gangster.

"I bet your pops was getting that Frank Lucas guap, wasn't he?" Cereniti asked Alexus. She was seated next to Alexus on the tan leather sectional, both of them curled beneath the same patchwork quilt that wash and-sewn by Granny Costilla.

"Yeah, he was," Alexus answered. *And I'll be doing the same thing real soon,* she thought.

Toward the movie's end, Alexus felt Cereniti's hand on her thigh, gliding over the thin fabric of her dress like melting butter in a hot pan. Alexus didn't say anything. She let her silence speak. And when Cereniti's wandering hand slithered under the dress and began to massage and finger Alexus' wet opening, Alexus spread her thighs and suppressed the moans and sighs that were begging to be released.

Kenya was animatedly describing a handsome college professor of hers to her aunt Rita; Rita was visibly vexed because she was trying to watch Denzel Washington on her new 42-inch flat screen television, and her inattentive niece didn't seem to notice.

Neither of them was paying any attention to Alexus or Cereniti.

Pushing her lips tantalizingly close to Alexus's ear, Cereniti whispered," I never knew a pussy could get so wet. I bet you can make a nigga come in three minutes flat." She shoved two fingers deep inside Alexus and wriggled them roughly.

Alexus bit down on her lower lip, unable to utter a single word, feeling as if at any moment she would succumb to the intense orgasm that was building up inside.

But Cereniti's fingers slipped out before that could happen, and Alexus was thankful; she knew that she would not have been able to remain quiet if Cereniti had continued.

As Cereniti's hand rose from under the quilt, Alexus saw that it was glistening with her vaginal juices.

Cereniti sucked her fingers dry.

"Let me show you my shoe collection," Alexus said, breathlessly. She pulled down her dress under the quilt. Then she and Cereniti went upstairs to her bedroom, leaving Rita and Kenya to their frivolous conversation.

Alexus locked the bedroom door.

Chapter 7

Standing in the middle of the large crowd of Dub Life Goons,
Blake King was in a state of worry. They were on the comer
of Eighth Street and Willard Ave, smoking blunts and sipping
from Hennessy-filled plastic cups. A few of them were shooting
dice on the sidewalk. Others were conversing with females, selling crack to the addicts who drove by or walked by; and watching
out for police, who were especially active today.

But the majority of them were being vigilant for another reason; they were expecting retaliation from the east Tenth Street
crew.

"Who went over there shooting in the first place?" Ashley
Joy asked Blake. She was leaning back against Blake, whose back
was pressed against the trunk of his brother's candy orange Caprice.

"I don't know," said Blake.

"Don't lie to me, Blake. You know damn well what happened.
And I know, too. Tim-Tim told Shannon everything. And he told
Britney. She stopped by my job and told me."

"I don't know nothing." Blake swallowed some cognac,
turning his head to look at the yellow house beside the vacant lot
where he now stood. He wondered if Bad Bitch was in there.

"You's a goddam lie and the truth ain't in you," Ashley
snapped.

"Can't wait to catch that punk-ass nigga," said Blake.

"Who you talking about?"

"Tim-Tim. I ain't know dude was that soft."

"You cannot be mad at him for running. I would have
run, too. Nobody wants to be involved with a murder. You killed
that—"

"I ain't killed nobody!" Blake hissed. "And don't *ever* let that
bullshit fall out yo' mouth again."

He was heated after that. Who on earth would boldly speak on
an unsolved murder? He thought. My dumb ass girlfriend, that's

who. May as well just call the police.

Blake smoked a blunt of dro to himself, wondering who else Tim-Tim had been running his big mouth to, hoping that 'no one' was the answer to that question. Blake had turned eighteen only three weeks prior and already he'd been arrested and sent to La Porte County Jail twice-once for possession of fifty-six grams of marijuana, and his second arrest stemmed from an assault at a party four months back. He did not want to be sitting in jail fighting a murder case, fighting for his life.

His older brother Terrence "Streets" King raised the volume of his Caprice's music system until Yo Gotti's gritty *Look In the Mirror* was shaking the car to its core. Then Streets got out and went to the rear of the car, beside Blake.

"Forgot to tell you," he said. "I caught that nigga Craig on the Boulevard earlier. Fly was with me. We was 'bout to shoot the rims off that 'burban." He laughed. "The law j'd down on us, though. Followed me all the way back to the 'hood."

"Fly wasn't going to shoot no damn body," Blake said. He looked at Fly, who was crouched over the dice game with a fistful of dollars. He was tall like Streets, but Fly was as bright as Prince. "I ain't never seen Fly shoot a pistol. Nigga got twenty guns and ain't never shot a bullet."

"Don't matter," Street shrugged dismissively. "Everybody can't be a goon. I'll shoot for that nigga. Last time I checked."

"Hold up bruh." Blake was looking up the dark street at an oncoming figure. "This weak ass..."

Blake stepped from behind his girlfriend and started hastily up Eighth Street, and as Tim-Tim crossed under a streetlight at the comer, Blake heard the voice of Bad Bitch's mother shouting from somewhere behind him.

"If you don't turn down that mess," she was saying, but Blake was not listening, he was pulling a compact .40 caliber Smith and Wesson from the rear of his denim jeans.

"S'up, bruh," Tim-Tim said as he and Blake finally reached each other.

"You wanna know what's—" Blake swung the gun at Tim-Tim's face, crushing his nose "—up, nigga? I'll tell you what's up."

"Ah, shit!" Tim-Tim covered his bleeding nose with both his dark brown hands.

"You broke my—"

Blake's powerful left fist collided with Tim-Tim's jaw, and that was all it took to render him unconscious. Then Blake was squatting over hischest, relentlessly beating him about the head with the pistol.

Bad bitch's mother was screaming again. So were Ashley and

Myrtle and a few other girls. Blake felt hands all over him, frantic hands,pushing and pulling him off of Tim-Tim.

King Rio

Chapter 8

"Alexus! Alexus and Tee-Tee!" Kenya banged on the bedroom door again. "Open the door!"

Alexus was stark-naked on her queen-size bed, lying on her back with her legs spread wide open. She was running her fingertips back and forth over Cereniti's corn-rowed head. Enjoying Cereniti's zealous tongue as it danced across her pussy as if had taken lessons from Shakira. The cute little New York girl was the truth at eating pussy, Alexus had to admit.

"I'm ... oh, shit ... I'm coming," Alexus moaned, a bit too loudly.

"What did you just say?" Kenya shook the doorknob. "What are y'all in there doing? Cereniti? Alexus?"

Alexus was gyrating her hips and Cereniti's lips were closed around her clitoris. As juice began squirting out of Alexus with the velocity of a high-powered water gun, Cereniti dipped her mouth downward and lapped it up, slurping audibly.

Feeling depleted of energy and out of breath, Alexus lay still after the phenomenal orgasm, regaining her mental equilibrium, gazing down at Cereniti's dripping chin as it hovered above her pussy.

"How do you do that?" Cereniti asked. "How do I do what?"

"Make your pussy squirt like that. That's crazy, yo. I never seen that shit before."

Alexus giggled innocently. "I don't know. It's natural, I guess, been that way since I was thirteen." She climbed off the bed and dressed hurriedly. Then she went to the bedroom door and opened it.

Kenya was standing there in the narrow hallway with her arms crossed over her chest and an expression of pure disgust on her face.

"Nasty hoes," she muttered as she turned her back to Alexus and started stomping down the stairs. "Sick ass, trifling bitches."

Alexus smiled. "What did you want Kenya?"

"Some boy just got pistol-whipped on the corner. Aunt

Rita's out there with my daddy, waiting on the ambulance." She paused on the stairs and glanced over her shoulder, glaring at Alexus with cold eyes.

"I'll be down there in a minute," said Alexus.

Sucking her teeth, Kenya snapped her head forward and continued down the stairs with an attitude.

"And she thinks I'm the nut case." Cereniti walked up behind Alexus and squeezed her fluffy derriere. "Kenya's the meaning of nut-case. Word to the mother." She took a step back, slapped Alexus on the ass, and watched it shake and wobble. "Damn, girl what's your measurements?"

"36C-25-48", Alexus answered with a grin on her face. "You're one to talk."

"My ass is big, but mine is only a forty-one. You got too much ass." "Can you make yours clap?" Alexus turned to face Cereniti and ended up with a tongue in her mouth. She could taste herself on Cereniti's tongue and lips.

Pulling back, Cereniti said, "of course I can make my ass clap. I was an exotic dancer in Harlem for almost two years, working at The Honey Dip. Juelz Santana's strip club."

"You were a stripper?"

"No, I was an exotic dancer." Cereniti nibbled on Alexus bottom lip. "I've been wanting to go back lately. But Kenya keeps talking me into staying in Lansing, Michigan to finish college."

"Why would you want to go back to stripping?" Alexus asked. "Exotic dancing." Cereniti corrected.

"Okay, exotic dancing."

"For the money. I was making good money as a dancer. Good money, yo. Two or three grand every night I worked. I got to hang out with superstars like Cam'ron, Juelz Santana, Jim Jones, Fat Joe. Lil Wayne and Baby even came though a few times. And they always requested me and my girl Tasia for their V.I.P dancers. Life was good then. Crazy good, yo."

"Well, what happened? Why'd you leave?" Alexus was curious.

"Tasia and me got involved with the wrong people, and

things wentbad quick. There was just too much money at stake for things to goas smooth as we'd planned. Some people got killed. Feds came sniffing around. Tasia flew to Atlanta-she wasmessing around with some nigga in Gucci Man's little entourage, and I ended up in Detroit with an old boyfriend."

Alexus sat on her bed to put on her stilettos, her eyes never leavingCereniti's.

"So," said Alexus, "what went wrong?"

"A drug deal with some Canadians in lower Manhattan. A millionXpills, seventy-five cents per pill. Tasia put up a hun-dred twenty-fivethousand; I put up the same, and this guy Tasia was with put up half amillion. We told him the fee was a dollar per pill. The plan was perfect.Tasia and me were to walk away with two hundred and fifty thousandpills apiece, sell them for three bucks apiece to hustlers in New York and NewJersey, and leave the game alone."

Alexus was shaking her head in awe, listening attentively. Cereniti continued. "The Canadians weren't playing by the rules, though, b word to my mother, they got to shooting as soon as we pulled up." She raisedher sweatshirt and the t-shirt under it, revealing two circular scars to the right of her navel. I caught two in the stomach, one in my right thigh; Tasia's boy-friend pulled his gun and kil]ed one of the Canadians before they blew half his head off. Tasia jumped out and left me to die, the yellow bitch."

"Wow," Alexus said, amazed. "I'm guessing they took the money?"

"Yup. Every dime of it. Can't say I blame them, either. Two strippers and a fat guy in a 750 BMW with close to a million dollars in the trunk, easiest lick ever."

"Would you ever do it again?" Alexus asked as she put on her fur coat. " Dealing, I mean."

"If I knew somebody like your pops, somebody who would give mea lot of product for cheap, then yeah, count me in. But I'm not risking my freedom selling ten and twenty dollar bags. I'd rather rob a bank, yo. Or a Brinks truck like them Chicago niggas in that Sweet Licks book. I ain't going to jail over no petty change."

A slow smile spread across Alexus' face. When she went inside her bedroom closet and returned with two cash bundles for Cereniti, who looked as if she was witnessing that second coming of Jesus that Ms. Rita was always talking about.

"Here you go," Afexus said. "That's twenty thousand. I want you to work for me and with me. You'll see at least double that every flip. I promise. Word to *my* momma."

Tears of joy formed along Cereniti's lower eyelids as she stared down at the money in her hands. She put it to her chest and held it there like a newborn baby.

Cereniti was in a state of bliss.

Chapter 9

When they finally made it to the front porch Kenya was wedged between Rita and Dennis on the sidewalk, a crew of paramedics were loading a bloody faced boy on a stretcher into the back of an ambulance and numerous police cars were lancing through the neighborhood again. "I see this little city has its fair share of problems, too." Rita said shaking her head. She had her hands on her hips and her eyebrows lifted, being nosey like the dozen or so others who were standing outside their homes.

Alexus walked to her brand new SUV and opened the drivers' side door, unmindful of all of the eyes that followed her. She was in a festive mood, ready to go clubbing, ready to shake her ass to a thrumming beat, and meet some new people. Maybe she'd see that fat little motherfucker named Blake at a club somewhere in the city, standing off to the side of the dancefloor whiles he grinded up on another nigga. Bet his ass wouldn't be late again.

Kenya was reluctant to join Alexus and Cereniti in the SUV, but eventually she did, and they ended up at The Swagger, a club on Michigan Boulevard. It was ladies night, which meant the girls got in free. The doorman was so distracted by Alexus' extraordinary curves that he didn't bother to check her identification close enough to see her age. He simply waved the girls through and kept his eager eyes on the back of Alexus' Versace dress. She had left her fur coat in the car on purpose. She wanted everyone to see how thick and cute she was. A fact that was overlooked by no one, as she walked through the club and found an empty table in the back.

Once they were seated, a pudgy redheaded waitress who looked to be the only white person in the entire club approached their table. Alexus ordered two bottles of Krug Rose at two-thousand dollars a bottle.

"You can't be serious," Kenya said to Alexus as the waitress was leaving. "Four thousand dollars on drinks? Have you lost your damn mind?"

"No, I have not," Alexus eased back on the comfortable red seat andglanced around the club. "There are some busted bitches in here tonight,""Niggas too, yo." Cereniti added. "It's like most of these niggas got

on star trek costumes or something. Look at that one right over there."She pointed at a broad shouldered man in a white Enyce fit who was standing at the bar gazing at them. "Don't he look like the kinda nigga you'd see peeking in your window?"

"Yeah, he'd rape something." Alexus smiled at the possible rapist and shifted her eyes to someone more visually pleasing: Lil Mike or was it Young-D? She wasn't certain which.

He was seated at a table that was far away from Alexus; a table that was surrounded completely by members of his crew. All of them were fresh dressed and scowling truculently across the club at another crew of young guys.

"Four thousand dollars," Kenya was saying, incredulously. "Not forty, not four hundred, but four thousand!" She shook her head. "I wouldnever spend that much money on some drinks."

Cereniti sucked her teeth and asked. "Kenya, are you going to complain all night long?"

"I know right? You're supposed to be telling us who those dudes are," said Alexus. "Who's living with their mommas? Who's rumored tobe snitch? You gotta let us know these things, big cousin. Can't have us choosing in the dark."

"Who cares if they've snitched or not?" Kenya said.

"What!" Alexus could not believe her ears. "A snitch is the worst kind of man you can possibly have. That's why all the real niggas locked up now. Its why my father facing life in federal prison. I'drather bedead than be with a rat."

"Preach, my half-Mexican sister!" Cereniti cheered. She high fived Alexus. "If son's a rat we can't get down like that in Harlem, yo, niggas get straight beat for talking to the jokes, For real, yo."

Kenya rolled her eyes. "Anyway... I don't know all these guys I onlyknow some of them. That's" she pointed at a man with gold teeth at the next table "Reggie, Duke's lil brother. Duke's in the feds now, and Reggie's the weed man."

"I like him," Cereniti said matter of factly.

The waitress returned with the Rose and three glasses.

When their glasses were full of bubbly, Kenya continued, "Thatshort light skinned guy by the bathrooms is Squeaky. He snitched on LilLord, got him thirty five years in Indiana State Prison."

"If he were in Mexico," Alexus said, studying the snitch, "he wouldhave gotten his tongue cut out and his head chopped off. His parents would have been killed, too."

Both Kenya and Cereniti were visibly shocked.

"Alexus" Kenyacleared her throat, sipped her champagne "have youever seen somebody get killed likethat?"

"I've seen a lot in Mexico. Once, when I was with my uncle Flako in Juarez, I watched a man and an old lady get murdered execution style in the middle of the street. They were caught stealing from the La Barbie cartel."

"That'spretty wild, yo." Cerenitisaid. "Aint never witnessed no shitlike that in Harlem."

"Stop talking about Harlem so much!" Kenya snapped. Alexus laughedbut choseto stay out ofthe dramaticargument that subsequentlytook place. Sheturned instead to LilMike or Young-Dor whatever the hellhis name was, he was on his feet pushing through the crowd of hyped

dancers on the floor. He was looking at Alexus, as she left her purse on her table and met him on the dance floor, turning down multiple dance offersin the process.

Trey Songz's "Bottom up" was thumping from somewhere overhead. It was so loud that Alexus had a difficult time understanding whatthe boy was saying until he put his mouth by her ear.

"Remember me? I'm LilMike!" He yelled.

"I remember your name," Alexus lied. "What's up? Where's yourlyingassfriend?"

"That's what I want to talk to you about. Blake couldn't get in. He'sout in the parking lot. He wanted me to tell you to leave. ASAP. And he tried calling to tell you why he couldn't make it to pick you up earlier butyou didn'tanswer the phone."

"Tell Blake he can kiss my fat ass."

"You needto leave, lil mama," LilMike warned.

But Alexus didn't leave. She spun around, swaying her hips, and found herself nose to nose with Reggie.

Slowly, and seductively, she began dancing against him, and she wasn't the least bit surprised when she looked up a moment later and saw that half the crowd was eying her.

"Man, bruh, I just told her twice. She's in here dancin' all on Reggie. Fuck that bitch, bruh. Let her stupid ass stay and get shot. We don't know that bitch anyway."

Blake shifted uncomfortably under the Suburban; he was lying on his back on the cold pavement with his AK-47 resting on his belly and a black and gray camouflage bandana tied around the lower half of his face. "It's alright," Blake said into his phone. "Just make sure y'all act a

fool in there. And let me know if Four-Five or AJ freeze up like Tim-Tim." "Mane," said Lil Mike, "you ain't even gotta worry 'bout that, you

hear me? The goons go'n ride hard, you feel me? On my dead brudda, mane. Shit finna blow in this hoe."

"Shit better." Blake pressed the End key, feeling both nervous and content at the same time.

He had great reason to be nervous.

Although Blake had reported his car stolen just minutes prior to the Tenth Street shooting, Michigan City police had still felt the need to search his girlfriend's apartment from top to bottom, and to question him nonstop for almost an hour, until he'd finally requested a lawyer, at which point they'd left.

The Caprice had been found exactly where and how Blake had left it: parked haphazardly in an alley five blocks up from where the shooting took place, three doors left open, fifty 7.62 millimeter shells casting sprinkled on the floor in front of the driver's seat. Blake wasn't worried about fingerprints being found; because the car was his and his friends were always in it with him, and the bullets had been wiped clean before being loaded into their guns.

Now Blake's every vein was tingling with adrenaline, and he was anxious to begin sending bullets through a few more niggas. Kevin "KG" Goldman, specifically.

Blake's girlfriend had a cousin named Danielle who was

always hanging around with the Tenth Street hustlers. Danielle had overheard KG conversating with some other TSH niggas about how he had participated in the armed robbery of Blake's crack house. During a brief phone discourse, Danielle had informed Ashley of this pertinent detail, telling her to keep it a secret from Blake because they both knew how he would react.

Ashley Joy could not keep a secret to save her life. She hadn't even gotten out of her Footlocker uniform before she started running her mouth.

"You do know that KG was one of the dudes who robbed y'all, right?" She'd said, shutting the apartment door behind her.

"Yup," had been Blake's sarcastic reply," I saw that right through the mask."

"I was only telling you, smart ass.""And I was only telling you."

Blake could not help smiling at the thought of his cute, statuesque spouse. They'd been together on and off for years and had a beautiful three year old daughter, Savaria Chanel King, who was the spitting image of her mother. Blake loved his daughter more than he loved himself. She meant the world to him. He'd watched her grow from infancy to the tiny little version of Ashley that she now was, and the experience had changed his outlook on life in general. He'd grown less violent, more approachable.

But the intrepid robbery of his crack house had left him livid. His respect was something he had killed for. Today, without remorse.

And he was itching to do it again.

Five minutes went by. Then ten more passed. Then twenty. With impatience closing in like an evening shadow, Blake called Lil Mike again.

"What's the hold up?" Blake asked.

"Mane, bruh, its like fo' poleece in here. They askin' niggas 'bout that Tenth Street shit."

Just my luck, Blake thought.

Lil Mike said," Muhfucka can't get to KG, no way. He been in the girls restroom with T-Walk, Reggie and that bitch you keep tryin to save for like fifteen, you hear me, mane?" Blake's heart swelled with jealousy.

The Rose had Alexus buzzed almost to the point of complete inebriation. Her knees were beginning to ache from resting too long onthe white tiled floor of the restroom. There were three guys huddled around her, their pants pooled around their ankles, their dicks erect andglazed with her saliva.

She went back to work on the muscular dark guy, sucking himfeverishly while masturbating the other two. She could see three ladies behind the guy she was sucking -*Reggie,* she thought, *that's his damn name*- peering down on the action with disbelief written all over their faces, but she didn't mind. Alexus dug the attention. It was arousing.

Stopping only once to warn them not to get anything on her dress,Alexus slurped each man until her mouth was overflowing with their semen, then shestood stretching her legs, and swallowed. Her expression twisted at the acerbic taste of all the semen and she had to swallow twicemore to get it all down.

"Girl," said oneof the female spectators, "you are one bold bitch, I'lltell you that much."

"Took the words right out of my mouth", another said.

As Alexus was rinsing out her mouth with sink water,the guy withthe ugly face and chipped teeth whose name she thought was KC left therestroom."

"I really just did that, didn't I?" Alexus asked no one in particular.

She looked at herself in the mirror over the ruby colored marble sink.

Reggie walked up behind her, locked his mammoth, veiny black handsonto both sides of her waist, gold teeth aglitter.

"Ay, T-Walk," Reggie said, "we gotta keep her wit' us all night bruh,real shit, my nigga."

"Idon't think so, players,"Alexus retorted, turning around to look atthe two men.

T-Walk was a high yellow nigga. His pale blue stitched Gucci jogging suit looked appealing and debonair on him, in Alexus' opinion, and his matching sneakers set off the ghetto rich ensemble.

He reached in both pants pockets and took out a duo of rubber banded folds of cash. "How much I gottapay?" he asked nonchalantly.

"If you can't hold it without a duffle bag," Alexus said, "it's not enough money for me. I can upgrade you sweetie. No Beyonce, get your weight up off the ground and feed it steroids."

Reggie began laughing. His attire was simple: new looking white t-shirt over a wife beater, clean baggy Evizu jeans, and a pair of fresh white and blue Air Force Ones.

Alexus gave the guys a cocky grin then started toward the restroom door. Then gunfire cracked through the sound of Waka Flocka's *No hands* outside the restroom. Instinctively, Alexus dropped flat to the floor.

The first bullet grazed KG's left earlobe. He stumbled to the side, holding his tom ear with one hand, reaching out towards the grimly determined gunman with the other.

A few young women had been engaged deeply in conversation with KG and Squeaky near the door of the women's bathroom, loudly discussing the possible reasons why a fine young woman in a Versace dress would bring a group of men into the ladies room. Their inquiring minds went blank with fear at the sound of gunfire, and they scattered away, screaming their lungs out, running and pushing toward the front door like most other club patrons were wisely doing.

Young-D squeezed the trigger of his .38 special again, hitting KG's shoulder. He shot KG a third time in the abdomen, then turned the revolver on Squeaky and sent two rounds through his wide forehead.

"Snitch.'' Young-D hissed under his breath at Squeaky. He observed the two men crumple to the red marble floor. They were both dead, Young-D guessed. *Dead like they were supposed to be. Punk-ass niggas.*

On the vast wooden dance floor behind him, a large fight had broken out between the Dub Life goons and the Tenth Street Hustlers, butthe explosions from Young-D's gun ended all the punching. Now they were rushing out of the club.

His bandana still hiding half his face, Young-D tossed the revolver and watched it skitter across the floor, through brain matter, shattered skull fragments and blood.

Then he removed his bandana and gloves and became one with the stampeding crowd.

"Somebody's holding the door closed!" Alexus whispered, looking back at Reggie, T-Walk, and three frightened woman. "I can't get it open!""Move out the way." Reggie stepped past her and, after putting his

ear to the door to check for any unwanted noises, he delivered a powerful kick to the restroom door;there had certainly been something or someoneon the door, but the sheer force of Reggie's kick had pushed it back.

Alexus trailed T-Walk and Reggie out the door, stopped to view Squeaky's lifeless body, which had been the door blocker, then continued toward her table.

There were only fifteen or twenty people left inside the club. A few of them were grounded figures, either due to injuries or because they werehandcuffed. Alexus saw one guy splayed under a table with a set of Taserprongs stuck in his neck. Two police officers were escorting a profusely bleeding man outside. Over half the tables were overturned. Chairs were kicked over. The Swagger looked as if it's name should have been changedto The War Zone.

Alexus was momentarily worried that her purse may have been stolen; it wasn't on the table where she'd left it. But when she made it out to the parking lot, Kenya was standing beside the MKX with the purseunder her arm, talking to Cereniti and a policeman.

"Oh, thank God." Kenya said as she ran to Alexus and hugged her. "I didn't know where the heck you'd disappeared to. Tee-Tee and I were aboutto send the police on a manhunt."

"I'm fine." Alexus took her purse. Behind her she heard angry shouts, and vulgar words expressed in dissonant tones. She glanced back and shook her head incredulously. "These niggas just won't quit. I can'tbelieve this shit."

The two cliques- The Dub Life Goons and The Tenth

Street Hustlers -were standing in a formation that wassimilar to the way 106th and Park's "Wild Out Wednesday" dance crews stood, only difference being that Terrence and Rocsi were substituted by a crew of Taser holdingpoliceman.

"Let's get the hell out of here, yo,[11] Cereniti suggested.

Alexus fished in her purse for her keys and gave them to Kenya. "Here, you drive. I'm too damn tipsy."

"I bet you are," said Kenya. "You drank a whole bottle of champagne. I barely got a sip."

"Just take me home," Alexus replied.

The three of them got in the Lincoln, with Alexus taking to the backseat sothat shecould stretch out.

Starting the engine, Kenya confessed to why she and Cereniti hadnot come looking for Alexus in the club.

"As soon as they started brawling and throwing chairs, we got up tofind you. But I swear, like ten seconds after the fighting started, we heardgunshots."

"And got up out that piece," Cereniti added.

"KG got shot up real bad," Kenya said, backing out of the parking space."He's one of Bookie's friends."

"I just met him. maybe twenty minutes ago," Alexus said. "Didn't remember his name,.though. I wonder why Bookie's friends keep getting gunned down? They must be real trouble makers. Either that or they've got the worst luck ever. I thought living here was going to be, like I don't know like living on a farm or something.'

"They're always shooting around here." Kenya was maneuvering around through the crowd.

"That snitch got shot, too," Alexus said.

"Who, Squeaky?"

"Mmm hmm. Two to the head. He's..."

Alexus went silent as the bone chilling sound of machine gun blasts interrupted the night.

Kenya slammed her foot down on the gas pedal.

King Rio

Chapter 10

"Dub Life, bitch!" Blake kept saying. He didn't care that there werepolicemen mixed in with his targets. He was in a blind rage. He wanted them all to die for even being associated with Bookie. So he went on shooting, waving the AK-47 from side to side, watching as tires flattened and windows broke and people dropped like flies trapped in a fog of bug spray.

One officer returned fire after taking cover behind a dark colored minivan. But it was to no avail. Blake King's "choppa" struck the young white man twice in his throat, once below his left eyebrow, and the cop collapsed to the pavement, the innards of his skull fanning out next to him.

A pair of crimson lights flashed in Blake's periphery, and he turnedthe assault rifle that way.

But it was not a law enforcement vehicle as he'd expected; it wasa silver Lincoln MKX, veering wildly onto Michigan Boulevard, almost crashing head on with an El Camino that wasexiting a gas station acrossthe street.

Blake quickly resumed firing the AK-47, backpedaling in the direction of the dull blue Honda Civic he'd stolen an hour earlier. He hadonly a few bullets left in the fifty round banana clip. A second banana clip,duck taped upside down to the first, held another fifty bullets. He put in the fresh clip once the first was depleted, snatched open the driver's door of the Civic, and sent a dozen more shots spiraling through a patrol car nextto which he knew two offices were ducking.

A barrage of bullets pierced the Civics' passenger side as Blake racedpast two Swiss cheesed MCPD vehicles and out of the parking lot. Then he was barreling north down the boulevard, through a red light, past a small scale rim shop, and another gas station. Past a low income housingcomplex. Heslowed at Eleventh Street's train tracks and turned left.

A patrol carwas comingrightat him inthe laneon the other side ofthe tracks. Blake used a leg to hold the steering wheel straight, picked up the choppa from the passenger seat, and destroyed the

Civic's windshield shooting at the oncoming police car. He was amazed at how quickly his weapon punched holes in the policeman's windshield, wounding him critically, causing him to speed up onto the sidewalk and clip a light pole in the process.

Two more blocks west and one south, feeling as gangster and invincible as Al Capone in the late nineteen twenties, Blake parked the stolen car inside his sister-in-law Nicole's poorly painted garage and hastily stepped out of it to shut the wide door; he pulled it down with every ounce of his strength.

Only then, squatting in the darkness, breathing heavily, did he allow himself a brief moment to think.

Outside, it sounded as if every cop in the state of Indiana was on their way to the new shooting scene with their sirens singing an opera like song of chaos.

"Now rob me again," Blake said, speaking as though his shooting victim were present. "I double dare you."

Chapter 11

The package arrived at 10:38 the next morning. Rita Mae Bishop was out shopping for things she needed around the house. She'd beengone since a quarter after seven and Alexus figured her mother wouldn'tbe home for at least two more hours.

Alexus had been on Facebook chatting with some old friends from high school, adding new pictures of herself, accepting only four of twenty-seven friend requests when the doorbell chimed.

She moved nimbly to the front door in her most expensive article ofclothing a fifty four thousand dollar brown mink Louis Vuitton bathrobe.She had showered minutes earlier and sprayed on mist of pleasingly scented perfumed after applying her make-up. A pair of four inch Louis Vuitton heels raised her from 5'4 to 5'8."

A burly, fat nosed white man with a Geraldo mustache was placinga fourth unmarked cardboard box atop a stack of three others on the porchwhen Alexus opened the front door. His UPS uniform made her smile gratefully.

"I have four boxes for Alexus Costilla," he said. "Bring them in for me, will you?" Alexus took a step back and moved to the side. "Just put them by the couch."

He lifted the top box. "You hear what happened at that club last night? Seven wounded, three killed. Then the shooter killed another officer a few blocks up."

"I know. I was there. Somebody else was killed in the club too, it was crazy."

"Yeah, I saw that on MSNBC. Cops say they ain't sure who killed the guy in the club or shot the other guys in there, but they are searching forthe psycho who killed those two officers. Hope they catch the bastard."

"I was just watching Val Warner talk about it on Channel nine. She said the second officer was only in critical condition." Alexus caught the older man staring at her as he stacked a third box next to the couch; sheturned away uncomfortably and said, "Let's hurry and get these boxes in here. My boyfriend's on his way over and he'll snap if he sees me alone with another man."

"Hell, I'd snap myself." He studied Alexus's robe for a moment, yanking up his slacks. "You're like a fine wine, young lady: you'll only get better with time. I've never in my years seen a woman with an ass like yours. I can see it through the bathrobe."

Alexus giggled shyly, embarrassed but not knowing why. She signed for the delivery and he was gone.

Her heart started pounding the very instant the UPS man departed. She went to the kitchen immediately afterward, located the can opener and a steak knife, and returned to the living room feeling light headed and thirsty for monetary gain.

Anxiously, Alexus cut though the tape holding the top of the box shut. Inside it she found twelve large cans of Campbell's tomato soup. She took one can to the glass topped coffee table, attached a manual can opener to it, and held her breath as she opened it.

The aluminum inside the can had a layer of Vaseline on it like a gelatinous skin, held in place by a second skin of cellophane. A compressed, football shaped, cellophane wrapped kilogram of cocaine was stuffed in the can.

In all, Alexus had forty eight kilos. She owed Savio $240,000 for the shipment- $5,000 per kilo- and there was no set time for payment.

Rolling the kilogram between her small hands, she looked up at the wall mounted television. The Wendy Williams show was on. Alexus silently admired Wendy's jewelry, that fat sparkling wedding ring, and wondered if she herself would ever get married.

But her iPhone rang before she thought too much about that. It was Cereniti, calling to let Alexus know that she was two streets from the house.

"So have the door open. I think my bladder is about to call it quits, yo," Cereniti said. "Have you been out yet?"

"No, not today." Alexus didn't want Cereniti around the shipment of drugs. Setting the open can back in the box, she stuck her phone between her ear and shoulder and was just readying to hide the boxes when the thought struck her. No one would be able to wrap their minds around the notion of drugs filled canned goods, and with the Vaseline covered inside, not even a drug sniffing K-9 could find the dope.

So, instead of moving any boxes, Alexus tucked the can she'd opened behind a couch pillow and left the kilo on the coffee table.

"It's a good thing you haven't," Cereniti was saying. "They got the FBI out here! Everywhere you look. Like we in Harlem or something, yo." "You love you some Harlem, don't you?" Alexus went to the living room window and peeked out the blinds. "I figured the Feds would be in town after last night. That was this city's deadliest day in half a century. And I heard that the other officer who was shot died, too."

"Kenya told me the same thing. She just made it back to East Lansing. I gave her five thousand and told her "I'll be gone till November." Cereniti laughed excitedly.

"Girl, you are too ratchet for me, "Alexus said. "Why didn't you go with her? Don't you have classes today?"

"I quit school."

"You what?"

"You heard me right, yo. I'm done. That nerdy shit ain't for me. I want some real money."

"Nuh uh. There won't be no dropping out. I need you in college," Alexus demanded. She wanted educated friends. A whole crew of them. Those were the ones Papi had always suggested that she hang around.

"I'm not saying I quit," Cereniti said as she parked a new looking Chrysler 300C behind Alexus' SUV. "I'm just going to give it a rest for a while. See how far you can get me."

"Nice car," Alexus said, eyeing the silver painted Phantom look alike. "It's the same color as my truck."

"That's why I bought it. So we can slide through back to back on these ignorant bitches."

Cereniti was out of the car, sprinting up the front steps in a hurry, her gray trench coat billowing out around the calves of her blue denim leggings. Alexus loved a woman in high heels. To her, it bespoke power in a woman, and Cereniti was rocking a pair of gray high heeled boots.

Alexus barely had the door open when Cereniti breezed and ran to the bathroom. A moment later as she stepped out to the living room and said, "What's that?" She pointed at the kilo, draping her coat over the arm of the sofa. "That what I think it is?"

"I believe so." Alexus was back at the window, staring out at two black Ford sedans that were parked in front of a church halfway down the block. "If you're talking about thirty six ounces of coke.

"You serious, yo?" Cereniti walked around the couch and picked up the dope. "Holy shit, son! This really is a fucking key! How in the hell did you get it so fast?"

"I have my ways. You know anybody I can sell that to?"

"Of course. But they're all in New York. That's a long ass drive." "Not an issue." Alexus joined Cereniti on the sofa, being careful to sit in front of the pillow that concealed the empty Campbell's can. "You can fly to New York and I'll have the coke delivered to you the next day. All I want out of it is fifteen thou' a key."

Thoughtfully, Cereniti fingered the dangling edge of one of her braids. She had a cashmere sweater on that was the same shade of gray as her heels.

"I'll have to make some phone calls," Cereniti said. "I know Tasia can sell them like crazy in the *"N"*, yo. She's out there in zone six. East Atlanta. They'll come for a hundred bricks at a time. That's Gucci Mane's hood."

"Help me with these boxes." Alexus stood up. "And tell me more about Tasia. I thought you said she left you for dead."

"She did. She was scared. That's still my bitch, though. We grew up together."

Cereniti then watched as Alexus shed the mink robe, exposing a Louis Vuitton bra and panties set.

"You trust her?" Alexus lifted the box she'd cut open and started up the stairs to her bedroom. "I mean, you have to really trust her. We need a solid, loyal team. A dedicated team,"

"I know that already, yo." Cereniti was close behind Alexus. "Tasia's down to get some money. It's all I've ever known her to do. Even when we were kids. Bitch used to sell kisses at recess. As soon as she hears about you. Tasia will be at your front door. No question about it."

"Nuh uh." Alexus set the box on her bedroom floor. "Nobody needs to know me. All you have to do is establish a steady clientele. I'll give you all the drugs you can sale. Just keep my name out of the mix."

Gazing down into the open box that Alexus had carried in, Cereniti said, "Bitch, I know you ain't got me moving around no damn tomato soup. And wouldn't' it make sense to put it in the kitchen?"

Alexus ignored the inquiry and went for the other boxes. Her mind was swarming with ideas. Would Craig hold true to his word and get rid of the coke like he said he could? She hoped so.

After sending Cereniti to Wal-Mart for a money safe, Alexus set to work opening the tomato soup cans in her bedroom. She placed the kilos side by side in one of the Louis Vuitton suitcases that Papi had purchased for their travels. She owned three of them.

As she was dropping the twentieth kilo into the suitcase and, tossing the nineteenth Campbell's can beside her bed- she had retrieved the other kilo from downstairs- someone began knocking at the door. "Who is it?" Alexus shouted. She zipped the suitcase shut, listening for an answer. There was none. Only more heavy knocks. On her way to see who was banging at the door, Alexus put on her robe again. She froze as the image of the black Ford sedans surfaced in her mind. Always the cautious one, she went to the living room window and snuck a glance at the front porch.

No one was there. And the Fords were gone now. "Crazy kids." Alexus said, automatically assuming some bored little rug rat as the culprit. But the knocking came again, reverberating from the rear of the house, and Alexus realized that it was somebody at the back door.

"I said, *who is it?* You deaf or something?" At the back door, which opened into the kitchen, Alexus stopped with her hand on the doorknob.

"It's me, Blake."

Alexus put her hands on her hips. "Sorry, but you are about twenty hours too late. I found a man who knows the value of keeping his word, you liar."

She heard him laughing through the door, and it didn't sit well with her. She unlocked the door and snatched it open.

"What the hell is so funny?" She snapped.

"What's funny?" Blake's laughter attenuated as his eyes absorbed the beautiful girl in front of him, she was a paragon of beauty in her flowing mink bathrobe, and a picture of Kimora Lee Simmons flashed in his mind for some reason.

"That's what I said, Einstein. Did I miss the joke? What's so damn hilarious?" Alexus said.

"Nothin just .... Nothin." Blake grabbed a few chips from his bag of Doritos and crammed them in his mouth. "Get me somethin' to drink."

"I don't think so, sweetie," Alexus said, but Blake pushed past her, anyway, and opened the refrigerator.

"Orange juice," he said, taking out a half gallon jug of Tropicana. "You got good taste. This my shit here." He twisted the top off and drank.

Crossing her arms over her chest, Alexus glared at Blake for a moment before closing the door with her heel.

"You know", she said, "I could shoot you right now and get away scot-free."

"You ain't gon' do shit," Blake said casually as he closed the fridge and seated himself on a white painted ladder-back chair by the kitchen table, holding the juice on his lap.

Alexus kept staring at him, like she wanted to kill him.

Consuming more of the juice, with his weary eyes locked on Alexus, Blake took his .40 caliber from his waist and slid it across the table.

"Start bussin," he said.

"Don't test me, cowboy. I'll pop one in your fat belly."

"I'll pop on yo belly and I ain't talking 'bout no bullet either." Blake grinned affectionately. "Pop one in you, too. Make you fat like me."

"Why didn't you come pick me up? I almost froze my butt off waiting on you."

"That ass ain't going nowhere."

Alexus sucked her teeth, scowling again.

"A'ight, a'ight," Blake said with a chuckle. "Somebody stole my Chevy. It's impounded now. Don't know when I'm gon' get my whip back."

"Okay hit me with the next excuse, 'cause you was better off saying the dog ate it."

"I don't do no lying." Blake put the gun back on his waist and finished off the juice. He pushed the empty container down inside a large garbage bag beside the refrigerator. "And what's up with you not answering the phone?"

"My fingers were too cold to press any buttons."

"Yeah, and my dog ate my car."

Finally, Alexus smiled. "I should've shot you when I had the chance. Bastard!" Blake stepped in front of her, and she rubbed her thumb tips over the bags under his eyes. "Boy, you look so sleepy. When's the last time you slept?"

Blake had been awake since around 2:00 am, when a battering ram had crashed his girlfriend's apartment door to pieces. They were searched and handcuffed, Blake caught a number of punches and elbows while being extensively groped then forced to lay and watch as uniformed officers tore their place apart. Savaria's screaming cries had attracted a few neighbors to the door of the small two bedroom apartment but by that time the mayhem was at an end, and homicide detective Neal Miller was escorting Blake out of Southgate apartments in back of a jet black Dodge Charger. Blake had requested to have an attorney present, and after a seven hour hold, during which time they failed to discover any solid leads or evidence on the club shooting, the MCPD had to release him.

On second thought, Blake decided against explaining the homicide investigations to Alexus. It was none of her business in the first place.

Instead of going into details, he said, "I'm tired 'cause I ain't had no pussy to put me to sleep. What happened to all that 'we gon' be fuckin' in a Lexus today' shit?"

Her smile grew steadily, as she spread her robe open, exposing her tan bra and her flat abdomen. "The dealership I went to didn't have a Lexus on hand." She separated the robe some more. "I'm Alexus, though. You can still fuck in Alexus."

Blake went to the sink to wash the Doritos crumbs from his fingers. Then Alexus grabbed a hold of his wrist and proceeded to her upstairs bedroom.

Chapter 12

Seventy four year old Vida Costilla sounded worried.

"How's Alexus doing out there? Does she need anything? Tell her I said to call me sometime today."

"I'll tell her when I get home, Vida. I would call her but that girl doesn't believe in answering her phone." Rita Mae Bishop was pushing a shopping cart through the electronics section of Meijers Department Store.

"So, what are you going to do in Indiana?" Vida asked. "And how much money do you have left?"

"I'm fine. I plan on getting a business loan and opening a jewelry store, maybe convince Alexus to go to college. She's spoiled like me, though. I haven't worked since Juan and I met." Rita dropped a coffee maker and a blender into the cart. "Hopefully the bank will accept my proposal and grant me the loan. If not, hey..."

"No no no no no," Vida said. "I'll give you the money, today. I'll wire it to you and ⎯ "

"No, I'll be fine."

"You won't owe me a cent, not one of 'em, you hear? Not one red cent."

"I said I'm fine," Rita said sternly. She had long since grown sick of

being supported by the Costilla's drug money, and the raid was the *very* last straw.

"I'll have my accountant wire the money to you," Vida went on, ignoring Rita's words. "If you don't want it, give it to my granddaughter. You know Juan wouldn't have you living with little money. Not for one second. And I'm not going to stand for it either, you hear?"

"Have you spoken with him?"

"I'm sending the money," repeated the persistent older woman.

"Okay..." Rita replied, but it was only to keep Ms. Vida from repeating herself again. "Have you spoken with Juan?"

Vida paused, and Rita knew the old lady was vexed with her for turning down money. Vida was used to lavish spending on gifts for Alexus and Rita and anyone else that she'd taken a liking to. She owned achain of nineteen Mexican restaurants in Mexico, Texas, and Arizona, anda five star hotel in Cancun, Mexico. Rita was uncertain as to exactly how much money Vida was worth, but she suspected eight figures at the veryleast.

While awaiting Vida's response, Rita waved over a male employee and requested his aid in loading a microwave into the cart; it took him several attempts but he eventually got it in there. As she was thanking him Vida finallyspoke.

"He called this morning. Said to tell you to get collect calling foryour home phone. And keep Alexus from spending all that money at once. You know she'llpractically give it away."

"All of what money?" Rita asked, but then she remembered her daughter's brand new luxurySUV.

"Now you know we can't speak freely on these devices," Vida reprimanded. "I'll have that money in your account within the next couple of hours. Make sure..."

Vida's last sentence was drowned out by a loud beeping sound thatRita surmised was a truck in reverse. Then the call was over, and Rita found herself praying again.

"Lord God in heaven, give me the strength and patience to deal with my daughter without me having to bust her pretty little head..."

Vida Costilla's young Mexican driver was like a husband in manyways, always there when she needed him the most, opening doors and carrying luggage and driving her around in her sleek Rolls Royce.

As they stood behind Vida's restaurant watching her grandson Savio back a nondescript semi-trailer up to the loading dock, the youngdriver covered her ears to ease the sound of the truck's loud beeping.

"Gracias," she said to him, then repeated herself a second later after

the tacit young gentleman raised a chilled bottle of Evian

water to her thin lips for a drink.

His name was Enrique Aleman, the estranged son of Felipe Manuel Aleman who was now president of the United Mexican States. Enrique was also a hired assassin or an "assassino" for the Costilla Cartel.

Enrique's sole purpose of employment was protecting Vida Costilla, because she was the oldest living member of the elite family of drug traffickers, which had been founded by her deceased husband, Segovia Costilla.

Standing beside Vida, wearing a white Canali business suit with a striped Burberry tie and pricey pair of Burberry loafers with a fully automatic Mac-11 handgun in one hand, Enrique carefully surveyed the area, as if someone was actually crazy enough to climb over the fifteen foot high brownstone wall, or attempt to crash through the solid iron gates.

As Vida shuffled forward, her vintage Prada pantsuit blowing in the dry breeze, she focused her aging mind on the shipment that was in back of the semi-trailer.

There were a thousand kilograms of cocaine, five hundred kilos of heroin, and one thousand pounds of Kush weed, all of which were concealed inside large odor-proof aluminum Campbell's cans. The cans were packed together inside tall boxes that were long enough to hold coffins. Soon the boxes would be removed from the semi-trailer on a forklift and taken through the family tunnel to Jennifer's house.

Savio and Santiago Costilla climbed down from the semi and briskly approached Vida in finely tailored white Armani suits and white alligator shoes.

Vida's wrinkled and age spotted hand and grabbed Savio,s ear and she pulled it close to her her. Alexus," she said in a hoarse whisper, "Do you think she's ready to join the family business?"

"I sent her forty-eight bricks,'' Savio said, shrugging. "Maybe she's ready. I don't know. We find out, though."

" You can give a bird wings, but you can't make it fly."

"Birds grow their own wings, grandma.''

"That's what I just said." Vida pinched Savio's ear. He winced and grinned simultaneously. "I think Alexus will be good for the business. Aslong as she ventures out of Indiana and gets a bit of that Chicago money.''

"But what about Aunt Rita? You know she's not going to allow

Alexus to do *anything* illegal. "

"I'll take care of that situation." Vida released her grandson's ear. She thought for a moment, and then said, "You ever hear of the divide andconquer strategy?"

Chapter 13

Alexus had her face buried in a pillow and her ass in the air, and Blake appreciated the view as he held on to her narrow waist, ramming his rigid dick in and out of her warm, dripping pussy with extreme speed. He was surprised at how tight and gushy she was down there, and he told her this.

"Shut up," Alexus moaned in reply. "Just keep going. Beat this pussy till ... ooh till I say stop."

Blake tried to push all of his eleven inches into Alexus, causing her to close her eyes tightly and scream into the pillow. He was holding her panties to the side, looking down in awe at his cream glazed member.

"Damn, this shit wet as..." Blake said, but he was so into pounding Alexus out, that he couldn't finish his sentence.

The doorbell chimed suddenly, and it seemed to be just what was needed to push both Alexus and Blake over the edge; her inner muscles began to spasmodically contract around his swollen muscle, and her sweet fluids belched out over him. At the same instant Blake dug in as far as he could and spilled a geyser of semen inside her.

"Ooo shit, boy," Alexus gasped as Blake rolled off of her and collapsed onto his back.

"That's gotta be the wettest pussy I done had," Blake admitted, slinging an arm around her, so he could caress her full backside. The doorbell rang again.

Alexus turned to face Blake with half her head sunken into the pillow. "I have to ...get that ... don't I?" She asked breathlessly.

Blake chuckled. "Go answer the door, lil mama. I ain't goin nowhere." He smacked her ass and rubbed it.

With a great deal of reluctance, Alexus got out of bed and put on her robe. "I've got something for you when I get back." She glanced down at her Louis Vuitton suitcase. "Don't go through none of my shit, either."

Pulling the sheets up over his lower half, Blake grabbed his .40 caliber from a wooden bedside table and laid it next to him.

"Lock the door behind you."

"You're safe here, fat man," said Alexus, but she did as Blake had asked.

Lying back on the bed, staring up at the white stucco ceiling, Blake King wandered how he'd managed to bed a girl as perfectly built and sexy as Alexus.

Blake looked over to the left of him, at a bunch of empty Campbell's Tomato sauce cans. "What the hell?" He said to himself as he picked up a can. A greasy material got on his fingers as he inspected it, and his mind couldn't fathom a single thought about why Alexus had grease coated cans on her floor. *Where they do that at?* His eyelids were heavy. He returned the strange can to its resting place and closed his eyes.

Cereniti entered the living room holding three big Burberry shopping bags in each hand. Bookie followed her, carrying a heavy looking box that had an image of a gray steel Remington safe with a digital keypad on it's top.

"Where'd you run into him?" Alexus asked Cereniti. Eyeing her cousin, Alexus noticed that he seemed sad again, and there were light traces of powder on his nose and the front of his pale yellow Coogi sweater.

"I stopped by your uncle's place to pick up some clothes and some other stuff I left in Kenya's room," said Cereniti as she plopped down on the sofa. "That's a high tech safe, yo. It's an upgraded version of the one I had when I was dancing. Fireproof, drill proof, changeable code. If somebody get inside that safe it's cause you let 'em."

"Hmm." Alexus was still watching Bookie. He sat on the arm of the sofa and began flipping through channels on the flat screen television.

He said, "I wish you wouldn't have moved here at a time like this, cuz." Tears filled his somber eyes. "Five people got killed last night. My nigga Mone died. My nigga Dave died. My nigga KG. got hit three times, Squeaky's police ass got killed. Two cops got knocked." He wiped his eyes, shaking his head. Cops think it was the same muhfucka who murked Johnny."

"I was there last night," Alexus said.

"I told him that," Cereniti said. "Shit was mad wild up in that piece. I couldn't believe it."

Alexus felt Blake's cum soaking through her panties, wetting her inner thighs. She pressed her legs together, lowered her eyes to the floor, and allowed a quick image of Blake's nakedness to skate across her mind. She felt bad doing this, thinking about Blake while her own cousin was so visibly distraught.

Cereniti was inconsiderate in the matter of Bookie's bereavement; she started pulling Burberry hats and scarves and belts and outfits from the bags, smiling radiantly as she showed then to Alexus.

"They got a Burberry outlet at that mall up the street, Cereniti said. "I went crazy in there. Spent damn near three stacks."

"I see." Alexus picked up her cell phone from the sofa. "Bookie, will you take the safe up to my ... um ... to the top of the stairs, outside my bedroom door? It's right across from the bathroom."

Bookie lifted the heavy box. "Want me to just put it in..." "No, the top of the stairs is fine."

As Bookie started up the stairs, Alexus' phone rang; the ring tone was Tupac's melodious "Dear Mama" let her know that it was her grandmother Vida calling. She took the phone to the kitchen to answer it.

"Hey, grandma!" Alexus exclaimed. "You around anybody, Lexi?" Vida Costilla asked.

"I know better than that by now, grandma. I'm by myself."

There was a pause, then Vida said, "Loose lips sink ships. You know that, right?"

"Here we go again." Alexus exhaled sharply. "Papi taught me more than you think."

"Si...si," said Vida. "So... you ready to join us? On this music business thing, I mean."

"I already have. I'm out promoting a tour now. The first concert starts in forty-eight hours."

"I heard about that. That tour's a small show. I'm thinking of expanding your stable of singers."

"Sounds good to me."

"You can't stay with your mother, though." "Huh?" Alexus's

eyebrows shot up.

"Rita's never been involved with the family business," Vida said,just verifying her previous statement. "She doesn't understand our way of living. She can't embrace our concepts, our ideas. Everything is about God with her. If he thinks something's wrong, so does she. We can't have that."

"I'm not leaving my momma." Alexus was vexed. "And please don'tbring religion into this, grandma. I goto church every Sunday, too."

"Will you be silent and use your ears, Lexi?"

Alexus sucked her teeth and poked out her lips, pouting belligerently. What the hell was grandma thinking? "You can't stay with your mother?" *This old bitch is trippin,* Alexus thought.

"Now, listen," said Vida. "I'm not asking you to move back to Brownsville, nor Mexico. You'll be right around the corner from Rita. It's the nicest house in the neighborhood, a four bedroom with two bathrooms, a finished basement, and a two car garage. It was just recentlyremodeled. How's that sound?"

Alexus was speechless as she twirled a ringlet of her long hair around her finger.

"How that sound?" Vida repeated.

"It sounds good, grandma."

"I've set up an account in your name at First Source Bank. Deposited two million in it."

"What!" Alexus leaped into the air, overwhelmed with excitement.

Bookie and Cereniti rushed to the kitchen to see what Alexus was soenthused about.

"Settle down, Lexi. Just settle on down, "said Vida. "Invest some of that in real estate."

"Savio told me how to do it, grandma. Thank you so much. I loveyou, I love you, I love you!" Alexus was all smiles. She sat at the kitchen table to keep from running through the house like a hyperactive child. As she jotted down the locations of the house and the bank Alexus couldnot stop fidgeting. *Two million dollars!* She thought, picturing herself in a Rolls Royce like Grandma's. Or maybe a Bentley like the one Papi once owned.

Alexus sat her phone down on the table after ending the call and looked over to Bookie, who was dumping the remainder of Blake's bag of Doritos in his mouth. Cereniti was behind him, hands on his shoulders, gazing intently at Alexus.

"Who was that, yo?" Cereniti asked.

"Nobody," Alexus stood, looking at her cousin. "I'm giving you twenty kilos to get rid of. Lay ten of them on your guy, and bring me that sixty thousand he said he had. After that you'll owe me two hundred and forty grand. Deal?"

Cereniti's mouth dropped open. "She wasn't bullshittin', Book!"

"Guess she wasn't." Bookie sealed the deal by shaking hands with Alexus. "I got you cuz."

"I'm serious, Bookie," Alexus said sternly, "I need my money.

There's no room for error."

"I said I got you."

"Good, because next time it'll be a hundred bricks, same price." She leaned down and hugged her sullen faced cousin; then grabbed a hold of Cereniti's wrist and yanked her out of the kitchen. "Stay there, Bookie."

As she was being dragged up the stairs by Alexus, Cereniti said, "Slow down, b. Fuck is wrong with—"

"Can't slow down," Alexus replied quickly. "Gotta go meet up with this real estate agent to sign some," she knocked on her bedroom door, "papers and get the keys to my house."

"Bitch, you made me hit my toe on that safe." Cereniti raised a boot and massaged the tip of it. "Why are you knockin on your own door? You got some nigga in there?"

Alexus knocked again. "Did you call that girl in Atlanta?"

"Yeah, I talked to her; she's ready whenever you are."

Blake opened the door in his boxers, looking half awake, with his gun in hand. He immediately returned to bed and was asleep before Alexus had even rolled her suitcase out of the bedroom.

The heavy suitcase thumped loudly as she wheeled it down to the living room, and she remembered how difficult it had been to move it off her bed before she had sex with Blake.

Alexus retrieved a heavy-duty trash bag from the kitchen. She and Bookie then carefully placed the twenty kilos inside the bag, while Cereniti stood off to the side with her hands on her hips, mumbling something about Harlem.

"I ain't never in my life seen this much dope," Bookie admitted, swinging the bulging black plastic bag over his shoulder as if he was Santa Claus. "Wait till Craig see this shit, He ain't gon' believe it."

"Just get rid of it, "Alexus said. "And please keep my name out of every conversation you have."

Bookie carried the forty-four pounds of cocaine to the front door. "I'm a street nigga, cuz," he said and opened the door. "Been sellin dope since I was twelve. I don't do no whole lotta talkin. I'ma slang these bricks and get that bread straight to you. That's my word."

Alexus leaned a shoulder against the doorframe and watched as Bookie stuffed the bag in the trunk of a deep maroon Cadillac Sedan Deville. When he was gone, she wondered if he'd return with the money. He could easily skip town with the dope. Pop back up months later with empty pockets and a mouthful of apologies. It was a part of the dope game. Happened all the time.

"Who was that upstairs?" Cereniti asked as she stepped behind Alexus, resting her chin on Alexus' back.

"He's a friend of mine." "You fuck him?"

Alexus shut the door and turned around. "I'm afraid I did." She giggled softly, gazing into Cereniti's eyes. "It was good too. First time I've ever had a boy in my bed. Papi would have snapped."

"I knew I smelled sex."

"Let's sit down for a minute," Alexus said, stepping around the sofa. "I need to run a few things by you."

They sat down, and Alexus turned off the television. She gathered her thoughts, trying to be as lucid and concise as humanly possible in expressing her plans.

"First off," she started, "what kind of car should I get ... a Rolls Royce, a Bentley or a Lexus? I really want a Lexus, but that's only because of my name."

Cereniti's eyebrows rose. "You got that kind of cake?"

80

"That was not an answer."

"A Rolls, I guess. I don't know. Rolls Royces are nice. And Bentleys, too. I'd get either a Rolls or a Bentley."

"What about the house? If you were about to start paying a contractor to fix up your house so you could resell them, how many estates would you buy to begin with? I'm thinking two or three. Four at the most." Alexus stood up again and commenced pacing in a tight circle. "What do you think about that?"

"Real estate ain't the best market to invest in right now, yo. For real. You might lose your money."

"Nuh uh. No, I won't lose a dime. I'll pay for a house with the money I have in the bank, then use drug money to restore it. That way I'll be able to launder the drug money, and even if I only make two hundred thousand off a property that I paid one fifty for, I'm still winning because I'll only be legitimizing my money. See what I'm saying? I could lose money and still win."

After a minute of thought, Cereniti nodded, agreeing with her friend. "That makes sense, I guess," she said, staring up at Alexus.

"I know it makes sense. My cousins became luxury real estate specialists in less than eighteen months. And they did it by following three basic rules: buy cheap; improve at low cost; and sell high. I'll be sitting on ten or twenty million in no time."

"Sounds like you got it all worked out."

"I do. I've been planning my come-up ever since I was fifteen. I can't even count how many times I studied online for my real estate license." Alexus picked up her empty suitcase, her mind reeling with ideas of how to get rid of the remaining twenty-eight kilos of coke.

"So," Cereniti said, leaning back on a pillow, "where do I fit into all this money you're talkin' about?"

"Right in the middle." Alexus stopped at the coffee table, grabbed the remote, and turned on the TV. She surfed through channels until she found CNN. "I don't want you doing too much right away, Tee-Tee. Let's see how Bookie acts with all that stuff first. I'm going to front Blake the same amount, and we can get your old stripper friend eight, if you trust her to pay up."

Cereniti sucked her teeth in angst. *"Exotic..."*

"Okay, okay, exotic dancer. We can send her eight bricks, and" Alexus mentally calculated the price she'd charge Cereniti for the cocaine. "You'll owe me only twelve thousand per kilo. That should give you enough leeway to sell them for fifteen or sixteen apiece and still make akiller profit.''

Both Cereniti and Alexus grew silent as two daunting sentences streamed across the television screen's bottom: *4 civilians and two policeman killed in deadly Northwest Indiana shootings, Local law enforcement and FBI ask for public's help in naming a suspect.*

"Wonder who in the hell that"suspect" is, yo", Cereniti said.

Alexus shook her head, sickened by the harsh reality of inner violence. "Truthfully, I don't even want to know what his name is. I just hope I never meet him."

"I know *that's* right!" Cereniti laughed. She high-fived Alexus.

Then Alexus Costilla zipped her suitcase closed and told her New York friend to follow her back up to the bedroom, so she could meet Blake.

Chapter 14

Homicide detective Neal Miller became elated when Timothy Trice's eyelids finally fluttered open; Tim-Tim's left eye was swollen shut, completely black in color, and there were twelve stitches surgicallyembedded beside it. The bridge of his nose was stitched as well, as his beaten in forehead.

He looked as if he'd flown through a windshield.

"Good afternoon Mr. Trice," said the beaming detective. "Been waiting on you to wake up. You ready to talk now, or do you want to restup a week or two in county jail?"

A pain filled groan crawled out of Timothy's throat. He tried raisinghis right hand, but it was handcuffed to the bedrail.

"Oh," said Miller, chuckling, "I meant to tell you, you're under arrestfor the murder ofJohnny Lay."

Timothy responded quickly. "I didn't even shoot him."

"I know you didn't. In fact, I believe I know who did. But none of that really matters. We pulled your fingerprints from a pistol that waslefton the murder scene. Got five eyewitnesses who remember seeing you jump out of Blake King's car and dropthe gun in the street. If you weren't the gunman, you were with him. That's all I needed."

Miller saw the fear register in the young man's eyes. Timothy was mulling over the notion of being charged with murder, an idea thatunnerved him. His chest expanded as he inhaled the lingering scent ofdisinfectants. He looked to the other side of his bed and saw a tall whiteman in a navy blue windbreaker with FBI stenciled over its breast pocket. "That's special agent Josh Sneed over there," Miller said. "I losttwo great officers last night. Some punk with an *AK* thought he was Scarface." Stretching his legs out before him, Miller adjusted his gray tie. "My FBI friends are anxious to find the punk who gunned down my officers."

"We certainly are." Sneed's tone was crisp and threatening.

Miller continued. "Right now, Mr. Trice, we have enough evidence to send you to prison for a very long time. Sixty-five years, to be exact. And once we connect Johnny Lay's murder to those slain officers, you'll becharged for those as well. They'll more than likely send you down to thatFederal prison in Terre Haute then, to wait your death sentence. TimothyMcVeigh was executed there back in '01. Maybe you'll be the next Timothyto getthe needle."

"Man I was in this hospital when that club shit happened," said Tim-Tim. "And I ain't shoot nobody."

"So, who did?" Miller leaned forward in the chair, his veiny brown hands clamping the knees of his gray slacks. "Who killed Johnny Lay? If you tell us who fired that AK-47, I'll take these cuffs off and let you go home to your mother. I promise!"

Timothy Trice's chest rose again as he took another deep breath. Hestared at the FBI agent, saying nothing. Then his eye went back to the homicide detective.

"What's it gonna be, Timothy?" asked Miller. "The decision is all yours. I can call the prosecutor and have your charge dismissed, and youcan be a free man in lessthan an hour."

"Man," Timothy said dryly, "all y'all bitches can suck my dick!"

Ten minutes later, Miller and special agent Sneed were in the detective's black charger. They were on their way to MCPD headquarters,conveniently located near a courthouse on east Washington Street.

Sneed finished his Marlboro cigarette before clearing his throat to speak. His voice seemed robotic and overly authoritative. "Surveillance teams were called off of Blake King's suspected drug house at noon. Theorder came from down from assistant director Charles Byrd," said Sneed."According to him, it's a waste of manpower that the Bureau can't afford withoutevidence."

Releasing a breath of frustration, Miller retorted, "What do you mean a waste of manpower? No evidence! King's vehicle was used in that first shooting. I've got twelve eyewitnesses who can testify to seeing his car speeding away after Lay was killed."

Sneed tossed up his hands in mock surrender. "Hey, don't shoot the messenger." He ran a palm over his short crop of Anderson Cooper likehair. "And besides, Byrd's got a point. There's nothing solid connecting King to any of this. He reported his car stolen before the shooting. Who's to say his car *wasn't* stolen? Who's to say he isn't actually free of guilt, a mere victim of circumstance?"

"That's bullshit, and you know it, Sneed."

"It's not bullshit. You may be pursing the wrong man, Miller. I understand that he's your only suspect, but we must be open minded with this investigation. We have to help each other."

It was at this time Miller remembered why he had never appreciated sharing pertinent info with FBI... they thought they knew everything. Intrinsically, they all seemed self-absorbed, a characteristic that Miller found supremely annoying. He'd been dealing with them on and off for nearly twenty years, and every one of them acted the same.

"Well," Miller said, "how do you explain Trice's involvement in all this? He's a close friend of King's. Why would he be in King's car if it was stolen, huh?"

"Didn't you see his face? I think King may have heard something about Trice being seen in his car after it was stolen. Maybe he kicked Trice's ass about it. Sounds pretty logical, doesn't it?"

Miller hadn't thought about that angle. "I suppose it does. But, Trice could have also been beaten for running."

True, but we don't know who it was he was running from. I mean, it *could* have been King, but that's only speculation. *Loosely based* speculation. Federal indictments can't be served on anyone as of right now, and we can't just go around accusing people."

"Listen Sneed," Miller said desperately, "I have two dead officers on my hands. I've got to arrest somebody."

The only significant lead we have is Timothy Trice. If he doesn't crack, and if no one else comes forward with information on these murders, we're looking at a cold case."

Miller was determined not to let that happen.

King Rio

Chapter 15

Sadness surrounded Rita Mae Bishop, as she gazed at a picture she'd just taken from her powder blue Coach purse. It captured her and Juan outside the Bellagio Hotel & Casino in Las Vegas, Nevada, hugged together in a lover's embrace beside a white Lamborghini they'd rented. The picture had been snapped on an ebullient mid-June night last year, anhour before Juan had finally admitted to being a drug lord.

Five days later Rita had filed for divorce.

For too many years, Juan Costilla had been deceiving Rita, telling her that hewas an executive of his mother's restaurant business.

And she'd foolishly believed him.

But Alexus had known of her father's misdeeds all along. She'd sat at dining room table with him at times when Rita wasn't present watching and sometimes even helping him open up tall aluminum cansof cocaine and heroin; learning the prices and how to traffic the drugs from stateto state. Papi had always told her to keep her mouth shut abouthis business. No one was to know, especially not Rita.

So Alexus had started a diary. In it she wrote liberally, expressing her thoughts on everything from boyfriends to the lessons Papi had taught her.

Rita had discovered the diary in a purse she'd borrowed from her daughter the night before she and Juan boarded the private jet to Las Vegas. She had read it from beginning to end in less than thirty minutes; she could have finished it in twenty, if she hadn't been crying.

Now, as she sat behind the wheel of the u-haul truck, parked at Citgo gas station on Michigan Boulevard, Rita found herself crying again.But this time she wasn't crying because she felt betrayed and hood winked. It was loneliness. Loneliness and anger. She hated Juan for leaving her alone, for not loving her and their daughter enough to say goodbye to the drug game when he'd had the chance.

Sniffling and wiping her eyes, Rita took a small bible from her purseand slipped the picture between its pages. She muttered a brief prayer, asking God to cure her of her loneliness. Then she put the Bible on the seat next to her and pushed open her door.

A middle-aged black man had been walking pass the u-haul at that very moment, and Rita's door slammed against the back of his black leather jacket.

"Oh God, I'm so sorry!" exclaimed Rita as she climbed out of the truck, shouldering her purse.

The thick bearded man turned to face her. "It's okay, ma'am. I'm fine." He had a professional look about him, like maybe he was a school teacher of some sort.

"I can't believe I did that", Rita said.

"It's nothing. I've been hit harder in training." He extended his hand to shake Rita's. "I'd accept an apology over dinner, if you'd allow me that honor and I must say, it would *truly* be an honor."

Rita shook his hand, checking his other one for a ring. There wasn't one. *Well,* she thought to herself, *God sure works fast!*

"I'm Rita Mae Bishop," she said, gazing into his deep brown eyes. She thought he looked a lot like the actor Morgan Freeman. "And I guess I'll be apologizing over dinner."

He smiled appreciatively." I'm Neal Miller, chief homicide de- tective of the Michigan City Police Department."

"Alexus, what in the world is *taking* you so long, yo!? I could've gotten pregnant and had a *baby* by now!"

"Will you be quiet and exercise a little patience, Tee-Tee," Alexus replied with a giggle. She found Cereniti to be quite humor- ous. "And, girl, if you get pregnant while my fat man's down there, we are going to have some serious issues."

Alexus was in her bedroom with the door locked, opening twenty more cans to retrieve the cocaine she was going to give to Blake.

She had already calculated her profits at $456,000, which would put her at $2.65 million total.

"I *love* my grandma!" she screamed exuberantly.

"By the time you get down here," shouted Cereniti, *"I'll* be a grandma! Now will you please hurry up?

A few minutes later Alexus went marching down the stairs with her suitcase in tow, looking like a Louis Vuitton model, smiling from ear to ear. She sat on Blake's lap, facing him, and kissed his lips, leaving the suitcase next to the coffee table.

"Twenty Kilos," she said to him. "How long do you think it'll take you to sell them?"

"Uh... I don't... wait a minute," Blake said, brows rising. "You said twenty kilos?"

"That's what I said."

"Shiiit...twenty kilos! I ain't never had *one* kilo."

Cereniti sucked her teeth, and when Alexus cast a casual glance her way, there was a jealous expression cemented on Tee-Tee's face that she had half expected but hoped would not surface. It permeated from Cereniti's eyes like steam from a teakettle.

"I can get 'em off to my nigga in Chicago," Blake said. "The one with the Kush. Nigga named Lil Cholly in Holy City. Fifteenth and Trumbull. I think he and his guy Reesie run shit out there, they keep some birds."

Alexus was relieved by Blake's interjection; she looked back to him quickly, interlacing her fingers behind his neck.

"Well," she said, "now, hopefully they'll be selling *our* birds. All I need from you is three hundred thousand. You can sell them for twenty- five apiece, put two hundred grand up, and come back for more."

"Aw, hell yeah!" Blake smiled ecstatically, slipping his hand inside her robe. "Yeah, we can do that all day." He grabbed her ass and squeezed, and his smile burgeoned. "I just spent my last lil bread on a lawyer. I need some money."

Again Cereniti sucked her teeth, with an attitude. She made no attempt at hiding her feelings. Although her eyes were trained on the television, it was obvious that she wasn't watching "Everybody Hates Chris."

"S'up with her?" Blake nodded his head toward Cereniti.

"She'll be a'ight," Alexus said, leaning forward to kiss Blake again. "Let's just focus on getting this money. If possible, I want all the dope gone in a few days. Then we can really start moving weight." She looked over to Cereniti. "Everbody cool with that?"

Cereniti never took her eyes off the television, "I'm with that ... wish you would have told me you dated men. Straight up b. Fucked me up with that one.'""You thought I was a *lesbian!*" Alexus laughed. "Never that baby. I want kids one of these days, and a woman can't give me anything but anorgasm."

"Damn!" Blake's eyes went wide. "Y'all be licking on each other? I *love* that kinda shit."

"I'm sure you do, nigga." Alexus playfully jabbed a fingertip against Blake's black hoody. Then she stood. "Let me go and clean all this nut out of me. I'll be dressed and ready to leave in ten minutes."

Alexus contemplated initiating some more freaky shit with Blake, but then she thought of her bank account and decided she necessitated at least a quarter million dollar shopping spree.

"Let's get this money," Alexus said, unzipping her suitcase slowly, to display the stacks of cellophane wrapped cocaine.

"All that's for me?" asked Blake.

"For us," Alexus corrected. "For my family and your family." She looked to Cereniti again. "And her family. We'll all live comfortably, drive whatever car we want to drive, live and mingle in mansions, vacation in Jamaica. As long as we stick to the street code, and we all know what that means."

"I'm a street nigga to the bone lil momma," Blake replied "Betta ask about Bee-Kay. I'm Blake King. Only other niggas out here goonin' like me is T-Walk.

Leaving Blake and Cereniti alone in the living room, Alexus Costilla went up to the bathroom mumbling the words to Gucci Mane's *Bricks* as she thought about the new Lexus she planned to buy herself. A Rolls Royce or a Bentley would be too conspicuous in such a hostile environment. A Lexus would undoubtedly draw attention, but not nearly as much as a car that cost twice as much as the houses in her neighborhood. She didn't want to splurge too much. She only wanted to be known and seen a little bit.

In the shower, Alexus pond,ered over beginning a relationship with Blake, she wondered if he'd be faithful, and if she could be faithful. Infidelity was a transgression that she did not want to encounter but her nymphomania compelled her to want sex all the time.

What he don't know won't hurt him she told herself, then she toyed with her clit until her body shook and trembled.

King Rio

Chapter 16

"Twenty bricks? Damn! She had 'em in her house?" Craig was surprised. He was pulling his Suburban into an alley on Chicago's Southside, 113th and Wentworth to be exact.

Bookie was seated next to him, his paranoid eyes darting all around the alley. "Yup," Bookie said, nodding his head. "I couldn't believe the shit my damn self. She brought 'em down to me in a Louis Vuitton suitcase. I wonder how she got it here that fast."

Craig glanced at his side view mirror as his friend Trintino "T-Walk" Walkson's candy yellow 1970 Chevy Chevelle turned into the alley behind him. "She must've had it sent through the mail. Either that or she got one of them Mexican cartel muhfuckas out here somewhere."

"Pro'bly," said Bookie. He shrugged nonchalantly, lifted a sandwich bag containing about an ounce of cocaine from his lap and dipped a pinky fingernail inside it. A small pile of the powder was hastily vacuumed up his right nostril.

"What do you mean *pro'bly*? That's some important shit to know, my nigga. We might be plugged in with the Costilla cartel! Didn't you see that shit on the news?" Craig was becoming incredulous. "They connected forreal! If we can keep gettin' bricks for fifteen, we gon' be damn near the richest niggas in the Midwest!"

"I was really thinkin' about robbin that bitch after I give her that three hun'ed racks," Bookie admitted as he treated his other nostril. "Throw some sixes on a Chevy like T-Walk."

"Hell nah, bruh!" Craig said. "We can get ten times that just sellin' bricks. That's how you gotta play the game with them cartels. Swear to God, joe, they'll kill yo' whole family." Bookie shrugged again.

"The longest I'll wait is till after the second shipment. She said next time it'll be hun'ed bricks. That's one point five for Alexus. Shit, I need that."

"Don't be stupid, Bookie..." Craig said, but then his words tapered off as a blood-red Mercedes Benz convertible swerved into the alley ahead of him. It was followed by a second, longer

93

Mercedes of the same color.

A slew of Conservative Vice Lords in black t-shirts began creeping out from beside houses and garbage cans. Although Craig had been born and raised here, he felt uneasy. Chicago's "Wild" Hunr'ed streets numbered in the hundreds are notoriously dangerous and merciless when it boiled down to a drug dealer's destiny, and Craig was leery of every gang member in the 'hood.

His edginess waned a little, however, when his gang's chief, Cooly stepped out of the long Mercedes with a pair of red duffle bags in his right hand.

Cooly was a bald headed, muscle bound man in his early thirties who wasrumored to have stabbed two men to death during an eight year bid in Statesville over a Bulls basketball game. He had on a dark brown bomber jacket, Girbaud jeans, and white and brown Gucci sneakers.

"I don't trust these niggas." Bookie said, as Cooly passed his door. "It's cool, bruh," replied Craig. He watched Cooly open the door behind Bookie and get in.

"Sup, yo." Cooly locked eyes with Craig as he placed the two duffelsbetween the driver and passenger seats. "I hear niggas been wildin out inMichigan City. Killin' cops and shit."

Craig nodded and opened one of the duffels, while Bookie unzipped the other. Both duffels were filled almost to capacity with rubber band stacksoftwenty dollars bills.

"Yeah," Craig said, "some cops got murked. AK-47 action. Couple ofmy lil niggas got it, too." He was flipping through a stack of bills.

Cooly lit a Newport. "It's all there, lil nigga. Six thousand twohundred and fifty bills in each bag, all twenties. That's a quarter ticket," "I trust you," Craig lied. He didn't really trust anyone in the dope game. Niggas were too devious, their motives too volatile, which is whyCraig's cell phone was on and connected to T-Walk's cell at this very moment, allowing T-Walk to hear everything.

Craig turned to Cooly. "Grab that bag from the seat behind you, man."

94

Cooly grabbed a cylindrical black gym bag from behind him, and a

huge smile spread over his face once he had it open "Ooooo-weee, Joe!" he exclaimed. "Man, this shit look *good!*"

"That shit is good," Bookie said. "I just whipped up fifty zips of hard off of one chicken. Got my nigga sellin' that shit right now. Fiends can't get enough of it."

After mooning over the cocaine for a full minute, Cooly shook up with Craig then departed without another word. Craig and Bookie left Chicago with $250,000 cash.

Chapter 17

"I knew you were lying to me, Alexus. I just didn't say anything at the time," Rita snapped through the phone.

"Momma, what are you talking about?"

"You know good and well what I'm talking about!" Rita chastised. "That god forsaken shoulder bag. You said Papi had *accidentally* left it over Jenny's house. I *knew* you were telling a bold faced lie. How could someone mistakenly take something that doesn't even belong to them in the first place and lose it? Especially *Juan!* He hasn't made a mistake sinewe met!"

"Calm down, momma." Alexus sighed heavily. She was walking past a row of Aston Martins at Michigan City Sportscars, a beachfront cardealership on LakeMichigan's shoreline.

"Why should I?" Rita asked. "Why should I be calm when my daughter islying to me? What kind of sense doesthat make? Since whendid westart being dishonest with each other?

"Mamma..."

"Don't you'momma' me. Not now. You may as well start calling me"stranger!"

"Momma, I'm sorry. Now will you please calm down."

Alexus stopped in front of a pearl white Aston Martin. She admired

it for a few seconds. *Nice car,* she thought. *Bet it's fast as hell.* She looked back at Blake King, who was standing before a black on black hummer H2,speaking into his cell phone.

"What wasin that shoulder bag?" Ritaasked."Some money," Alexus replied.

"How *much* money?"

"Two hundred and fifty grand, momma. Okay? And I'm sorry fornot telling you. I just didn't want you all stressed out about the money. You're already dealing with Papi's situation."

"Chile, please. He's my ex-husband. When you break the law, sooner or later you're going to have to face the consequences, and that's what he's doing. Keeping *you* safe and out of that sort of trouble is my goal."

"I'm a grown woman, momma. I can take care of myself."

"You're supposed to be in college, Alexus. You have a lot more to learn. A high school diploma can only get you so far."

"I'll be fine," Alexus said, then she told Rita about the two million dollars that Vida had deposited into an account for her, and the house on Seventh and Lincoln Avenue that she now owned. "I'm going into the real estate business like Santiago and Savio. It's what I've wanted to do for a long time."

"Every dime of that money belongs to the devil, Alexus. Thousands and thousands of men, women, and children in Mexico were viciously murdered for that money."

"Whatever, momma. Listen, I have to go. Be home in a bit."
"I'll be here waiting," hissed Rita.

Alexus angrily threw her phone inside her purse, and again her eyes settled on the white Vanquish. Twenty minutes prior, when she and Blake were leaving first source Bank, she had been all smiles; now, she wasn't so happy. Rita's words had her vexed.

She was able to regain some excitement, when Blake approached her from behind and slipped his arms around the waist of her fur coat.

"I got four of them sold already," he said, planting a kiss on her neck. "Nigga named Pat outta Gary coppin' em from me for twenty two apiece. He said his guy Rube might grab a couple, and he knows a Naptown nigga who'll want some, too."

"Just get rid of them," Alexus turned around to face Blake. "Don't you just hate when other people's opinions go against yours?"

Blake shrugged his brawny shoulders. "Depends on if their opinion makes sense or not. If it's good advice, it's best to take heed to it.

"But what if... what if their advice was good, but you know if you followed it you'd end up broke? What would you do then?"

"I pro'bly wouldn't listen, I got a daughter to take care of. Aint nobody else gon' do it for me.

Alexus squinted her eyelids at Blake. "You never said anything about a *baby.*" She stepped back, studying him with a look of contempt.

"I can't be a deadbeat daddy, lil mamma," Blake said defensively. "I love my babygirl. She's the best thing that ever happened to me."

"You still could have told me."

"You didn't ask," he reminded her.

Alexus turned her back to Blake and watched as a blond haired carsalesman walked towards her.

"Good afternoon," the salesman said, extending his hand to Alexus. "Can I help you?"

Stepping around Alexus, Blake shook the salesman's hand. "She's looking to buy a Lexus."

"Great choice." The sharp salesman rubbed his palms together in anticipation of a sale. "We have twelve in stock now. If none of them fits your taste, you can—"

"Forget the Lexus," Alexus said. Taking her new checkbook from her purse, she pointed at the white Aston Martin coupe in front of her. "I want this one."

"Ma'am, that's a two hundred and seventy thousand dollar car," the salesman informed her.

Blake was speechless.

"So what?" Alexus went to the Vanquish driver door and opened it. "I want this one," she repeated, scrutinizing the exotic car's luxurious white leather interior. "I don't care how much it costs."

As Blake was trailing Alexus back to her new home, he found it difficult to keep his eyes off the Aston Martin she was entising so effortlessly in. It was definitely an eye-magnet. After a while he reached leaned back in the MKX and called the law offices of Bostic and Staples to speak with his attorney, a chocolate hued beauty named Britney Bostic.

"I was just about to call you," Britney said once they were connected. "Timothy Trice has been charged for the murder of Johnny Lay. He's been moved from Saint Anthony's Hospital to the county jail's infirmary. Word is they're trying to get him to pin the murder on you."

"On me?" Blake quickly became paranoid. "He can't blame it on me!

My car got *stolen!* Whoever stole my car killed Johnny." "I understand that, Mr. King."

"I'm *serious.* I don't know why they tryna blame *me.* "

"Mr. King, you have nothing to worry about at the moment. No charges have been filed against you. The case against Trice isn't even solid. They have some eyewitnesses who've testified to seeing him hop out of your car after the shooting took place and drop a pistol. Evidently,

though, his weapon was never even fired. Unless someone comes forward with information on *who* the actual shooter is, Trice's murder charge will be dismissed. He'll do maybe a year for the handgun and be home in no time."

"Oh." A feeling of relief overcame Blake. "So, I'm in the clear, right?

They gotta leave me alone now?"

"Technically, yes. But I doubt they will. You're suspected of killing two police officers. Nine times out of ten they're going to be following you everywhere you go. They're going to have every snitch they know trying to befriend you. They may even try framing you."

Blake instinctively checked the rearview mirror to see if he was being tailed. He really couldn't tell. There were too many vehicles.

"Detective Neal Miller wants you to come in for questioning," Britney Bostic said. "Of course I said hell to the no. I don't want you anywhere near those policemen. In fact, I'd rather you left you left town for a few weeks at the very least. Or stay indoors for a while.

"I'll be cool. I'm just gon' walk light and stay out of everything," replied Blake. But he wasn't sure if he could voluntarily exile himself from the 'hood. He wasn't sure if he even *wanted* to. He'd just ran into the sweetest drug connect ever. Now was not the time to become crime free.

He got off the line with his attorney when his girlfriend Ashley called. She sounded frantic, and he could hear his daughter crying in the background.

"It's over, Blake. I can't take it," Ashley cried. "I'm taking

Savaria to my mom's apartment in Indianapolis, and we're staying there."

"What!" Blake nearly rear-ended the Aston Martin as he turned onto Willard Ave. "You ain't takin' my daughter *nowhere!*"

"It's too late for all that," Ashley confided, "because we're already on the highway. Goodbye, Blake."

Alexus didn't feel like being chastised by her mother. Her brand new Vanquish had her feeling elated and she wanted to enjoy this feeling. So instead of going to her mom's house, she voice commanded her navigation system to lead her to her new house, a sky blue two story clapboard masterpiece that had cost Vida Costilla $237,500.00 for her to purchase for her granddaughter.

As Alexus turned into her fresh paved driveway, she noticed a posse of Blake's dudes posted up on the corner. She saw lil Mike and Young- D among them, staring down her Aston Martin. Then their eyes were trained on her Lincoln MKX as Blake pulled in beside her and parked.

They all rushed to her driveway and crowded around Blake's door.

Since being nosey wasn't on Alexus to do list, she left Blake with his guys and went inside her new home.

The living room walls were clean and white, the floor, a polished hardwood. Alexus liked the gentle clicking sounds her Louis Vuitton heals made on the floor as she crossed the room. She stopped at a side window and gazed out at Blake.

He was shaking hands with a tall light skinned boy.

"Fat bastard," Alexus said with a smile. Her heart warmed at the sight of him. She admired the way he'd spoken of his daughter. It made her not regret having sex with him without using protection, which was something she had never done before.

She walked into a large bedroom that connected to the living room: the master bedroom. It had a bathroom, a walk-in closet, and was roomy enough for two people to reside in. Alexus hung her coat on the doorknob. She had on black and gray checkered Chanel leggings with a matching halter top. Simple yet stunning nonetheless.

She was examining herself in the bathroom mirror, wondering if Cereniti had made it to Chicago's Midway airport and onto an Atlanta bound plane yet, when she heard Blake's boots on the living room floor.

"I'm in here, fat man," she said, fixing her hair.

Blake knew the house well, he told Alexus that he'd been a close friend of the previous owner, Mr. George "Boogie" Trig. Boogie had been a numbers runner and a heroin dealer until lung cancer took him at fifty four. He had taught Blake many things, things like how to cook eighteen ounces of cocaine into twenty two ounces of crack, and how to turn one gram of heroin into four or five grams. Important things like that.

"This was the only room without a camera," Blake said as he entered the bathroom behind Alexus. He leaned against the oak door, studying her reflection in the mirror. "Boogie's son fixed it up real good when the old man passed away."

"I love it," Alexus said. "And I have three extra bedrooms... well with Cereniti staying here; we'll have two extra bedrooms."

Blake took a pack of Swisher Sweets cigarillos from his hoody's front pocket. "You smoke weed?" he asked, lowering his gaze to Alexus's ass.

"Occasionally," she said. "I'd rather have a drink, though."

"Shit, I need some drank. My baby momma just left town with my daughter. Somebody shot through her apartment window about two hours ago. Lil Mike told me about it. I'm guessing that's why she left."

Yes! Alexus thought. She'd been subconsciously hoping for Blake's baby mama to be removed from the picture ever since he'd mentioned her and the baby at the dealership.

"You're good, baby," she said, turning around to face him. "I'll never leave you like she did. And look" she spun around as if she was presenting the house to a potential buyer. "We have our own place here. Your daughter can live here with us. I'll fix up a bedroom for her."

"Ash ain't goin' for that,"Blake said as he dexterously split a cigarillofrom top to bottom. "That's why I've been staying with her. I just wantedto be there with Vari."

"Her name is Vari?"

"Savaria." Blake took a quarter ounce of strong scented weed out ofhis sweatpants pocket and opened it with his teeth.

Alexus watched him roll his blunt expertly. Saliva from his quick tongue sealed the blunt together instantaneously, and she wondered howit would feel to have his talented tongue on her pussy.

"So", she said, "can I count on you to stay here with me? To protectme? I have way too much money to be living alone." She lifted herself upontothe granite countertop.

"I noticed that when you spent down near three hundred racks onan Aston Martin," he replied, putting fireto the end of his blunt.

Blake silently toked his weed. Alexus hoped that he was thinking about staying with her. She scooped up the cigar tobacco he'd dumped on the sink and dropped it in the toilet.

"My lawyer advised me to stay in the house for a while," Blake said finally. "I guess I can stay here. Kick it for a lil bit. At least till the feds leave."

"Good." Alexus smiled and hopped offthe sink. "I'll cook and clean.

You can scratch your balls and watch Sports Center all day."

Chuckling, Blake raised his middle fingers and presented them toAlexus. "You talk a whole lotta shit, I see."

"I do, don't I?" she said as she stepped in front of him. She leaned inand pressed her lips against his. Then she turned her back to him." I canback it up, though."

"Well," Blake retorted wittily, "let me see you back it up then."

Never one to disappoint, Alexus peeled her tight leggings down andshowed Blake King what *backing it u*p was all about.

Rita Mae Bishop stirred her mug of coffee with a straw then sipped from it. She was standing before a tall mirror she'd hung on her bedroomdoor, visually scrutinizing her dark green sequined Dolce and Gabbanadress. It hugged her every curve, accentuating her generous legs, and her ample D-cup breasts.

"I hope you like it," she said, thinking of Neal Miller as if he were present.

He *had* been there. He had unloaded the U-haul and brought everything inside for Rita, but now he was gone, and Rita was waitingfor him to return.

She had kept herself busy after Neal left. She'd taken the u-haul back to the rental company, then boarded a city bus to a used car lot,where she purchased a seven-year-old Escalade that was merely a shade darkerthan the dress she now wore.

Rita's watch read 5:30 pm. "Come on, Alexus," she said stepping into a pair of black Manolo Blahnik heels. Spinning around to further observe herself in the mirror, she tried focusing on her date with Neal Miller and forgetting aboutthe three milliondollarsthathad been wiredto her bank account earlier that day.

She wasn't going to spend any of it. *I'm sending it back*, she'd told herself after receiving the call from a bank manager. "On Monday I'm sending it all back. That's three million dollars of Satan's money. It belongs to the unrighteous, the wicked, the hellbound."

But her brother's opinion was different. Dennis had called her anhour ago, while he and his children's mother were on their way to East Lansing, Michigan, to attend one of Kenya's basketball games. Once Rita had told him about the money, Dennis had taken a moment to ponder hisreply.

"Imagine the good you could do in New Orleans with three million dollars," he'd said. "Imagine how many homes you could rebuild, howmany Katrina victims you could help. Giving it back to that old lady, doesn't make any sense. You can make something positive happen with thatmoney."

"No Dennis, I will not spend blood money on anyone."

"What are you going to do with it then? Send it back to the

same people who killed to get it? Nah, sis, that ain't the solution. It'll be used to buy guns and dope. That's all those cartel, are known for. You could do so much for yourself and the family, and you'd still have enough left over to donate to a helpful charity, or like I said, to rebuild a few homes in honor of our parents. You would give Daddy and momma permanent smiles in Heaven, and you know it. Can't twist my nuts and tell me different."

Rita had giggled then, and now, eying her tense reflection in the mirror and drinking from her steaming mug of coffee, she found herself snickering again.

Being comedically entertaining was a gift of Dennis'; he had been making Rita laugh ever since they were kids. He'd been a staple at family gatherings, simply due to his well-placed seeds of seemingly unintentional comedy, seeds that never failed to blossom into fits of laughter.

A small brown bird landed suddenly outside Rita's bedroom window. Reflexively, she turned and went to the window a front window. She watched the little bird hop along the ledge, its neck jerking sporadically from left to right.

"You're a free little fella, aren't you?" Rita whispered to the bird. "I wish I were like you." She tossed back her head and laughed, and when her eyes settled on the window again the bird was flying away, soaring around the front of the house next door.

Following the bird with her eyes, Rita saw something that caught her attention—Neal Miller's black Charger. It was parked across the street, three houses east, and detective Miller was dressed inconspicuously in oilspotted overalls and brown work-man's boots, hunched over the charger's open hood. He seemed to be toiling over the engine, at first glance. But then he raised a cam-era and snapped a picture of some young guys who were standing on the corner of Eighth and Willard.

"What in God's name are you doing?" Rita muttered aloud. She made a mental note to ask him later.

King Rio

Chapter 18

"Bookie, we need to go, bruh," Craig said impatiently, his face a thundercloud. He was incredulous.

He and Bookie had just returned from Detroit, Michigan, where they'd sold five kilos to a huge man named Big John, one of the leaders of the Gangster Disciples.

Now, while Craig sat behind the wheel of bis suburban, countingthe cash out, Bookie had some crackhead woman bent over a large green garbage can in the alleyway on Sixth and Cedar, and he was eagerly fucking her from behind.

"Hold up a minute, nigga," complained Bookie. "You fuckin' up my concentration."

"You should be concentrated on..." Craig started. But then he said fuck it and continued rummaging through bills, twenties and fifties and hundreds. If not for Alexus being Bookie's cousin, Craig wouldn't need Bookie for much of anything. Why attempt to save him, when he'sstanding in front of a Mexican drug cartel leader's daughter. Better to let Bookie's ship sink and pass by. So what if Bookie demise came from him sliding bis raw dick into the rank pussy of a crackhead who could bean AIDS victim? So what if Bookie snorted up one gram too many and overdosed?

"This shit good, bruh!" Bookie said, holding on to Diana's ashy elbows and slamming himself in and out of her frail body. He looked backwith a smile and peered through Craig's passenger's side window. "You might as well buss her down next."

"I'm cool," Craig said quickly. He turned to his left at the sound of ascreen door.

Tiffany "Tiff-Tiff" Jenkins, a beautiful, caramel hued chick thatCraig had been bedding for going on two years, came sauntering downthe back stairs of her house with a big smile on her pie shaped face. She looked like she belonged on the cover of Straight Stuntin' magazine, as thick asshe was.

Her friend Danielle- an equally gorgeous twenty two year old whocould easily pass for Tiffany's sister- came down the stairs behind her. It was normal to see the two of them dressed alike, and today was no different. They wore black Chanel sunglasses, peach colored cashmeresweaters, tight blue jeans, and pink high heel Timberland boots. Theirhair and nails were impeccably done up.

Bottom line, both of them were certified dime pieces.

"Hey baby," Tiffany cooed as she approached Craig's door.

Bookie opened the passenger's door and got in just as Tiffany pulled Craig's door open.

Buttoning and zipping her tattered pants shut, Diana hastily disappeared around a garage, clutching the twenty dollar bill Bookie had given her in one hand.

"Ugh" Danielle's face twisted in disgust. "Bookie, what the hell wasyoujustdoing with Diana?"

"Girl," Tiffany said, eyeing the two cash filled grocery bags betweenCraig and Bookie, and a pile of fifties in Craig's lap, "you know Bookie will fuck anything with a pussy."

"Bitch, don't worry 'bout Bookie," Bookie said. He then fired up acigarette, leaned back and closed his eyes, apparently content after havingfucked a dope fiend.

Craig kissed Tiffany's succulent lips in a passionate manner, and tucked a hand inside one of her back pockets to hold her softness.

"Pack some clothes up, some summer outfits, and be ready to take that trip you been beggin for." Craig said.

"Cali?" Tiffany grabbed her hips. "Or are you talking about the cruise ship to Jamaica?"

Danielle, peekin gover Tiff-Tiff's shoulder at the moneylying on the front of Craig's jeans, asked, "Damn, boy how much money is that?"

"Jamaica," Craig chimed, ignoring Danielle's inquiry. "Just pack enough for two weeks. We should be leaving next Friday, seven days from now."

"Can I come with y'all?" Danielle asked.

"I'm on some romantic shit with my baby." Craig said. He removedTiffany's shades to see her pretty eyes. "Don't need nobody else there with us, fuckin' up our sextime."

"I'm on some romantic shit with my baby," Bookie cut in

mockingly and laughed. "Nigga think he Ray-J now. I guess Tiff-Tiff s'posed to be Danger."

Tiffany raised a middle finger at Bookie. "Nigga, fuck you. You just mad 'cause you ain't got the money to go."

"Round here fuckin crackheads," Danielle added.

Craig decided to end the bickering before it got serious.

"Y'all, shut that shit down," he intoned and kissed his lovely lady again. "Baby, let me go take care of some business. I should be back in about thirty minutes. We going shopping soon as I get back."

"Hoes just don't know," mumbled Bookie, *"I'm* the one with the bread now."

Simultaneously, Tiffany and Danielle sucked their teeth. Neither of them had ever liked Bookie; they merely tolerated him because he was always on Tenth Street, where they generally hung out. Plus, he wasn't as hustle savvy as other niggas in the 'hood. The majority of Bookie's money went to supporting his many habits.

As the girls headed back inside, Craig turned to Bookie and shook his head disapprovingly. "Let's drop the money off to Alexus. Then all we'll have to do is grind off the last five while we wait on that next package to land."

Nodding, Bookie went for his bag of coke and treated his nose. Then he passed the bag to Craig, who indulged in a bit of snow himself on rare occasions.

"A hun'ed birds," Bookie said, staring off into a majestic blue sky. "Fifty for you, fifty for me... that's gon' be a helluva sight." He paused to swallow two triple stack ecstasy pills. "Man, I can't *wait* to see that hoe ass nigga Blake. I'm thinkin' about stayin with my Auntie Rita on the westside for a few days, just to catch that nigga."

"Wait until after we flip that next shipment," Craig advised. "We got the ultimate connect right now. And you know it's *way* too hot out here to be on some gunplay. Feds in town, joe. I ain't even gon' sell no workout here."

Driving to the west side, to deliver $300,000 to Alexus, Craig contemplated shooting Bookie in the head and keeping all the money for himself. He knew he could more than likely get away with it. As long as Tiffany and Danielle kept their mouths shut about seeing him and Bookie together before he...

Craig shook away the thought and snorted some coke. Now wasnot the time to contemplate betrayal. Definitely not over a few hundred grand.

But for a few *million...*

Chapter 19

The Dub Life Goons, and their chicks, embraced Alexus like family. She enjoyed their company. Both genders showered her with compliments on her looks and her Aston Martin coupe.

She was sitting atop the hood of her new whip with her thighs spread wide open to accommodate Blake's wide back as he stood languidly between her legs, his back pressed against the front of her fur coat. They were watching a dice game on the sidewalk a couple feet ahead of them.

"This right here is Patrick Street," Blake was saying. "Crack city. I done made so much money on this street, it's pitiful. I started sellin' dope 'cause I found three eightballs of hard in a brown paper bag down the street. My nigga, Blubby, taught me how to weigh up the dope in twenty dollar rocks. I made seven hundred off that and I ain't looked back since."

"Promise me you'll never do that again," Alexus said. "I can't have you doing twenty years over twenty dollars."

Blake cast his eyes downward. He twirled the strings of his hoody around his thumbs. He stomped an already flattened sprite can, and kicked it to the side.

"Thinking about your daughter, huh?" Alexus asked.

He nodded somberly. "I need to be on my way to Nap-town to see my baby. Ash won't even pick up the damn phone."

Alexus began massaging Blake's shoulders. Cautiously, she scammed the side street, searching for signs of danger.

Last night's club shooting was still vivid in her mind. The dead man outside the restroom. The overturned chairs and tables, and the warning from Lil Mike.

"I just remembered something," she whispered suddenly into Blake's ear. "Lil Mike *knew* what was about to go down last night. He *had* to have known. In fact, he said something about you wanting me to leave. And that you were in the par... the parking lot!"

Blake spun around quickly. His expression turned from warm to thirty below in half a second. Alexus felt her heart pounding as if it was a jackhammer.

"Oh shit!" She gasped. 'You're one of the guys who tried to kill my cousin..."

"Blake" shouted Lil Mike, he sprinted past the dice game, pulling hisRuger from under his blueCubs jacket.

Young-D appeared from beside a blue one story house, cradling a shotgun, running up Patrick Street behind LilMike.

A millisecond later, Blake's .40 calibers was drawn, and he too was racingtoward the comer of Patrick and Willard Avenue.

When Alexus turned her head to see what or who they were chasing down, her eyes and mouth went agape. Dread filled goosebumpsspread over her body.

Craig's suburban was crusing byon Willard. "Nooooo!" Alexus screamed at the top of her lungs.

But her scream went unheard, eclipsed by cacophony of gunfire that resounded throughout the neighborhood like thunder on steroids.

Bookie noticed them first.

"Speed up, bruh!" Hescreeched nervously.

As the driver's side off the Suburban started getting abused by myriad of bullets, Bookie and Craig ducked low in their seats. Jagged pieces of glass rained down on their backs. Craig put the gas pedal to the floor, propelling his SUV forward. A bullet penetrated his left wrist. Another tore through the door behind him and became lodged in Bookie's left leg.

"Shit, I'm hit, bruh!" Bookie yelled, as he clamped a hand down overthe wound, watching as his bloodstarted saturatingthe blue denim of hisCoogi jeans.

"Me, too!" Craig raised his head cautiously and braked to avoid colliding into an old Civic at the stop sign on Eighth and Willard. He veered around the Honda turned left onto Eighth, and gassed it half a block before stopping and glancing over to Bookie. There was an unspoken bond established between them.

"Alexus was right there with them," Bookie said, snatching a 9mm Glock from his waist. "Swear to God she was. Saw her sitting on the hood of a car talking to Blake."

Craig reached down between his Nikes and picked up his formidable chrome pistol. Blood from his dripping wrist was splatting everywhere. The cash from the Aldis bags littered on the floor behind him. He heard police sirens closing in, and in his rearview he saw a black Charger with blue and red flashing lights built into its headlights zoom off towards Blake and his crew.

"We gotta go back around there," said Craig. Bookie only nodded.

Homicide detective Neal miller could not believe his luck. His diligently thought out plan had paid off handsomely. Figuring that a retaliatory response to the club shooting was as predictable as rain in April, he had ordered a six car team of police to stay out of sight but within a ten block radius of the area where Blake King and his friends hung out.

The officers chased and tackled Blake and numerous members of the Dub Life goons as though they were practicing at an NFL training camp. Neal parked so that his car was blocking one end of Patrick Street, and a patrol car secured the other end. As he stepped out of his car, gun in hand, eyes fluctuating from left to right, thug to hoodlum, he caught sight of the bullet riddled white suburban he'd witnessed the Dub Life Goons shooting at.

It was idling in front of the J. Cooper Community Center, a small building on Grant Avenue and Patrick where the elders of the neighborhood gathered every two weeks for neighborhood watch meetings.

"Hey, Officer Swizz," shouted Miller to the policeman who was roughly handling Blake King against the side of a patrol car, "go check out that SUV, see if anyone's wounded. "I'll tend to my friend Mr. King here."

"Bitch, I ain't yo' mufuckin' friend!" Blake snapped.

"You are now." Miller walked up behind Blake as Officer Swizniak started off toward the shot up Suburban. "You see, Mr. King, your little streak of luck with the system has come to end. I just witnessed you empty an entire mag into that SUV. You're going down.

Skiiiirk!

The ear-piercing sound of tires churning compelled Miller and Blake to snap their heads to the right. The Suburban was speeding away'on Grant. "Catch them!" Millerscreamed.

Relaxing to the peaceful sounds of Gladys Knight and the Pips, Rita Mae Bishop was sitting quietly at her dining room table, reading her Bible, when Alexus entered the front door with a tear streaked face.

Rita looked at her daughter briefly, then went back into the Book ofProverbs without uttering a single word.

"Bookie's been shot," said Alexus in a weak tone. She was shaking asshe took off her coat and draped it over the back of the sofa.

"I already know that, Alexus." Rita closed the Bible and set it on the table. "I just spoke with his mother. Evon said he's fine. She and Dennisare driving back from Michigan now. The police have arrested him for unlawful possession of a firearm, possession of cocaine and Ecstasy, and a domestic battery warrant. They found him limping through a hospital parking lot. Some guy namedCraig's SUV—"

"They shot it up ma!" Alexus shrieked hysterically. "My boyfriend and two of his boysdid it."

"Yeah, I know that, too. They have all three suspects in custody, police found Craig's SUV a block away from the hospital, and they're looking for him as wespeak."

Sitting across the table from Rita, Alexus planted her elbows on thetabletop, dropped her face into her palms, and tried vehemently to calmher nerves. *What have I done?* She thought. *And how did momma know everything?*

"Alexus Denise Costilla. Relax, and tell me about this boyfriend of yours. What's his name?"asked Rita.

Excluding the sex and drugs, Alexus told her mother all about Blake King, explicating everything from his daughter to the Patrick Street shooting. As the words flowed, she realized how little she knew about him. She didn't even know his *age*.

"Are you listening to yourself?" Rita asked, shaking her head."Basically, you just described 0-Dog from *Menace to Society*. Is that thekind of man you want to start a life with? A career criminal? Come on now, Alexus. As intelligent as youare, I know you can do betterthan that."

"I know, momma, I know. Give me a minute to sort out my thoughts. This isn't easy."

"It isn't easy?" Rita gave a sarcastic laugh. "What's so hard about leaving him alone? You met him yesterday, for Christ's sake and already he's shot your cousin. Lord knows what other simple minded atrocities he's intentionally committed."

"But, momma..."

"Don't *but momma* me," Rita said as she stood up and pushed in her chair. "I guess I'll have to be your personal assistant in the relationship department," she stepped around the table, hugged Alexus as if she were an American soldier about to head off to war, and whispered, "I love you, Alexus. More then you'll ever know. Some things are just not meant to be, and your relationship with Blake is one of them."

Alexus sighed discontentedly.

"Go and get your face fixed," Rita said, walking to her bedroom. "Our double date is due to start at nine o'clock tonight."

"Double date? What double date?"

At her bedroom door, Rita turned around and smiled. "I ran into a fine young club owner at a car dealership earlier. He's twenty four, handsome, college educated. He owns that club where those officers were killed last night."

Studying her mother's exquisite little dress, Alexus cracked a smile.

Momma looked damn good, like Angela Basset in her prime.

"Well, what's my date's name?" Alexus asked.

"You'll find out when we get there."

"An Aston Martin?" mused Rita.

Alexus saw the shock register in her mother's eyes as they went down Rita's front stairs. She half expected a windy lecture on money management to follow, but that wasn't the case. Rita circled the Vanquish, silently admiring its sleek curves, its exotic features.

"Papi should have driven one of these." Rita said, running a thin, manicured finger along the expertly designed hood of the car.

"It is his style," Alexus agreed. Her mind wasn't on the

Vanquish, though. Nor was it Papi's taste. Bookie's gunshot wound was also out of the equation.

She was deeply worried about Blake, wondering how he was faring in jail. When Cereniti phoned Alexus from Hartsfield International Airport in Atlanta a bit earlier, Alexus had been upset to learn that her cousin had been shot; Kenya had called Tee-Tee with the disheartening news. But the arrest of Blake King, weighed heavier on Alexus's heart, because she hadpledged her loyalty to him not even two hours before he'd opened fire on Craig and Bookie.

Now she was about to go on a blind date. *Some loyal chick I am,* she thought, yanking her white asymmetrical Louis Vuitton dress down over her thick thighs.

"So, where are we going with our dates?" Alexus asked. "And whosewhip are we taking? I kinda like your Escalade. It's long and spacious."

"Nuh-uh, child," Rita said as she went to her SUV, which was parkedin front of the Aston, and opened the driver's door. "If my date strikes the right chord, I may be pushing out baby Cadillac in thirty six weeks." She laughed her soothing laugh, and it relaxed Alexus to see Rita so happily anxious. "We're going to the theater to catch *The Takers*, that movie that "

"Chris Brown!" Alexus said excitedly, snatching her own driver's door out.

"I was going to say Idris Elba, but I forgot, you're more into the violent ones." Rita climbed up inside her dark green SUV, shut the door,and started the engine. She rolled her window down and said, "We're coming back here for a quick dinner."

"I'm *not* into crazy men," Alexus retorted. *I'm just into Blake who* happens to be a crazy ass man!

The entire theater was redolent of butter, cheap perfume sweat and overpowering chocolate when Rita and Alexus stepped through the front glass doors.

Instantly, about a hundred male eyes bombarded the mother daughter duo. Fifty more followed them in from the parking lot.

Rita's watch read 8:47 the movie was to begin at 8:50.

"Your grandma Rosie always instilled in us the importance

116

of punctuality," Rita said, leading the way to a set of wooden doors with an advertisement poster for The Takers hung above them.

"We should get some snacks," Alexus suggested."Let's meet up with our dates first."

Alexus wondered momentarily if she was going to be stood up by a man she'd never even met before. How embarrassing would that be?But the daunting notion dissipated as she and Rita sauntered into the darkened viewing room and down a long aisle to the right of the movie screen.

"There," Rita whispered, pointing an index finger at two guys- anolder man in a dark suit and tie; and a young man in a white and yellow pinstriped shirt-- who were conversing beside the fourth row of seats from the front. "The dark one's mine."

"And the white one's here for me?" Alexus inquired.

He isn't white, he's mixed. Black and white. Like President Obama. And he has that ... what do you call it...wag?"

"It's called *swag,* momma."

"Yeah, he has *that*. Now listen up, there will be no sexual healings tonight. Be a lady and—"

"He's my date!" Alexus was about three feet away from her ''date",. who was staring her down, when she realized who he was. Her expressionfaltered, but she quickly regained her composure. Smiling coyly, she reached out and shook his hand. "Hello, I'm Alexus Costilla."

"Trintino Walkson," he said, still embracing her hand with his, ''Buteverybody calls me T-walk."

King Rio

Chapter 20

Ten weeks later, on Friday, December Twenty Fourth, Alexus Costilla's eyelids fluttered open at exactly 8:30 am, thanks to Cereniti's loud singing in the shower.

"This bitch thinks she's Keri Hilson," Alexus mumbled groggily.

"That girl needs counseling, *serious* counseling." T-Walk said, turning over onto his side to gaze into the sheepish, innocent looking green eyes of his girlfriend.

"Makes me want to throw a pretty girl rock at her damn head!" Giggling joyfully, Alexus mounted Trintino beneath the expensive white silk sheets and thick blanket on the king size bed in their hotel suite.

They were in a luxury suite on the eighth floor of Chicago's Trump International Hotel and Tower, a masterfully furnished, marble flooredpalace that offers a spectacular view of the windy city from a downtown vantage point. The floor to ceiling windows held Alexus spellbound every time she stood before them, looking down a snow glazed Wabash Avenue.It was an $8,500 a night suite, an exorbitant price for most, but to Alexus, who had vicariously pushed over two hundred kilos of cocaine throughout the ghettos of Indiana, Illinois, Georgia and New York, since the middle of October, the price of the room was chump change.

"I can't believe how far I've made it already," Alexus said, staring down at T-Walk. "This shit is crazy. The money's coming *too* fast."

"Ain't no such thing as too fast, baby," he said, "I fixed up my club with drug money. Bought all my cars with drug money. Shit, you just bought two half a million dollar homes and fixed them up with drug money.Look at what you made off those estates— eight fifty off of one, nine seventy off the other! Plus the fifty bricks of boy went so fast; that's where you *really* struck gold. I ain't even mentioned the hundred pounds ofKush."

"Ssshh." Alexus laid her index finger on his lips. "If

the room wasbugged, they'd already have enough to bury us."

T-Walk moved her head aside and leaned forward to kiss her neck. Then he took her rigid nipple into his mouth and sucked it. "If they bury us together," he tongued her other nipple, "I wouldn't have a single complaint."

Well I would, Alexus thought. She threw the covers back and spun into a sixty-nine position, and she stayed that way for a while, until her body was convulsing and his dick was twitching in her mouth.

***

With perspiration oozing from his every sweat gland, Blake King continued to plow through a hundred count set of push-ups with a look of grim determination painted on his dark, dripping face, exercising away his anger and frustration.

"Fifty-six, fifty-seven, fifty-eight..." The fire he felt in his chest and arms consoled him. He had been working out every day since his arrest seventy days ago; in a way, it was a remedy for his sanity.

Blake had been alone in the dayroom of North-8 cell block for more than an hour, working out and watching ABC 7 news, when old school Remo, a fifty year old man with light streaks of gray in his wavy black hair, pushed open his cell door and shuffled out with a plastic cup of coffee in one hand and a folded woolen blanket in the other.

"I see you up early again," Remo said, placing his blanket on a cold steel stool at the table outside his cell door. "Hell, it ain't nine yet, and youalready woke?"

"...eighty-six, eighty-seven..."

"That fine young girl of yours must be comin' up to see you today." Remo sat atop his blanket, grabbed the remote control, and turned to WGN9 news. "Mmm, mmm, mmm. Look at the smile on that black angel. Finest news lady I ever seen."

Blake completed his final set with an agonizing groan. Getting to his feet,he glanced up at the TV for Remo's sake. Valerie Warner was live in a newschopper, flying over a three car pileup on the Dan Ryan Expressway in Chicago.

"Yeah, she's a piece." Blake headed to one of the three small shower stalls that were situated in the corner of the dayroom. "My lawyer favorsher a little. Both of 'em sexy. My lawyer's dark skinned, though."

"You talking 'bout that Bostic girl?"

"Yup. Britney Bostic. She's supposed to be up here to see me in about twenty minutes. Said she had some good news."

"She probably does. Her old man, Niemann, beat a dope case for meback in seventy nine. Their law firm is the most prestigious in the city."

"I sure can't tell. She can't even get my bond lowered," Blake complained as he stepped in the shower.

The fact that Christmas was merely a day away and he still had not bought anything for his daughter really bothered him. It bothered him more than his lack of freedom, more than missing an opportunity to flip twenty kilos of cocaine.

Well, at least I'll get to see Vari today, Blake thought.

A vivid image of Alexus and her friend Cereniti sailed into his mind and had him hard instantly. He wondered what Alexus had done with the dope. A few people in his neighborhood had told him that she, Cereniti, and somenew bad bitch named Tasia were out there in the free world getting big money.

Blake couldn't wait to get his hands on Alexus again.

"And I bet I keep everything next time," he whispered aloud to himself. "I'll never make that mistake again."

Five minutes later the dayroom intercom emitted the drab tone of officer Joe Roberts: "King, you got an attorney visit."

"A'ight," Blake said. He finished stroking and scrubbing himself, rinsed off the foamy soap, and exited the shower with his bath towel wrapped around him, wondering what kind of titillating attire Britney would bedonning today.

She wore an enticing pair of black leather, high heeled boots beneath a black pantsuit. Her hair was short and choppy, giving her face an angelic frame. She smiled at Blake through the sheet of glass that separated them.

Blake waited until the officer who'd escorted him to Britney left before returning her smile.

"They lower my bond?" He asked immediately.

"I'm afraid not." Britney's optimistic smile grew wider. "It's still set at

$150,000. I've tried everything."

Ain't this about a bitch! Blake thought. He wanted to punch the concrete wall beside him, but he didn't want to frighten his attorney. He wanted to ask her what she was so damn happy about, but he knew the inquiry would have been just as detrimental as a sudden wall punch, so he decided to keep quiet and drop his head.

"Your daughter's mother called me yesterday evening. She wanted to know if you could still receive visits. She's bringing your daughter here to see you today."

"I already know," Blake said. "My brother told me she was coming. Now, can we get to the good news? I ain't in the holiday spirit like you."

"You're not?" Britney put on a look of mock surprise and brought her lefthand up to her chest. An engagement ring – a nice sized white diamond set in platinum – shined brilliantly on her ring finger. "Well, you should be. If I could trade places with you for just this day, I would do it in a heartbeat."

"I'm waiting…"

"Okay, here's the news: some eighteen year old Spanish girl dropped by my office after I went home yesterday. She gave a new lawyer at my firm – Nikkia Staples –a few things for me to give to you, the first of which was this note."

She dug in her pants pocket and retrieved a small, folded piece of perfumed paper. She pushed it through an opening under the window.

The name Alexus was bouncing around in Blake's head like that green blob from the movie Flubber. *I know it's her*, he thought to himself as he unfolded the note.

And it was.

Fat man (LOL!),

I apologize; I should not have left you in jail like that. Words can't express my apology, no matter how I try. Hopefully, my x-

mas gifts will cheer you up!
    Check the only one that didn't have one.XOXO,
    Alexus Costilla

"Gifts? What gifts?" Blake said, speaking more to himself than to Britney.

"She left a check for a hundred fifty thousand for your bond, two sets of keys, and an iPhone. And the car. How could I forget the car?"

Blake conformed to his attorney's holiday spirit in a hurry. "When do I leave?" he asked, balling up the paper.

"Very soon. They're downstairs getting your release papers ready, so youshould be out of here within an hour or so. And, please take my advice this time and stay off the streets. That pretty little Spanish girl must be crazy in love to spend all her money on you. Either that or she's plain crazy. Andthat car! Wait till you get a glimpse of it. You're going to pass out."

King Rio

Chapter 21

The photo shoot for Black Men magazine went well. It was Alexus's firstever shoot for a magazine, and she was surprised at how respectful and considerate the photographer and his elaborate team of stylists and make-upartists had been. Although the photo shoot was actually for Chicago rap artist Lupe Fiasco, Alexus got the feeling that she was just as important as he.

She'd worn three different bra and thong sets in the photos, which were taken inside the luxury suite across the hall from hers. Her body had been oiled from top to bottom, especially her ass, which faced the camera from one angle or another in nearly every picture.

And to think, this is all because of Blake King, she thought, eyeing her reflection in the rearview mirror of her brand new 2011 Bentley ContinentalSupersports convertible. She had on a long white leather Louis Vuitton coatwith matching gloves, hat and boots. A pricey pair of diamond flooded platinum hoops weighed down her lobes. Her eyes, tucked behind a white diamond framed pair of LV shades, were unwaveringly fixed on the slick road ahead as she drove down I-94.

Beside her sat Cereniti, whose fascination with the youtube video of Alexus that Blake had posted online months prior had yet to wane; both sheand her exotic dancer friend, Tasia, who was seated behind her, wereYouTube fanatics.

"You just passed two million hits, yo!" Cereniti said from the edge of herseat. "That's mad crazy, b! People are going wild about watching your ass shake up three stairs. You're a YouTube sensation."

"She ain't even lyin' b," said Tasia. Like Cereniti, she was surfing the net on her iPhone.

"My Facebook and Twitter pages are loco, I swear," Alexus said. "Modeling contracts, music videos, commercials; I'm being offered every kind of deal you can imagine."

"You don't seem too excited about it," Cereniti said, her eyes scanning a list of YouTube comments." They're calling you the new and improved Cubaña Lust. I'd be buggin' out right now, yo."

"I don't like the attention," Alexus admitted. "My father and his mom do not approve of the entertainment industry either. It goes against our morals to mingle with clientele, and more than likely they'll fold when they come under pressure. I'm not trying to get fame. I only want the fortune."

"So, why'd you do the Lupe shoot?" Cereniti sucked her teeth indignantly.

"I don't know," Alexus admitted. She hadn't really given any thought to why she'd accepted the offer from Black Men magazine. She guessed that maybe it was her childhood dream of one day becoming a famous actress that was compelling her to want a piece of the limelight. Maybe it was because, with the abundance of cash she had at her disposal, she hadalready started living like an A-lister.

Alexus had recently spent $587,122.47 on Louis Vuitton clothes and purses for herself and the girls. The Bentley had squandered away another three hundred grand, which was basically the combined price of the three white Jaguar XJ's she'd bought for Bookie, Craig and K.G.. Plus, she had just purchased two more residential estates, a burned out corner store and a small foreclosed beauty salon in Michigan City.

And not to mention the cash she'd spent on Blake.

"You should get us a photo shoot with you," Cereniti suggested. "We've already taken a thousand pictures for Facebook."

Tasia disagreed. "We're not the Kardashians, Tee-Tee. Being in thepublic eye isn't exactly the best thing for either of us. We're making good money in the streets. Too many people poking their noses in our business could jeopardize everything."

"She's got a point," Alexus agreed, her interest piqued by the wisdom in Tasia's words.

Tasia was Bookie's girlfriend now, a light skinned cutie whose work ethicwas awe-inspiring. She was truly all about the Benjamins. She and Alexus had finally met on Thanksgiving Day over dinner at Rita's place and, the very next day, Tasia bought five kilos of cocaine from Cereniti for $20,000 each. Impressed by Tasia's hustle, Alexus had told Cereniti to give Tasia fifteen more kilos on consignment. A week later, at around the same time that she and Bookie were moving into their luxury condo, Tasia had come back for another twenty bricks.

Alexus had been keeping her close ever since.

"Tee-Tee," Alexus said as she turned onto an off ramp, "I'm going to have to leave you with Tasia when we get to her place."

"You ain't leaving that ugly hoe with me," Tasia protested.

"I gotcha ugly hoe in my mirror, want to see her?" Cereniti shot back, turning to glare at her ex-colleague. They both began laughing.

Shaking her head, Alexus turned up the heat and hoped T-Walk wouldn't task a bunch of questions pertaining to where she'd been all day when she made it home.

She also hoped that Blake would accept her apology.Chapter 3

"Shannon proposed to me this morning. It took him seven years." BritneyBostic was gazing down at her engagement ring, her expression an amazed one as she strolled out of LaPorte County Jail beside Blake, impervious to the cruel eyes of the many officers who hated seeing the man suspected of slaying two of their fellow officers going home for Christmas.

"If you didn't want to wait," Blake said, "you should have proposed to him. Life's too short to be timid about anything. Sometimes you gotta take risks."

"It's a man's job to propose."

Blake shrugged and stuffed his hands deeper inside the front pocket ofhis black hoody. His mind was on Savaria. His eye was on a long 70's model Chevrolet Caprice that was parked behind Britney's small silver Mercedes.

The Caprice was painted candy red, with a tan leather Louis Vuitton convertible top. Chrome twenty-eight inch rims glistened beneath its meticulously cleaned frame.

"That's yours," Britney said, dipping her head further back into the fur- lined hood of her coat. She handed Blake a set of car keys. "Your house keys and the iPhone are on the passenger seat. I checked that suitcase in the backseat, but that's only because attorney Staples"— she motioned toward areddish brown faced woman in the passenger side of her Benz –"drove it here. I didn't touch anything, though. Alexus wants you to text her as soon as possible. She said she'll call you back immediately if she's available."

"If she's *available*?" Blake laughed, creating a cloud of fog before his face. "That bitch ain't wrote me in two months; she's lucky if I call before Valentine's Day."

"Don't call her a bitch," Britney chastised as she hastily trudged to her driver's door. "The least you could do is *thank* her. I'll call you on the first of the year. And please, this time, try to stay out of trouble. Merry Christmas."

"Merry Christmas." Blake was still stuck on the Chevy. He looked insideand saw that its interior was tan Louis Vuitton as well. "Merry Christmas tome."

He got behind the wheel and took in his surroundings. The Chevy's engine sprang to life. After turning on the iPhone, he turned and studied the Louis Vuitton suitcase on the seat behind him. Then he opened it, half expecting a pile of clothes or maybe twenty kilos.

"Daaaaammn!" he exclaimed.

The suitcase was filled with cash. More dollar bills than he'd ever seenup close. Twenties and fifties and hundreds, all bundled together neatly in rubber bands.

He shut the suitcase, and the biggest smile he'd ever smiled lit up his face. He was envisioning Savaria kneeling before a Christmas tree encircledby a thousand gifts, her little hands tearing away layers of wrapping paper.

He pulled away from the curb slowly, adjusting his seat, pushing buttons on the center console. A kaleidoscope of excited smiles— the majority of them white— met his eyes as he lanced the Caprice out of LaPorte and into Michigan City.

The iPhone started ringing as Blake was entering the parking lot of aToys "R" Us. Alexus's face appeared on the screen.

Blake contemplated pushing ignore. It would have made

him an even happier man if he'd followed through on the thought. But his attorney's suggestion made more sense. He had to thank Alexus for bailing him out.

He took a bundle of hundreds from the suitcase and stuffed it in his hoody's front pocket.

Then, stepping out of the Chevy to the jam packed parking lot, he lowered his head against the cold and answered the phone.

Alexus was still amazed by the iPhone's video chat feature. She waslying naked atop a plush white faux fur blanket. Her makeup was on, her long hair straightened and splayed out around her head. Her phone, proppedup against a silk encased pillow beside her, offered Blake a jaw dropping view of her from the waist up.

When he answered his phone, she turned onto her side to look at him. "Put some clothes on," Blake ordered. "I'm walking into Toys "R" Us, and I don't want no lil kids seeing you naked."

"What?" Alexus hopped off of her large circular bed and crossed the plush white carpet to a Carrera marble Jacuzzi in the corner. "Mind if I ask why you're at a toy store? And did you get the money? There's fivehundred thousand in there."

"Yeah, I got it. Damn, that's a half mill?" Blake was entering the store.

Bright lights shined above him.

Alexus picked up her Louis Vuitton robe from the Jacuzzi's edge and slowly, lasciviously slipped into it. Blake was watching her every move.

"I put a hundred grand in that Caprice," she said proudly.

"I can tell. Thanks."

"Well, come and thank me. I'm not standing here all dolled up fornothing. You can stop by Toys R Us later."

"No, I can't."

"Yes, you can and you will. I have about four hours until my family arrives from Mexico. We're going to dine here at the mansion with a bunch of important people, and I want to spend some time with you before then."

"I'm spending time with my daughter today," Blake said. "And I heard you got a man, anyway. Heard you fuckin' my nigga T-Walk."

Alexus released a sigh of disappointment. This wasn't how she'd plannedfor things to go.

"T-Walk and I are an item, Blake. He's my man now, but that doesn't have to change anything between *us*. I mean, you were here first, right?"

"Why didn't you write me?" Blake asked. "Why didn't you come visit me? Ash brought my baby all the way from Nap almost every week, and you couldn't..."

"I was busy."

"I gotta go. I'll be at you tomorrow."

"I'm pregnant, Blake." The words fell from her tongue like icicles. She stepped closer to the bed, closer to the phone. "I'm ten weeks pregnant."

"Tell T-Walk I said congratulations," Blake said, and hung up.

Ashley's forrest green Taurus was parked in front of Blake's mother Carolyn's house when he got there. Christmas lights were strung up across the short metal fence. Blake's entire car was filled with bags full of presentsfor his family. To keep them from seeing their gifts, he left them in the car and, aplomb, stepped out stuffing bundles of twenties in his sweatpants pockets after parking behind the Taurus.

Lincoln Avenue was alive with colorful lights and plastic, flickering lawnornaments. Blake noticed that Boogie's old place across the street— the house Alexus had taken him to shortly before his arrest— was the only unlithouse on the block.

"Lil bruh!" Streets shouted, smiling hugely as he rushed out of his Chevy, zipping up his black Girbaud jeans. He had on a black Pelle Pelle jacket over a white Girbaud shirt. A blunt was secured between two fingertips.

"Yeah, I'm back, bruh. Full throttle goon mode." Blake embraced his brother, feeling better than he'd felt in a while. "That bad bitch bonded me out. Bought me the Chevy too."

130

"Nigga, you better *marry* her."

"Nah, bruh," Blake laughed. "She fuckin' T-Walk. Plus, I heard she sucked like ten niggas off in the club the night that shit went down at The Swagger."

"Come on," Streets said.

Blake pushed open Carolyn's gate, and he and Streets started up the cobblestone walkway. Ashley's cousin, Danielle, got out of Streets' car withher head down. The proverbial walk of shame. She followed them through the front door.

Elated screams, tears of joy and a whole lot of hugging ensued. Savaria had been stretched out on the sofa sleeping with her head in her mother's lap. Dale 'Big Streets' King, Blake's father, had been reclined in his lay-z- boy chair, reading one of James Patterson's novels. The moment Blake entered the door, they all seemed to hop up at once.

Savaria ran into his arms, shouting, "Daddy, Daddy!" He lifted her onto his waist, and her little lips pecked his face a hundred times. Ashley began crying even before he had an arm around her, planting a soft kiss on herlips.

"Boy, how did you get out?" Ashley asked.

"Daddy, you goin back to jail again? 'Cause I don't want you in jail again, Daddy," Savaria said. "Momma got a boyfriend at my granny Nana'shouse. His name…"

Ashley pinched Savaria's ear to shut her up."Ouch!" Vari giggled and massaged her ear.

Blake looked into Ashley's eyes, giving her the 'you must wanna get choked' look. He pulled a knot of hundred dollar bills from his hoody and put it in Vari's hands. A bundle of fifties went to Ashley. And when Carolyn and Streets' eight year old twin boys, Jaime and Jason, appeared from the kitchen, the three of them each received hundred-count bundles of fifties.

"Son," Dale said, slapping Blake on the shoulder, "it's good to see you home. But where's all this money coming from? Who came up with your bond money?"

"Leave my baby 'lone, Dale," Carolyn cut in. "The boy ain't been here two seconds and you already messin' wit' him. You ought to be prasin' the Lord."

"Police done searched this house twice already. I don't need them findingno whole lotta money up in here that we can't explain," Dale said.

But Blake paid him no mind. Dale was always cantankerous when he waswithout a bottle of Seagram's gin or a bag of crack to soothe his troubled soul. Standing there in his dingy blue trash man uniform, with a Newport cigarette hanging precariously from the right of his mouth, Dale couldn't stop himself from staring at the cash in his wife's hand.

Carolyn tucked her five grand away in her blouse. "I'm almost through cookin'," she said, "so don't get far." She turned and headed back into the kitchen.

"I ain't goin' nowhere," Blake confided, even though he was thinking of Alexus and how damn sexy she'd looked naked on that bed. *And hadn't she mentioned something about a mansion?* Blake gave his poor father four bundles of twenties. Then he gave Streetsa bundle of hundreds and the keys to his Chevy. "Pull it around back and put all that stuff in the basement. Everything except the suitcase." Blake said. "Grab some bread out thesuitcase for yourself. I'm about to go upstairs and change clothes."

"Ha!" Ashley laughed, taking Savaria from Blake's hip. "You're about todo a lot more than change clothes."

In the affluent Long Beach area of Michigan City, a long line of multimillion dollar mansions line the shore of Lake Michigan. One fancy, 16,000 square foot palace of blue marble and glass had happened to be on the market when Vida Costilla made up her mind to visit Alexus for *Christmas*. Apparently, Vida had taken a liking to the mansion and all its amenities. She purchased it for nine million dollars.

Alexus loved every mesmerizing inch of the high ceilinged, blue marble floored beachfront property. The indoor swimming pool was a favorite of hers. All except two of the mansion's seven bedrooms had white fur from wall to wall, and Alexus liked the way it felt beneath her bare feet. It was like walking on warm snow.

After Blake had hung up on her, she'd dived into the pool and practiced her backstroke until her legs and arms ached. She thought about the factthat she had failed to warn Blake of the danger he now faced as a free man. Craig wanted him dead. Bookie wanted him dead. Even Neal, the detective who was Rita's new man, disliked Blake King with a passion, and wanted him dead. Alexus mulled over a plan to keep Blake safely out of harm'sway during her relaxing swim. Then she went back up to the bedroom she'dchosen for herself and got some sleep.

"Mamacita! Lexi, get your lazy ass up." Savio Costilla's deep voice was warm and inviting.

Alexus rolled over, and even before her eyes opened she was smiling in Savio's direction.

He was dapper in an expressive black business suit, twirling a set of keys around an index finger. Tall, bronze-skinned and gentle-faced with cheery gray eyes and a well-groomed, low fade haircut, he looked the part of an excessively rich young Mexican bachelor.

But his seemingly pleasant appearance was only a front. Savio's bellicosetemper had ended the lives of many men in Mexico. She rememberedwatching him fatally shoot an older white man in Brownsville for staring at her a second too long. Another incident, in June of 2005, had resulted in thebeheadings of seventeen rival cartel members in Monterrey, Mexico; according to his brother Santiago he had murdered them with the ease of a "mother slicing bread."

Dropping the keys into his pants pocket, Savio approached the bed and kissed Alexus on the forehead.

"'Please tell me you're not driving that white Bentley out there," he said in Spanish.

"I'm not driving that white Bentley." Alexus sat up, fixing her hair. "There, you happy?"

"Not exactly. I figured you'd at least have a Phantom. Santiago and Ihave the new Bugatti Veyrons. Max speed in those is 260. Speedy Gonzalezcouldn't catch us."

"I'm not rich enough to spend two million on a car, Savio,

and I'm not trying to go that damn fast, anyway."

"Two million's chump change." Savio went to the large, white fur curtains of one big window and opened them, "I moved two million througha jeweler a few years back. And wait until you see how easy it is to launder money through the casinos in Las Vegas."

"I'm interested in learning about that...whenever you free up some time in your schedule."

"We can't rush things, Lexi," Savio said as Alexus joined him at the window, tying her robe shut. "You'll be fine after today. There's twenty-sixmillion in it for you.

"Sounds like a start!" Alexus replied, flabbergasted. She was gazingdown at five blacked out Rolls Royce Phantoms that were parked in the circular driveway out front. "What's with all the cars out there? Are these yours?"

"Security. For the family. I keep them with me at all times, and today I felt they needed to be here in full force. We're plugging you in with the Traveling Vice Lords in Chicago. These guys are treacherous, but they're a source of major income. They were Papi's loyal customers back when you were in middle school."

"So, what's the deal?" asked Alexus.

"Look over there." Savio pointed at a white semi-truck that was inconspicuously resting beside Alexus's Bentley. "Got five hundred bricks of coke and two hundred bricks of H for the Vice Lords in there. There's some guns, too. And five hundred pounds of California Kush."

"Why are we arming them? What if they turn against..."

"The guns aren't for them, Lexi. Neither is the weed. Give them to that cousin of yours and his crew, and keep them around you. You're in the big league now, little cousin. You need protection."

Alexus was gazing at the Phantoms again. Black windows, black paint and black rims... as black as her thoughts. She didn't want to put more weapons into the hands of Blake King's enemy. What if someone was killedwith those guns? And what if that someone was the father of her unborn child?

"We don't need guns," she said, crossing her arms defensively.

"We all need guns, Lexi. I just got a call from Moammar Ghadafi in Libya. He thinks his people are about to rebel against him, and he's lookingto spend more cash on weapons because of it."

"I've never been to Libya, and I don't particularly care what Ghadafi needs."

Savio clamped his hands down on Alexus shoulders. His intense eyes stared deep into her green ones.

"If grandma loved you like she loves us, you would have a hundred Mexicans for security," he said.

An intense silence followed his statement. Alexus started crying. What did he mean IF grandma loved you like she loves us'? What kind of bullshit was that?

"Don't go getting all upset," Savio said, softly squeezing her shoulders. "Grandma has never liked blacks. She was pissed when Papi came home with your mother, said he'd tarnished our family tree with that misstep."

Alexus ripped away from Savio and set her sights on a silver, ice filled bucket that was sitting on the Jacuzzi's mahogany edge between two ten ounce crystal stem glasses. She'd originally planned to sip on a bit of Aceof Spades champagne with Blake before retiring to the bed for an apologetic fuck, but now she simply needed a drink. She snatched the bottleof bubbly from the bucket and filled a glass.

"I can't believe you just said that, Savio," she said in a tone of disgust. "Don't kill the messenger, okay? You know I love you, Lexi. I wouldn't be here if I didn't." Savio watched her down her drink and pour anotherone. A full minute of deafening silence passed. Then Savio said, "I'm flyingthe cash to Las Vegas today. We're pushing it through the Cosmopolitan Casino Spa Tower, the casino owned by the Gandolfini family. They're charging us four million for the laundry. Twenty two million will be wired to your account once the transaction is complete. It'll be listed as a businessloan, but you can do whatever with it."

Alexus remained silent, looking down into the heated Jacuzzi's churning water. She heard a toilet flush somewhere nearby, but there were too many bathrooms in the mansion to know which one was occupied.

"You got company?" Savio asked. Alexus turned and saw that he was staring out into the hallway.

"Nobody was here but me," said Alexus. She still wouldn't look directly at him. How long had he known of Vida's ill feelings towards blacks? Maybe he was the same way.

A short, serious-faced Mexican man appeared at the bedroom doorway. He had on a long black trench coat, and he was buckling his belt tightly around his corpulent waist. "Nachos we had in Chicago, vato," he said, rubbing his belly, "didn't agree with me."

Two brief puffs of air—*pyoo-pyoo*—sounded in Alexus's ear. At the same instant, two .50 caliber bullets burned through the fat man's forehead. He dropped like a sack of potatoes.

Glancing over at Savio, gasping reflexively, Alexus saw her cousin tucking a gold plated Desert Eagle inside his suit jacket. The gun had a longgolden silencer screwed into its barrel.

"Savio!" Alexus screamed, her frantic eyes sweeping back and forth,from the dead man's grotesque, exploded head, to Savio's emotionless face."Get some clothes on," Savio said, leaving the bedroom. "The family's downstairs waiting on us. And watch your step, there's a dead guy out here."

Chapter 22

When she was not talking on the phone with Dennis or speaking with the elder neighbors about reducing the west side's crime rate, when she was notcleaning the house or cooking up some scrumptious meal for herself and Neal Miller, when she was not lecturing Alexus on how to walk righteouslywith God, or at the Progressive Womanhood group meetings, then Rita Maecould usually be found at the First Baptist Church on the corner of Eighth and Willard.

The church was Rita's place of refuge whenever she needed spiritual up- lifting. The congregation was a wonderful mix-ture of people who praisedthe Lord together on almost every day of the week. When Rita had joined the church a month and a half prior, it had been in dire need of a renovation,inundated in overdue bills and on the brink of foreclosure. Rita's kind heart had succumbed to the church's needs, and she had purchased the building for a little less than a hundred grand and put an ad-ditional thirty eight into the renovation.

She was sitting in the front pew next to Pastor James Harvell, hashing over tomorrow's Christmas plans, when Neal Miller stormed into the church. His anger was palpable.

"Rita, we need to talk," he said. "Okay, give me a few minutes.""It's urgent," he shot back.

Rita told the pastor she would be back in a moment. Then she put on her coat, shouldered her purse and followed Neal out-side, wondering what it was that had him so upset.

She did not have to wait long to find out. As soon as they settled into his Charger, Miller cut to the chase.

"Your daughter posted Blake King's bail earlier today, and I'm nottalking ten percent to a bail bondsman. And not only that, we think she mayhave also helped the families of his other friends acquire the cash needed to bond them out. As of now, nine of them have been released. Nine of them. The mayor's been chewing my boss out all day."

Rita looked down at her purse, massaging her forehead with

her fingertips. *What the heck has my baby gotten herself into this time?* She thought to herself, resenting the fact that she had yet to inform Neal about the millions she and Alexus had been given, and of Alexus's connection to the one man Neal detested so intensely.

"You have to tell me *something*, Rita," Neal continued," because this investigation has just deepened. Your daughter's name was ran through the federal database. Wanna know what we found?" He didn't give her time to answer. "Juan Costilla, Mexican drug lord...ring any bells? *Mrs. Rita Mae Bishop Costilla?"*

"That's not my name anymore," she replied, raising her guilt stricken eyes to meet his. "And what does that have to do with anything? Neither menor Alexus were involved with the criminal side of my *ex* –husband's life. When I found out about it, I divorced him."

"But you didn't leave him. You lied and told me that you moved here to be closer to your brother."

"I didn't lie, Neal." Her words sounded weak. She shifted uncomfortably in her seat and stared straight ahead at a half dozen young girls who were standing near two big rimmed Caprices at a burned out convenience storeup the street.

"I spoke with DEA agent Dewitt Larkson," Neal said. He, too, waspaying attention to the crowd of youngsters. "He told me that Juan Costilla was the leader of Mexico's second largest and most deadliest cartel—The Costilla Cartel. Their war with the Zeta cartel is devastating northern Mexico, and now we have reason to believe the Costilla cartel have come here."

"What would make you think that? And what does Alexus have to do with any of this? She's a real estate investor. Every cent of her income has come from either home sales or her..."

"Grandmother, I know. And that's what's puzzling us all. Vida Costilla made four billion dollars in the Mexican stock market last year alone;which is why we can't understand why her boys are involved in the drug trade. Two of her grandchildren are real estate moguls. Her restaurants are prospering."

Neal shook his head. "I don't know what it is about her, but something is definitively wrong. The FBI tried tapping her phones andcame up with nothing but a stream of static; evidently, she has scrambling devices on every line."

"Please get to the point, Neal. I have important business to discuss with Pastor Harvell."

Miller reached around to the backseat and grabbed an iPad. Later an image appeared on the screen that made Rita cringe.

It was a picture of a corpse, a short Mexican man with two big holes in his forehead. He was stretched out on a bed of snow in front of a tree.

"He was found in the woods near Krueger Middle School. A twelve year old found him." Neal zoomed in on a tattoo on the dead man's neck. There were two small, interlocking letter C's. "Ever seen this particular tattoo?"

Rita couldn't believe her eyes. It was the exact same tat that Juan had behind his left ear, a tat that every member of the Costilla cartel received upon their initiation into the lucrative drug gang.

"Oh, my God," she muttered vacantly as her heart plummeted to the pitof her stomach, "they're here. The Costilla cartel is here."

King Rio

Chapter 23

At 6:45 p.m., T-Walk's cloud gray Denali whipped into the Long Beachmansion's driveway with enough speed to cause his thirty two inch tires toslide an extra five feet across the blacktop as he parked beside Alexus's car.She was standing in the foyer behind the tall glass doors that served as the mansion's main entrance. Her eyes were full of tears. Her body wastremulous, and her full length leather coat was not warming her chilled flesh the least bit.

T-Walk stepped out of his pimped out SUV. He stopped dead in his tracksas all four doors of one Phantom were flung open. Suddenly, he found himself staring down the formidable barrels of four Mac 11 submachine guns, guns equipped with red laser beams, titanium silencers and 32 round clips.

"He's here for me!" Alexus shouted frantically. She barged outside and ran to her boyfriend. "Put those fucking guns down!"

"Don't warn 'em baby. Let 'em find out the hard way." An expertmarksman, T-Walk could take down four targets in under two seconds… and he was prepared to do just that.

But the gunmen lowered their weapons and retreated back into the Rolls Royces.

Amorously, T-Walk cupped Alexus's face in his palms and kissed her softlips. "Baby, what's wrong?" he asked in a tone that was so considerate it made her green eyes cry harder.

"I'm afraid to stay here by myself," she said, burying her face against theside of his neck. "I mean, my dad's family is here, but I still feel alone. Andthey scare me. They're all a bunch of angry sociopaths with no regard for human life."

T-Walk embraced her firmly, rubbing her back, letting her pour her heart out in one poignant moment of emotion. She felt comfortable in his strong arms. Even though he knew that she was possibly pregnant by another man,he was still there for her, and that mattered a lot. Especially to Rita, whowas under the impression that T-Walk was a godsend for Alexus.

"Thank you, T-Walk," Alexus whispered into his ear, "for being so real. Besides my father, I've never trusted a man the way I trust you."

"I'm real all day and all night. You ain't never gotta worry about that changin'. Are we stayin' here or not?" He cradled her face in his hands again, thumbing away her tears.

"My grandmother wants my mom and her brother to come over fordinner tonight," Alexus said, regaining her emotional equilibrium. "She wants to ask my mom why the majority of the money she gave her is still sitting in the bank."

T-Walk's nose was as red as Rudolph's in the frigid breeze. So were his ears. Alexus interlaced the fingers of her right hand with those of his left, and together they walked into the mansion. To Alexus, this moment was theepitome of picture perfect. She reveled in the warmth of his strong hand, feeling a sense of companionship that she had never felt before.

In the beautifully floored foyer, she stopped in front of a double stacked row of four foot long wooden crates. There were twenty crates in all.Behind them sat ten 50 pound bales of high grade Kush; the potent scent of the weed was barely detectable, due to the multiple layers of baby powder scented wipes, cellophane, and Vaseline that had been methodically wrapped around the bales before they were boxed in cardboard.

"I met up with some Vice Lords at another mansion up the road," Alexus said, discarding her coat atop a crate. "Taxed them a hundred grand a-key for two hundred bricks of boy and twelve a-key for five hundred bricks of girl. They're pledging to spend at least twenty five million with me every three months. Here, open this crate."

"Damn, twenty five!" T-Walk's eyes were cast upwards, and he seemedmesmerized by the crystal chandeliers above him. He took off his gray leather Gucci jacket and laid it over Alexus's coat. Then he snatched the topoff the crates she had pointed to.

It was filled with Kalashnikov AK-47's and fifty round banana clips. He picked up one, slipped in a clip full of bullets, and cocked it in one fluid motion.

"My cousin Savio is on his way to Vegas in my grandma's private jet right now with the money," Alexus said, intrigued by the expert way T-walkheld the weapon. "I'll have twenty two million dollars in the bank! Legit cash. We can …"

"I can bet you a hundred racks," T-Walk interrupted, aiming at a chandelier, "that Bookie is going to end up whacking Blake with one of these. Craig told me his girlfriend, Danielle, saw Blake earlier. Said he was flexin' in a Chevy on eights, blowin' money on everybody." He turned to stare into her eyes. "Wonder where he got all that money from. He couldn't even afford to pay fifteen thousand to bond out of jail."

"Don't look at *me*," she said, crossing her arms defensively. "I didn't accuse you of anything."

"Your eyes did, and for the record, none of these guns are going to Bookie. I'm thinking about having Tee-Tee and Tasia sell them in New York and Atlanta. Two hundred guns, everything $300 apiece…"

"Nuh-uh." T-Walk laid the AK-47 back in its former resting place. Then he pried open a second crate… Heckler and Koch MP-5 submachine guns with sound suppressors. "We need these guns. And you'll will only make about fifty or sixty thousand off these. What is that going to do for you, buya pair of earrings?"

"Does it matter?"

"You're trying to save Blake's ass, and it's not going to work. He's too wild; I've been dealing with that young nigga since he was eleven. Only thing gon' calm him down is a gunshot to the head."

"It's not gonna come to that," Alexus said, hopefully. "There's a possibility that he's the father of my unborn child. I can't allow anything to happen to him."

T-Walk eyelids slowly squinted close together, as though he had inhaled five blunts of Kush. He fished in the side pocket of his blue velour Gucci pants and came out with his smart phone.

"You fucked him today, didn't you?" He coldly asked. "Bitch, you betternot have sucked his dick."

"I haven't been with any other person since we met," Alexus

replied. His words were like punches to her heart. *It's my fault he's feeling this way,* shethought, holding his taut gaze.

He brought the phone up to his ear.

"Hello? Streets? Man, I heard lil bruh got out today… Yeah, let me get a word wit' 'im."

Chapter 24

"I can't even lie, Tim-Tim, I thought you was gon' end up rat-ting about that one," Blake admitted, honestly, as he steered his Caprice into SouthgateApartments behind his brother's car.

Thuggishly decked out in a snow white Coogi sweat suit, with a matching skullcap and white Timberland boots, Blake King *felt* like a king. The four 15" speakers in his trunk had his entire car shaking with Birdman's "Fire Flame" remix, and the video was playing on all twelveTVs in the Chevy's cabin, which was densely clouded with Kush smoke.

In the rear seats, there were three sexy young ladies, a slim bodiedchocolate flavored Lakiesha Brown; her half-sis-ter, Lakita Thomas, a thick redbone bordering on obesity; and Tiffany "Tiff-Tiff" Jenkins. The girls were sitting on the laps of Lil Mike, Young-D and Blubby, all of whom hadbeen bonded out of jail earlier in the day with Blake's newly acquired fortune.

"I could never be a snitch," Timothy Trice confided. He hit the blunt and instantly began coughing, then passed it to his left, to Blake. "That punk assdetective tried to get me to talk at least twice every week. I know he gottabe mad as hell about me getting bonded out."

"Fuck that cop. He gon' fuck around and get it next," Blake said, glancing down at the forty caliber glock in his lap; he'd just bought it from Blubby for an even grand.

Blake parked between his brother's car and an oak colored Escalade EXTon thirty two inch Lexani rims. He was parked near the front door of an apartment that belonged to Dawn, a pretty-faced hustler who'd just recently completed a five year federal prison sentence in Lexington, Kentucky.Streets had sug-gested a spur of the moment Christmas Eve party at her place, and since Ashley was out doing some last minute Christmas shopping, Blake had decided to join the fun… at least for a little while.

With eight bottles of Remy Martin, five fifths of Hennessy, a hundred ecstasy pills, and four $800 ounces of Kush to party with, an exhilarating night was inevitable for everyone involved.

As Blake and his passengers were piling out of the Caprice, he noticed Kiesha eyeing him; Kita was staring him down, too. But he had his sights set on Tiffany, who had yet to cast even a causal look his way.

Streets interrupted Blake's freaky thoughts. "Lil bruh, somebody wanna talk to you," Streets said, stepping around the front of his car with his arm outstretched, phone in hand.

"Who is it?" Blake was watching Kiesha's peach-shaped ass shake as shesauntered up the stairs to Dawn's apartment door.

"It's T-Walk."

Blake cracked a smile as he accepted the phone."What it is, high yellow?" he quipped.

"Shit. You seen Alexus today?" T-Walk's words exuded a repressed but thinly veiled fire that didn't go unnoticed by Blake.

"Nah, I ain't seen that bitch. Niggas been tellin' me she yours now. That true? You handcuffin' buss downs?" Taking a toke from the blunt, Blake threw his head back and laughed up into the darkening sky. "Didn't shesuck you and some other niggas off in the club? I heard she gave Craigsome head, too. Man, on some for real shit, I wish I would've knew she wassuckin' dick like that... I would've had her slurpin' all day."

"Who bonded you out of jail?" "Some nigga named Johnny Lay."

"Ha ha ha. Real funny," T-Walk said sarcastically. "I talked to Craig and Bookie. They wanted me to squash that bullshit between y'all. We got too much to lose and nothin' to gain from this lil war. Niggas makin' *millions* out here, lil bruh. *Millions!* Feds just indicted thirty somethin' niggas the other week. They popped off Sneezy, Cheese, Raw-B, Jay— shit, theydamn near got *everybody!* And whoever slipped through the cracks got statecases."

All of this was not breaking news to Blake. During his stint in the county jail, he'd been housed with several others who'd been arrested in a threecity sting that stemmed from the fatal shooting at The Swagger. Many of them had supplied Blake with drugs at one time or another and all of them respected him; after all, he had *allegedly* shot and killed two cops, and to those caged in hustlers, he was as much a hero as Hancock.

"I'm done shooting if they are," Blake said. "I didn't start that drama, anyway. Them niggas shouldn't have robbed me."

"Well, it's over now. Give me your word.""You got it."

"I'm *serious*, Blake."

"Nigga, I'm *serious*, too! Have I ever lied to you? I said I'm done.

D.O.N.E. Now let me slide off into this lil party real quick before my baby momma hit me."

Handing the phone back to Streets, Blake studied the denim covered backslides of four more girls who had just got out of his brother's car. They were carrying the drinks into Dawn's place.

He and Streets followed everyone inside. Dawn was sitting at a small glass topped dining room table next to a brown skinned man who looked to be about 6'3" and 250 pounds. She was giving him a tattoo on his forearm; he was checking out the girls while simultaneously observing the guys.

"Y'all go ahead and get started," Dawn encouraged. "Plastic cups are under the sink, and I got two bags of ice in the deep freezer. Make yourself at home. Turn on the CD player. Just make sure none of my shit comes up missin'."

She went on to say that the big guy was a Blood from Cincinnati named Jazzy, but no one offered their respective names to the Ohio native; instead,they all turned their uncertain eyes to Blake.

It was then that he realized the level of respect he'd attained in thestreets. For a few tense, wordless seconds, he stared at Jazzy, and Jazzy stared back.

Finally, after careful thought, Blake asked, "Who you know out here?" "He was just in the joint with Lil Lord," Dawn cut in. "They're tight like this." She twisted two fingers together.

"Yeah," Jazzy concurred, "my lil nigga introduced me to Dawn a couple years ago. I'm out here to drop off some killer and twenty cell phones to hismule."

"You got his phone number?" Blake asked, skeptical.

Jazzy produced his cell phone and within seconds had Lil Lord on the line, a feat that astonished Blake, because there weren't many guys outside of Indiana State Prison who Lil Lord considered, worthy of his friendship. Lil Lord was the realest nigga Blake ever met, the highest caliber of hood nigga, and Blake idolized him in many ways.

So, when Lil Lord said, "He's solid, lil bruh. Fuck wit' him. Dub Life or no Life. Get at me later," Blake walked over to Jazzy, shook his mammoth hand, then sat in the black steel backed chair beside him and dropped an ounce of Kush on the table.

"If you know how to roll blunts" Blake said, lifting a fifty count box of Swisher Sweets cigarillos from a bag that Tiff-Tiff had just set down near his chair, "Start rollin. Kita, bring me two bottles of Remy. And sit that Buffie on my lap when you' done."

Everyone broke into a recess of laughter. Then the drinks began flowing, the music... a Lil Boosie and Webbie mixtape... started playing, and Kush smoke filled the air. Tiffany and Danielle sat juxtaposed on the livingroom's Aztec-patterned sofa, snorting up grams of coke, ingesting Blue Dolphin x-pills, gulping down mouthfuls of cognac and ignoring Blake.

But it did not bother him at all. With Lakita's thick derriere on his lap, and her half-sister's long thin fingers massaging his shoulders, he quickly became horny enough to achieve a raging hard on.

Before long, Kita and Kiesha were pulling Blake down the creaky wooden steps that led to the basement.

He laid back on a king sized bed, pushed his sweatpants and boxers downaround his ankles , and watched as the two pretty young ladies crawled up onto the bed like lionesses stalking their prey.

"Tell me how this feels," Lakiesha said in a husky purr. She slid her sumptuous lips down his dick until its thick crown was lodged deep in her throat. Then, slowly her mouth attacked his thick dick, and her flickering tongue bathed it in spit.

"Sensational," replied Blake.

Sipping his Remy straight from the bottle, he attentively watched the twogirls as they alternately sucked and licked him. Minutes later the sisters stripped naked and took turns riding him— both his tongue and his dick. Hethirstily tongued their sweet tasting, creamy centers and wholeheartedly enjoyed the wet tug of their pussies on his manhood.

LaKita gyrated her way to an orgasm on Blake's mouth before tumbling to the side of him, breathing heavily, giggling merrily. Then it was Lakieha's turn to climax—for the fourth of fifth time, Blake noted— as shebit her lower lip and dropped all her weight downward, completely impaling herself on his erection.

"I can't take no more of that monster," panted Kiesha. She climbed off ofBlake, joining her sister next to him. "Boy, somethin' must be wrong with yo' dick. Why can't you come?"

"He got too much energy for me." Looking physically drained, Lakita started to dress.

The clicking sound of heels on the basement steps made Blake glancethat way.

"Too much energy?" It was Tiffany, smiling at him as she preceded Danielle and Streets downstairs, "I think I can take care of that little problem."

"Girl," Danielle warned, "Craig gon' fuck you clean up if he finds out about this."

"He won't find out." Tiff-Tiff took out an extra-large condom from her Alexander McQueen shoulder bag, tore it open with her teeth, then approached Blake and rolled it down his glazed dick. She waited for Kita and Kiesha to leave before taking off her jeans and heeled boots.

Face down, ass up, she moaned as Blake slid in and out of her juicy insides.

He came in no time.

King Rio

Chapter 25

At precisely 9:00 P.M. sharp, the seemingly endless procession of Audis, Beemers, and limousines began filling the circular driveway in front of the mansion.

Many of the arriving guests were top echelon celebrities. Tyler Perry wasamong the first to show up. Jennifer Hudson and her WWE wrestling star boyfriend pulled in behind Sofia Vergara. Penelope Cruz came with her friend, Salma Hayek. A number of politicians, Democrats and Republicans, were also in attendance.

From her vantage point at her second floor bedroom window, Alexus watched, unfathomably stunned and awestruck, as the celebs handed over their keys to the red vested valet parking employees and disappeared beneath the hastily constructed gold and black striped awning that led to thefront door.

"So, this is the big meeting, huh? Grandma Vida's coming out with her own damn TV channel? Who does she think she is Oprah?" Alexus turned away from the window, and her indignant eyes landed on her aunt Jennifer's.

Statuesque and buxom, with a thick mane of straight black hair andoverly rouged cheeks, Jennifer Costilla was still a fairly attractive woman atforty-six. She stood up, smoothing away a wrinkle in her black Armani dress.

"You know," said Jenny, in Spanish, because she did not know a lick of English, "my mother is personally responsible for every designer dressyou've ever worn, every meal you've ever eaten. It would be nice if you expressed just the tiniest amount of appreciation."

Sucking her teeth, Alexus looked down to inspect her own attire. Hersoot colored backless Louis Vuitton dress fit her elegantly. Her black diamond clustered tennis bracelet, watch, necklace, and teardrop shaped earrings shined brilliantly; her four inch LV heels, drowning in an ocean of black diamonds that brought the price of the gaudy shoes up to $120,000, were certain to be the talk of the industry after tonight's ballroom celebration.

"Excuse my bad disposition, Aunt Jenny, but it bothers me to know that my grandmother halfway hates me because of my ethnicity"

"*Hates* you?" Jenny's hands slapped on to her hips, and her voice rose anoctave, "You think Vida Costilla hates you? I wish somebody hated me enough to buy me a million dollar pair of shoes. You sound foolish. We should be downstairs congratulating her on her success as an international businesswoman. She's directed, produced, and executive produced showson Mexican television for decades. Now she's finding her riches in the television society of America, and she has celebs of every level jockeying for a talk show or a sitcom on her network. Our only job is to support her."

Alexus rubbed her pregnant belly with both her palms and turned back to the window. She felt a thousand emotions tumbling around in her chest like pebbles in a washing machine.

"Aunt Jenny I'm...I'm curious to know, exactly how much is she worth? I mean, I'm no financial genius, but doesn't it take tons of millions to buy a television network?"

Outside, Rita Mae's dark green Escalade pulled up.

"I have the latest Forbes magazine at home. They estimated Mother's networth in an article devoted to the world's richest women. She's reportedly accumulated forty-three billion dollars over the past thirty some years, mostof which came from huge, risky investments in the stock market."

"Shit, that mean she's richer than Oprah," Alexus mused. She was watching Rita, Neal Miller, Dennis and his wife, as they exited the SUV in their Sunday's best. "All that money and all I got from..."

Alexus grew silent as Aunt Jenny's youngest son, Santiago Costilla,entered the bedroom with an ingratiating smile on his clean shaven face andan arm draped around T-Walk's neck.

"I like this guy, Lexi. He's got elephant nuts, you chose well," said Santiago as he slapped T-Walk between the shoulder blades. "Papi would love him."

Aunt Jenny frowned. "No he would not. Papi would kill

him."

"Have either of you heard from him?" Alexus asked, hating that she had to use Spanish in front of her boyfriend. "Neither me nor my mom have heard from him since his arrest. We've written him a hundred letters and have yet to receive a single reply; Papi would never be so inconsiderate."

Jenny and Santiago locked eyes quickly. The suddenness of this made Alexus suspicious of them, but she didn't show it. A morsel of dubiety had just been dropped onto her brain, and later on, preferably with the assistance of her prudent mother, that morsel would be thoroughly dissectedand analyzed.

But what would her conclusion...*their* conclusion...be?

"I don't know, I don't know," Santiago said, turning to leave, motioning for everyone to follow. "What I do know is that Salma Hayek's down there without a date. That's all I *need* to know!"

In the blue marble floored ballroom, fifty circular tables, covered byblack silk tablecloths, gold cutlery and crystal stem glasses, were set up to accommodate 190 guests. A wooden stage, complete with a glass podium and looming black stage curtains, had been erected against one wall.

Waiters and waitresses in black blazers designed by Louis Vuitton dispensed sushi, oysters and vintage champagne. With their good looks theycould have been Rip the Runway models.

Alexus and her family were seated closest to the stage. At her table sat T-Walk and Neal; the two of them stuck out like sore thumbs in the roomfulof black suits and dresses. T-Walk had on the same blue velour and mesh jogging suit, and Neal wore the suit he'd worn on their first movie date.

Rita Mae and Vida were quietly conversing at the table to the left of Alexus.

"Baby," T-Walk said softly, reaching across the table to squeeze Alexus'shand, "you look amazing, way prettier than any of these other women."

"Thank you, and you don't look too bad yourself." She smiled, then turned her attention to Neal Miller. "Isn't this the most memorable Christmas Eve ever? I had no idea my grandma was so connected. This little..." she glanced at a black and gold banner that read *Minority Television Network*, "...MTN channel could turn into something big. My Aunt Jenny said the NBA has already contacted the network about the showing of primetime season games."

Detective Miller eased forward "You're a smart young lady, Alexus. I really believe that. T-Walk's a lucky man to have you."

"I'm the lucky one," Alexus corrected. "I never expected him to be so loyal to me."

"His father, B-Walk, was the same way. But that's neither here nor there.If you're as smart as I believe you are, you'll answer all these questions as honestly as possible."

Alexus stiffened. She looked over to her boyfriend for buttress; he was staring at the detective, eyes narrowed.

"First off," Neal began, "I'm interested in knowing why you decided to bond Blake King out of jail."

"*What!*" T-Walk snatched his hand back and glared at Alexus. "*So,* you *did* bond him out! And I bet you bought him that Chevy, too. I can't believethis shit." He stood, his demeanor tumultuous, and stormed out of theballroom.

As Alexus was getting to her feet, feeling embarrassed, scowling at Neal,he grabbed her hand, effectively halting her.

"Don't think for one second I'm gonna let you get away with what you'redoing," he threatened. "You're playing with fire. Blake King is a cold blooded monster, a modern day serial killer. Now you can either help me bring him down, or you can continue to finance that criminal's little wannabe gang until you're brought down with them. I'd advise you to cooperate."

"And I advise you to let go of me," Alexus said tightly. "Blake is simplya friend of mine. He's not a killer, Neal. Get that out of your head."

Miller released her hand. "I'm only trying to help you."

"I don't need your help. Next time you decide to put me on blast, please don't do it while my man's present."

Chapter 26

Check the only one that didn't have one.

Sitting on his mother's living room sofa with Ashley and Streets, watching his daughter and Streets' twin boys as they impatiently ripped intotheir gifts, Blake kept mentally going over the note his attorney had given him.

What did that last sentence mean? He'd conducted a thorough search of the Caprice, but he had found nothing other than some insurance papers, registrations, and an unopened bag of Jolly Ranchers.

"I've never in my life owned a piece of jewelry this expensive," Ashley said, gazing down at the watch's yellow paved diamond drizzledface. "A nine thousand dollar watch. Hmmm." She turned to Blake with suspicion filled eyes. "I want to know who dropped that fifteen thousand foryour bond. And who paid for all these gifts."

"Stay out of my business. You didn't see me askin' you about that nigga you got laid up all around my daughter." Blake leaned to the side and kissedAshley's cheek. "Merry Christmas."

Savaria leaped to her feet and went over to the iPad Santa Claus hadbrought her and the twins. There were also iPads and iPhones for Ashley,Streets, Mr. and Mrs. King, and Ashley's mother; a myriad of play station3's, Xbox 360's, and Nintendo Wii's with a vast collection of games;clothes and shoes and jackets for everyone; and a bunch of toys for the kids. "Blake, you have truly outdone yourself this time," Carolyn King said.

She was tired looking but clearly happy for her grandchildren as she stood by the tree in her threadbare red robe, sipping from her cup of coffee. "You and Santa must be good friends now, 'cause that fat bastard ain't never leftus with this many gifts."

"Daddy you know Santa?" asked a bright eyed Savaria.

"Yup. I loaned him the money he needed to pay his elves to

build all this stuff." Blake was recording video of Vari's indelible smile with his new cellphone. He had never seen his baby girl so excited and full of energy.

"Nuh-uh, Daddy, Sanna Caus got all the moneys. Him don't need *your* moneys; *me* and *Momma* need *your* moneys," Vari emphasized. "We need itfor the *recussion*." She said it matter of factly, as though she was the parent and Blake was her son.

"That's right, Vari," Ashley encouraged with a giggle. "But it's notrecussion, it's a recession."

"Don't teach my baby how to be a gold-digger like you," Blake admonished, playfully pushing Ashley's head to the side.

By the time all the gifts were opened it was well past midnight. Streets retired to his upstairs bedroom, drunk and high off Kush and X pills, alone because he and Nicole, the mother of his twins, had broken up a few weeks prior over gossip of him cheating on her with Danielle.

Blake's phone rang again. Alexus, calling for the fifteenth time in less than an hour. She'd also texted him thirty-seven messages.

He had yet to read any of them. Just as he'd done with her previous calls,he pressed ignore on the screen.

"Damn, you got her whipped, huh? Who is that bitch?" Ashley inquired, picking a piece of wrapping paper from her white cotton Burberry bodysuit."Is she the one giving away all that money? If she is, tell her I said thanks for the down payment on the CTS Cadillac I'm about to get."

"A Cadillac?" Blake laughed incredulously as he logged onto Facebook on his phone. "Alexus whippin' a Vanquish, baby. I was with her when she bought it. She would laugh at that 'Lac."

Ashley sucked her teeth. Then, in an attempt to induce jealousy in Blake, she dug in her new Burberry bag, took out her cell, and began scrolling down her lengthy list of missed calls; somebody named Lorenzo was responsible for most of them.

"I can't believe I ditched my nigga on Christmas for *you!*" She hissed. "Hope you enjoyed yourself earlier. You'll be jackin off tonight."

"It won't be the first time," Blake said dismissively. He was checking outhis Facebook friend requests; *Britney Bostic, Alexus Costilla, LakieshaBrown, and Lakita Thomas*. With a subtle grin pointed on his face, he accepted the requests; contemplated browsing the girls' pictures, but changed his mind when he glanced over and saw that Ashley was nosily eyeing his phone, her then lips poised in a belligerent pout.

That's when it hit him.

"The note," he said, and jumped to his feet. *The bathroom at Boogie's oldplace,* he thought, cursing himself for not thinking of it sooner.

"What note?" Ashley looked up at him.

Quickly, Blake pushed his arms into the sleeves of his brother's jacket and headed for the front door.

"I'll be back in 'bout five minutes," he yelled over his shoulder.

The black Dodge minivan had cost Bookie a gram of crack to rent for thenight. Parked behind the J. Cooper Community Center on Lincoln Avenue,a block down from the King's residence, the dope fiend rental was as inconspicuous as a yellow needle in a haystack.

With their black ski masks rolled up to their foreheads, Bookie Craig and

K.G. were passing around a bag of cocaine, snorting small piles of the drug from a pen cap, when Bookie, noticed someone jogging across the street in front of Blake King's parents' house.

"I gotta give it to him." Craig said. "The nigga got nuts. T-Walk said Blake threatened to kill all of us. Ain't that some shit! That nigga got adeath wish."

"Look." Bookie pointed over the steering wheel. "I think that's him, rightthere, under the streetlight."

"That is him," K.G. said from the backseat. "Pull up on the side of him.

Let me blow his muhfuckin' head off."

Starting the engine, Bookie gripped his pistol in a warm embrace and inhaled deeply. He silently hoped that the hit would go as planned. He had alot to lose. His burgeoning relationship with Tasia was most important. Their upscale condo was his dream home. The bone white Jaguar XJ that Alexus had bought him was his dream car. He had money in the bank, cash in his bedroom closet.

Frankly, he had everything he'd ever wanted, and he secretly wished Blake had come home in a peaceful state of mind.

Bookie left the headlights off. He pulled his mask down, then hit the gas.

As Blake was crossing the street, Alexus called again. This time, heanswered.

"You must be bored," he japed. "Why the fuck you keep…"

"Didn't you get my messages?! They're coming for you! T-Walk sentthem to kill you!" Alexus was hysterical.

There was movement to the right of him. A dark colored minivan,moving fast—without headlights.

"Damn," Blake intoned, fearfully drawing his Glock; he ran to the side ofan old Ford pickup truck and ducked beside it.

The minivan slid to a stop on the other side of the truck. "Blake, where are you?" Alexus screamed through the phone.

"At the house that was s'posed to be ours," he whispered, and ended the call.

He heard the minivan's sliding door open. Someone said, "Where he go?

He was just here a sec…"

Like a jack-in-the-box, Blake popped up from beside the pickup and started firing shots into the minivan. Due to the sliding door being open, theinterior light was on, allowing Blake to see as his bullets tore through the rear passenger's mask.

But he was not quick enough to take them all out. Their gunshots were like camera flashes before Blake's eyes. His entire body felt like it was being stung by a determined swarm of bumblebees. He tried applyingpressure to the Glock's trigger, but his attempt was useless; he was too weak.

The minivan sped away as he crumpled to the snow laden ground next to the pickup. He landed supine, his right cheek grounded, and his eyes on the screen of his iPhone, which was still in his hand.

He had not logged off of Facebook.

His attorney, Brittney Bostic, had just typed something that would be Blake King's last thought before the darkness enveloped him:l

If I walk backwards, I wonder if things will go back to the way they usedto be.

King Rio

Chapter 27

Alexus awoke with puffy eyes and a nauseated stomach on Christmas morning. She had slept in the bedroom she still had at her mom's house, because the idea of staying at the mansion sort of frightened her.

After all, Savio had murdered Rolando Garcia simply because he found the man too talkative.

Spending the night with T-Walk had not been an option. He hadn'tcontacted her since he'd left the mansion ranting and raving about how he planned to send his goons to properly do away with Blake. And after what had subsequently happened to Blake, Alexus didn't feel like being with T- Walk, either.

So she'd ended up in bed with Cereniti, who had cared enough to hold and console her while she cried her eyes out.

An episode of morning sickness sent Alexus stumbling sleepily to the bathroom, where she kneeled in front of the toilet and regurgitated last night's sushi.

"You okay, Lex?" Cereniti stepped into the bathroom, stark naked like Alexus, and shut the door.

"I'm fine, Tee. Start me some bath water.

"How many times was Blake shot?" Cereniti asked as she bent over the claw foot tub and turned on the water.

"Ten times altogether. Two bullets went through his jaw and out the otherside of his face. All the others hit his chest, stomach, arms and shoulders. He's in critical condition."

"And you know who did it?"

Alexus's throat muscles contracted as a second wave of vomit lurchedout of her mouth, searing her throat. But this time it was not morning sickness that had her throwing up. Macabre images of Blake's bullet riddledbody filled her head.

Immediately after hearing the gunshots, she had rushed out to her Bentley and high tailed it to the house she owned on Lincoln Avenue. Thereshe had found Blake lying in a mass of red snow, surrounded by people she'd occasionally seen around the neighborhood but had never spoken to. Perhaps the most disturbing memory of all was the woman in the ancientred robe; the woman had been crouched over Blake, sobbing uncontrollably, screaming at God as if he were deaf in one ear and half deafin the other.

Once they carried Blake to a dark colored Taurus and loaded him into its backseat, Alexus had followed them to St. Anthony's Hospital, where she had eventually learned of his condition from a passing doctor.

"That's what you deserve for getting pregnant, yo," Cereniti joked, bringing Alexus back to the present. "Wonder when you're gonna start showing. I can't wait to see you all fat and lazy. And I bet it's a boy, too."

"Don't jinx me like that. I'm having a girl, and I'm naming her Astonia."Alexus stood and flushed the toilet. Grabbed her toothbrush and layered its bristles with Colgate.

"Astonia? Are you fucking crazy, yo? You can't be serious. Where'd youfind a dumbass name like that?"

"I'm naming her after the first car I bought. The Aston Martin, hater."

"You might as well name the baby after the first TV show you ever saw. Name it Barney or something retarded like that."

"Shut up, Tee-Tee," Alexus said through a mouthful of foam. She wasn't in the mood to be joking around. Not with Blake in the hospital, fighting forhis life. Not with Detective Know-It-All sticking his fat nose all in her business.

Cereniti stepped out to put on her sweatpants and a small white Louis Vuitton shirt. When she returned, eyes fixed on her smartphone, Alexus wassoaking in the tub.

"They're calling us the Louis Vuitton Team on Twitter now, Lex. All myfriends in New York are."

"Louis Vuitton Team. I like the sound of that." Eyes shut, Alexus smiled. "Get on Facebook and check out Britney Bostic. She's Blake's lawyer. I added her to my friend list yesterday. She posted something last night that I still can't get out of my head."

"Oh yeah? What did she say?"

"I don't remember it verbatim. Something about walking

backwards to change things back to how they were before. It sounded good, whatever it was. It's what I was commenting on when you showed up."

Chuckling derisively, Cereniti sat on the side of the tub. "What is so amusing about walking backwards?"

"She didn't mean it literally, Einstein. She meant, like going back in the past, to the good old days, I guess. Sometimes I feel like I'm walking backwards in time. The bad thing is that I'm not going back to the good times. I feel like I'm turning into one of those cold-hearted cartel bosses who will kill the world for drug money. Those killers I used to be around in Mexico, with Papi and Uncle Flako. Nothing good can come from walking backwards if all that's back there is negativity. I don't want to end up like my father. I have a kid on the way."

Cereniti's response was delayed. She sat there playing with her phone,chewing Big Red gum, saying nothing.

"So, Alexus," Cereniti said, "I think I'm getting the gist of what you'resaying. I hope I'm wrong though."

"You're not wrong, Tee-Tee. I'm done selling drugs."

Rita Mae Bishop financed a huge Christmas banquet for the church's congregation and her Progressive Womanhood group. It was held at the J. Cooper Community center.

When Alexus and Cereniti arrived the banquet was in full swing. Alexus found her mom in the vast basement serving thick slices of turkey at a long table covered with an assortment of foods.

Seven other women were on the serving line with her. The crowd consisted mostly of women and children, the majority of them carrying plates, sodas and toys. Nearly all the adults were seated in eight rows of chairs that faced a white dry erase board with Progressive Womanhood written across the top in red marker.

"I've been meaning to get down here to your little office," Alexus said toRita.

"Merry Christmas" was voiced by everyone, even the

children. Alexus was surprised by how many people knew her name. She walked around the table to a chair behind Rita and sat down, keeping her black fur coat on so that no one would see the bulky, gold plated .45 caliber Smith and Wesson she had concealed in a shoulder holster beneath it.

"Did you get your gift from under the tree?" Rita asked as she slapped some turkey onto a little boy's plastic plate.

"Nuh-uh. I wasn't thinking about any presents." Alexus flicked her eyes around the room. A dangerously thin man in a tweed turtleneck sweater andslacks was gazing intently at her from his seat across the room. He looked away, unnerved. "Where is Neal, at work?"

Rita nodded. "They called him in at about four this morning, said they'd found some guy named Kevin Goldman dead in an abandoned minivan. He's interrogating the owner of the minivan. They suspect Blake King may have killed Goldman during the shootout that left him critically injured, but no one knows for certain. He's hoping the man he's interrogating willbreak."

"K.G.'s *dead*?" Alexus was shocked. She had not heard about his death until now. But then again, she hadn't spoken to Bookie or Tasia since the previous morning.

"I know that whole mess is the devil's work," said Rita. She turned around to study Alexus. "Your grandmother wants me to take the positionof president with MTN. She promised to donate a hundred million dollars tothe charity of my choice if I accept the offer. She also promised to keep the family—all the *Costilla's*—out of any evil activities. And I believe her... Neal may not believe her, but I think she's being truthful."

Alexus lowered her head. A moment of meaningful rumination, during which time Rita thoughtfully recounted every bit of information Neal had given her the day before outside the church.

Alexus stood and stepped about four feet behind her chair, where no one, besides the fairly insignificant presence of two little girls, was situated. Alexus had her mind on the twenty two million dollar deposit that had been placed in her bank account the night before.

"So, what if Neal and his officers are looking to imprison Papi's family," Alexus said, being careful to remain calm voiced while speaking of her mother's lover's intentions. She set her eyes on Rita's. "If granny Vida's clean, and if Savio and Segovia stick to managing the sales of their multimillion dollar estates, together we'll be able to recreate the Costilla image, to turn it around to something both positive and progressive for *all of us.*"

Again, Rita nodded, pulling up the plastic enwrapped fingers of her gloved hands. Her hands went immediately to her hips. She wore a white apron over her black skirt and blazer.

"I think you should accept the offer," Alexus suggested. "We can rebuild homes in New Orleans' Ninth ward neighborhood in memory of your parents, Granny and Grandpa Bishop. And how much would your annual salary be as president of MTN?"

"Somewhere around fourteen million every year after taxes."

Alexus stood and hugged Rita.

"Too positivity," Alexus said. "To moving forward." She said as if she were giving a toast to an Obama like political figure.

"To moving forward," Rita Mae said.

King Rio

Chapter 28

Light skinned and bow legged, with a slim waist and pretty face and longhair and thick as Maliah Michel, the third member of the newly coined Louis Vuitton Team, Tasia Olsen wandered through her and Bookie's plushly furnished condo in a skimpy pink Victoria's Secret teddy, lighting lavender scented candles, preparing to give her man the Christmas presentof a lifetime.

Tiff-Tiff was there, too, but she wasn't being much of a help, as she was too busy applying makeup to her face, incessantly reinspecting the results inher small portable mirror. She also wore an alluring teddy. Several lines of cocaine were spaced equally apart on the glass top coffee table in front of her, and every minute or so she leaned forward on the burgundy leather semicircular sofa and sniffed up a line.

"We should fly to New York for New Year's Eve," Tasia suggested thoughtfully. She was lighting candles on the mantel over the fireplace. "The whole Cash Money/ Young Money family are supposed to be on 106 and Park."

"You can count me in if Drake gon' be there," Tiffany said. "I need another vacation from this small ass town. Especially with all the bullshit that's been going on." Dejectedly, she shook her head. "I've known K.G. since I was lil girl in Harborside Projects. That was my nigga."

"Honestly, I'm sorry for your loss, Tiff. K.G. was a cool nigga. But we are not about to dwell on his death. Craig and Bookie should be here any minute now, and I plan on dislocating my jaw before the day is over."

Tiffany chuckled dryly at that. "Girl, you are just as deep fried as that crazy ass Cereniti."

"Get off my bitch." Tasia went to a window that overlooked the street out front, searching for Bookie's Jaguar. All she saw was her emerald greenCorvette, and Tiffany's gray Hummer H3, which she received this morning from Craig as a Christmas gift.

"Why didn't you just tell them that we're here waiting for

them?" Tiffanyasked.

"It's a *surprise*, yo. Know what that word means? It means something notexpected, something..."

"I know what the hell it means, Tasia. It means we're gonna be sitting here all day while they're out partying, celebrating their little victory over Blake."

Tasia turned away from the window, pondering the text message she had gotten from Cereniti moments earlier. //: *The Mexican says she's out of the football league, b. For good!* it read. Which translated to the end of the football shaped kilograms, a daunting notion for Tasia, a daunting nation forthe entire clique.

Tiffany inhaled a thick line and fell back on the sofa.

"I wonder where Alexus keeps all that cash," Tasia mumbled to herself, regarding her wide eyed guest with a look of disgust.

"What did you say?" Tiffany snapped her eyes to her left and focused herdilated pupils on Tasia. "Did you just say what I think you said? Because if you did..."

"I didn't," Tasia said quickly, thinking, damn, this cokehead got spidey senses! I barely even whispered!

"...I've been thinking the same thing about Craig," Tiffany finished.

Tasia grew silent, shifted her eyes back to the window. Already she was contemplating sending her cousin Beeyo and his crew from Harlem to rob Alexus.

But Tasia had not intended to let Tiffany in on her plans. "Let's forget this conversation ever happened," said Tasia.

"Let's not and say we did." Tiff-Tiff rose slowly from the sofa and walked to the window, beside Tasia. "Listen... I know you don't know Craig like I do, so allow me to let you in on a tiny secret: he's tighter than a rat's pussy with his money. He rarely buys me anything. He never gives meany money. And, yeah, he got the Hummer for me, but it's not even in my name. What if the Feds get onto him and snatch every car and truck he owns? Huh? What if they freeze his bank accounts? What if they find his stash before I do? I'll be flat broke and moving back in with my momma. "

"Here's a suggestion: stop snorting up all the dope he's been giving you and start selling it. He is not the government and you need to realize that. You're actin' as if he owes you welfare checks. Don't be a dumb ho, okay. Be a smart lady."

"I'm not selling dope, Tasia. I ain't no damn drug dealer. That niggaowes me and, one way or another, he's going to pay up. If you won't help me, I'll find somebody who will."

Tasia's iPhone vibrated on the mantel, a welcoming interruption. She rushed over to answer it.

"Baby, where you at?" It was Bookie.

"I'm out shopping with Cereniti and Alexus," Tasia lied in her sweetest voice. "I need you to stop by the house and grab my purse off the bed. Meetme at Applebee's."

"We're pulling up at the crib now. Give me 'bout forty-five. We gotta count this money. Love you, bae."

All who knew her called her Fat Krissy for a reason: she was 5'2" and weighed 300 plus pounds.

But Bookie didn't care about her weight, nor did he mind the way she made the right side of his Jaguar sag close to the ground as he parkedbehind Tasia's Corvette. The only thought on his mind was getting Fat Krissy indoors so that he could get a quick nut off before his rendezvous with Tasia.

Craig's identical Jag pulled in beside Bookie's. Craig had his girl's best friend, Danielle, with him.

Infidelity was on his mind, as well.

"We gotta be quick," Bookie told them as they headed towards thecondo's front door. He has his arms wrapped around the waist of the fat woman's dark overcoat, kissing the ample flabs of exposed flesh at the napeof her neck.

Next to him, Craig couldn't seem to keep his tongue out of Danielle's mouth, or his hands off her ass. He and Bookie wore white leather Louis Vuitton jackets and skull caps over baggy blue Red Monkey jeans and custom made Louis Vuitton Jordan sneakers. Five carrot square cut white diamonds sparkled in their earlobes. Currently, they were the most sought after hustlers in town. Craig was taking full advantage of this fact,

169

fucking every pretty girl that looked his way; Bookie was bedding women of every shape, size and color, and he didn't give a flying fuck if they were pretty or not.

Bookie turned the doorknob and found it unlocked. He pushed open the door...his mouth dropped open.

Standing there in the foyer was a half-naked Tasia and a similarly dressed Tiff-Tiff. Tasia had a large glass bowl of melted chocolate balanced in the palm of one hand, a bowl of strawberries in the other. Tiffany held two bottles of Krug Rose champagne.

"What the hell!" Tasia snapped. "Baby, I can explain," said Bookie.

Tasia struck first, launching the bowl of chocolate at Bookie's head. The thick brown liquid splattered all over him, the fat woman, Craig and Danielle. The bowl missed its intended target and smashed to pieces against the wall, but the second bowl hit Bookie's forehead, opening a gash above his right brow.

A feeling of vertigo overcame him and he dropped to one knee.

"Don't run, you fat bitch!" he heard Tasia scream. When he looked up, Craig, Tiff-Tiff and Danielle were all slipping and sliding across the slick linoleum, with Craig trying earnestly to stop Tiffany from killing Danielle with the Rose bottle.

Straddling Fat Krissy's back, Tasia was punching Krissy's head like a proboxer, slamming Krissy's face on the floor.

This bitch done busted my head, Bookie thought. He stood and retaliated with a well placed kick to the side of Tasia's face. Then he clamped a hand onto the front of her neck, pulled her up to her feet, and forcefully threw her a good eight feet across the foyer. She landed harshly on the bottom step of the staircase.

Fat Krissy scrambled out the front door on her hands and knees, leaving behind a tooth and a blond streaked weave. Craig was planted on the floor with Tiffany on his lap and his arms wrapped tight around her struggling body; she was trying to kick at the unconscious head of Danielle, which remained just out of the reach of Tiff-Tiff's four inch Jimmy Choo heels.

"You hit the wrong bitch," said Tasia. She massaged her jaw where Bookie had kicked her, glaring at him. "As good as I've been to you, nigga, you wanna go out and cheat on me? With a fuckin' whale! And here I was trying to be all sexy for you on Christmas. Yo, you ain't…you ain't shit, son. You're a fuckin' lame."

Covered in chocolate, Tasia turned and ran up the stairs before her tears became evident. Bookie was trying to think of something…anything…to say in his defense, so he took his time going up the spiral staircase.

Behind him Tiff-Tiff was yelling at Craig, telling him to let go of her. But he was not hearing her request. "Tiff, you gotta calm down a lil bit first," he kept saying, as if she was going crazy for no reason.

Suddenly, just as Bookie was approaching the top step, an eighteen man team of heavily armed policeman swarmed through the front door with their
guns drawn.

Bookie recognized his Aunt Rita's boyfriend at the forefront of the MCPD team.

"Put your fucking hands up and don't move!" shouted Detective Neal Miller, his gun trained on Bookie's back.

King Rio

Chapter 29

Alexus gobbled down two bacon cheeseburgers and five Snick-ers bars while she drove to the law offices of Bostic and Staples. Once there, she settled the Bentley next to a silver Mercedes, the only vehicle in the parkinglot, and sat quietly, nursing a va-nilla coke through a large straw... and staring quizzically at the black Denali in her side view mirror.

She had first seen it as she and Cereniti were walking out of the community center, it had been parked three blocks down, and Alexus wouldnever have noticed it if one of Blake's guys— some crooked nosed boy named Tim-Tim—had not pointed at the Denali.

"I think they're followin' you," he'd said. "They pulled up right after youdid and ain't moved since. I'm only tellin' you 'cause I know you fuck withmy nigga Blake."

She had taken his phone number and promised to compen-sate him for thewarning, Then she and Cereniti had slipped into the car and left, stopping atthe gas station, stores, and three res-taurants en route to the law firm.

The Denali had followed them every step of the way. "Please, God," Alexus prayed, "don't let me end up like Papi. I'm only eighteen, forChrist's sake. Life in prison can't be my destiny. It *can't* be.

"Yo, that has to be the feds," said Cereniti. "Your cousin Bookie is a certified retard, Lex. He's mad retarded. How do you explain to the judge why you had eighteen ounces of co-caine laying on your backseat? Nobody can blame him and Craig for carrying around pistols, but there's no excuse for the dope. Now he's got *us* all hot, b. Getting followed around and shit."

Alexus popped a stick of Doublemint chewing gum in her mouth. "Neal told my mom that he believes the guns they re-covered from Bookie and Craig are the same ones that were used to shoot Blake."

"Blake won't live to testify, so that shouldn't be much of a problem," said Cereniti.

"He's not a snitch, anyway," Alexus retorted snappily. "We need to be worried about your homegirl, and Craig's girlfriend. Neal said they found over an ounce of coke in Tiffany's purse and three duffel bags full of cashin Tasia's closet. Tasia and Bookie are probably going to the feds. Even if Bookie doesn't go to the feds, he and Craig still have gun and attempted murder charges to deal with."

"Shit wild, yo."

As she and Cereniti stepped out and headed into the law firm, Alexus fought the urge to look back at the Denali. Was it an FBI agent? A DEA agent? MCPD?

Attorney Britney Bostic greeted them at the door in a soft gray conservative pantsuit. Britney's gloomy blood shot eyes didn't match her sweet smile.

She led them past a large secretary's desk, down a brief hallway and into her fastidiously organized office. Manila folders were open and spreadacross her mahogany desk. A dozen or more cardboard boxes with *NiemannElements* printed on them were stacked perfectly next to a steel filingcabinet behind the desk.

"I know this may be a bit personal," Alexus said as she sat across thedesk from Britney, "but what are you doing working on a holiday? It's Christmas."

"My fiancé and I had a...how do I put this? ...a major disagreement. He wants to spend our savings on the wedding; I think it would be wise to invest in the small business I started a year ago." Britney spun around in hercomfortable looking swivel chair. She placed the toe of one Manalo Blahnik heel shoe against the side of one of the cardboard boxes. "I've always aspired to be something more than a lawyer. When my girl Nikkia and I passed the bar exam and became lawyers here at my fathers' firm, we put together twenty grand and started a line of hair care products...shampoos, and conditioners, gels... hair stuff, you know? Niemann Elements."

"So, what's the problem?" Cereniti asked. She was standing behind Alexus with her arms crossed over her chest like a bodyguard.

Britney turned to her Dell computer and began typing on the keyboard. "The problem is Shannon's afraid we'll lose our money. See, he's a street guy trying desperately to transition to the businessman he dreams of being one day, and the idea of failing sends his brain into overload. He was a drugdealer when I met him, fairly popular in his neighborhood, and he's determined to hold on to that senseless level of popularity. He fears losing money will downgrade him in some way."

"Hmm... sounds silly to me." Alexus dug around in her Louis Vuitton shoulder bad and retrieved her checkbook. She grabbed an ink pen from thedesk, leaned forward, and started filling out a check. "I'm going to be in Miami for a few weeks. I need you to represent my cousin, ReginaldNelson, on an attempted..."

"Can't do it," Britney said. "You've already hired me to represent Blake King in a case where Nelson's a victim."

"Well, I'm hiring you to hire someone else. Just get him an attorney. Andbesides..."— Alexus pushed a $8,000 check toward the lawyer and began writing on another— "I'm hiring you for me, too. I may be in some trouble soon, and I need to be prepared."

"This eight grand will take care of the both of you."

"I figured that. This next check is for my friend, Cereniti Stingley...""That's me," Cereniti murmured.

"...Tasia Olsen, Craig... I don't know his last name. And that Tiffany girlwho was arrested with them. Make sure they're all taken care of." Alexus slid the second check to Britney, then stood to leave.

Picking up the check, Britney gasped. Her eyes widened "A milliondollars!" Britney said, shocked.

Alexus cracked a smile. "Get your company off the ground. No more walking backwards."

Immediately after leaving the law firm, Alexus stopped for gas andsnacks then hit I-94, on her way to Chicago.

"That Denali stopped following us about ten minutes ago," said Cereniti. She had her seat reclined, her gold sequined Louis

Vuitton mules propped up on the dash.

"I noticed," Alexus replied.

"Yo, why'd you give that lady all that money?"

"Because she needed it and I had it to give. Plus, she's a member of my momma's Progressive Womanhood group."

"You've never given *me* a fuckin' million dollars," Cereniti complained. "Do I have to sign up for a group?"

Alexus cast a seething glance at her friend, thinking *Bitch, this is not the time nor the place.*

"Dang, yo," Cereniti laughed. "If looks could kill…"

"I'm not in the mood to be playing around. If any one of them snitches, I'm done. You'll be done, too," Alexus said. "Now take your feet off my dashboard and start thinking. That lawyer had a business plan. What's yours?"

Cereniti dropped her feet to the floor and sucked her teeth indignantly. "First of all, we have absolutely nothing to worry about. Even if somebody out of the crew breaks under pressure, the feds won't be able to prove a single thing. They'll try to set up a buy, but that'll be useless since you're not dealing anymore. Oh, and as for my business plan, I'm going to take the money I've saved up… about $400,000… and open an exotic dancing studio in Harlem. A lot of women out there want to learn how to dance on a pole, and it would be an honor for me to teach them everything I know."

"Now, you see," Alexus said with a subtle smile, "that's what I like to hear. We knew coming in to this that dealing wasn't something to make a career out of. It's a get-in-and-get-out type of business, and now's our time to get out and move on to the legal hustle. I might even be able to get you a reality show on my grandma's new cable television network."

"Your gramz got a TV channel?"

"MTN consists of over three hundred TV channels, actually in five different countries. At least that's what my aunt Jenny claims." Alexus veered around a behemoth semi-truck; its driver, an older Hispanic man wearing a weathered John Deere cap and an oversized moustache, smiled down at the Bentley and offered Alexus a thumbs up.

"He looks familiar," Alexus said thoughtfully, as she flicked on herwipers to clean away the lingering flakes of snow from her windshield.

"Yeah?" Cereniti leaned over Alexus to catch a glimpse of the semi's driver.

"Yeah," said Alexus. "As a matter of fact, he looks just like one of my Aunt Jenny's old boyfriends." She struggled to remember the name of AuntJenny's ex, but it eluded her mind's grasp. She hadn't seen him since she was eight or nine... maybe ten. The more she tried envisioning his peculiar features, the more she became convinced that he and the man in the John Deere cap were one and the same.

"You are thinking *way* too hard, yo," Cereniti noted with a short giggle. "So what if he looks familiar. Everybody looks like somebody."

Alexus's phone emitted the ringtone she'd assigned to Granny Costilla; still feeling a little vexed about Vida's disparaging perception of blacks, Alexus let it go to voicemail.

"Was that T-Walk?" asked Cereniti.

"Nuh-uh. It was nobody. Turn on some music, and *please,* no more Keri Hilson. If you play that damn "Pretty Girl Rock" one more time, I'll be

forced to pop a cap in your ass." Alexus laughed as she finally relaxed enough to loosen her grip on the steering wheel and rest her back on the seat.

"Yo, this Bentley rides mad smooth," Cereniti muttered contentedly. She put in a Gucci Mane and Yo Gotti mix CD, turned up the volume, andbegan bobbing her head to the thrumming beat of "Take 'em to school."

Minutes later an Indiana state trooper came speeding by, lights flashing, and sirens blaring. Cereniti hastily fastened her seatbelt. Alexus already hadhers on.

"Keep that seatbelt on," Alexus said, checking her rearview mirror. "At least until we get to Chicago. If you get me a ticket on Christmas..."

The remainder of her friendly threat became lodged in her throat as she glanced in the rearview again.

The man in the John Deere cap was speeding toward the rear of Alexus's car; his congenial smile was gone, replaced by a scowl that was as gelid as the wind that was flowing through his female passenger's long black hair.

Jennifer Costilla was hanging halfway out the passenger's window with an Uzi machine gun cradled in her small hands.

As bullets started pinging through the Bentley's trunk, Alexus stepped down on the gas, wondering why her aunt was trying to kill her.

Tiny flakes of icy snow were stinging Jennifer's face, so she pulled her head back inside the semi's cabin and kept her arms out, not once letting upon the trigger.

Alexus was a better driver than Jenny had expected her to be; the Bentleywas going over 100 mph on the snow slick highway, swerving from left to right between cars and SUV's.

"Damn you, Paco!" Jenny screamed heatedly. "Run through them!"

Forty eight year old Paco Ramirez picked up speed, slamming into the back of an Explorer, which fishtailed then rolled twice in the air before landing on the back of an F-150 that was pulling over to the side of the highway like a bunch of other shell shocked drivers.

Paco's next vehicular victim was a fire truck red Challenger full ofcollege aged white girls. It flipped twice thorough the air, crushed top first onto the blacktop, then tumbled three more times.

Jenny ejected the depleted thirty round clip from the Uzi and pushed in another one. She quickly went back to firing out the window, but could onlymanage to hit all the wrong cars.

The Bentley was getting away!

"Come on, Paco. Come on," Jenny chanted venomously. "She's heading for that off ramp! Step on it!"

"We got four hundred kilos of coke in back of this thing, Jenny! Cops geton it we're screwed!" Paco retorted.

But he veered sharply to the right, anyway, attempting to pursue the speeding Bentley. He literally sliced through a magenta colored Maxima, cutting it in two…as a result, the semi's trailer swung to the left like a baseball bat. Its thick tires skipped across the blacktop several times.

Then the semi jackknifed, landing on the drivers side, sliding thirty feet and leaving a gleaming trail of shredded metal and shattered glass in its wake.

Jennifer Costilla was thrown onto Paco. She lifted herself quickly, flexing her extremities to ascertain if any of her bones were broken. Shewas fine.

Paco was not. Blood was spilling profusely from the nape of his neck where a broken bone protruded.

"I can't...feel...any...Jen," he groaned, gazing vacantly ahead at theflames that were leaping from the hood of the semi.

Lifting the Uzi, Jenny closed her eyes and sent a spray of bullets through the side of Paco's head.

"I'm so sorry, Paco," she murmured, taking the gun inside her large alligator skin Versace bag, "but mother would have had me killed if I'd left you to get arrested with a shipment."

She reached upward up and out of the sides of the passenger window, andhoisted herself up and out of the burning wreckage. Without looking back, she hopped down and ran to a white Pathfinder that had narrowly escaped being swiped by the semi-trailer. Its driver, a middle age, penguin shaped white man in a tweed overcoat, was standing outside his open door, cell phone to his ear, reporting the crash to 911 operators.

Jenny shot him in the face, climbed into the Pathfinder, and sped away from the carnage, strategically plotting her next move.

King Rio

Chapter 30

Following a two hour long Christmas service at her church, Rita Mae went home, bathed and washed her hair, then donned her negligee and retired to her Glade scented boudoir to engross herself with a Denzel movie... Déjà Vu.

A half hour into the movie she heard the front door opening, the thud of Neal stomping snow off his boots. He paused in the bedroom doorway, taking a moment to admire Rita's body.

"God could not have possibly created a more beautiful woman," he said, stepping over to the bed. He leaned over her, kissed her lips, then walked around to his side of the bed and laid beside her, taking off his badge and P-90 Ruger handgun. He placed them on the bedside table, releasing a breath of finality. "You want the good news first?"

"Not again." Rita paused the movie and turned to him with a glint of fear in her eyes. "Is it Alexus?"

"Good news, it is. Alexus is fine. She's at the Trump in downtownChicago with her friend Cereniti. She's a bit shaken, though." Neal slipped his arm under her neck. "Bad news is, someone just peppered that Bentley of hers with twenty bullets from, according to eyewitnesses, an Uzi. Happened on I-94. Turn off this movie and flip to the news."

Rita was almost too afraid to shut off the DVD, let alone turn to a news channel. But she dug up the courage and did it, selecting abc7 news.

"...grisly scene on I-94, where nine people, including one suspect, were killed in a brutal incident that took place at approximately 12:30 p.m.central time. DEA agents recovered almost nine hundred pounds of cocaine from inside the trailer of an alleged suspect's semi-truck..."

Neal muted the television. "It'll take them all day to tell you whathappened," he said. "Some dark haired woman started firing on the carfrom the passenger's window of that semi, while the driver slammed through other vehicles as if they weren't even there. When the semi flipped over, the woman killed the driver, climbed out the passenger window, then shot and killed a second man and sped off in his SUV."

Rita thought: Please don't say what I think you're about to say.

But Neal said it. "The slain driver of the semi was a member of the Costilla cartel. He had the tattoo inked on the inside of his right wrist."

"Where does it end?" She covered her face with her hands and fought away the tears were begging to flow freely. "Essentially, you're telling me that the cartel has a hit ordered on my *child*?"

"We're not yet certain, Rita. That may be the case. The thing is, Alexus doesn't seem to be cooperating with the federal agents who were sent to question her. She claims to have seen nothing. Hell, if the valet at theTrump hadn't notified the Chicago Police Department about the bulletriddled Bentley he'd parked, we would never have known she was even in danger."

Momentarily, Rita Mae was paralyzed with fear. What in God's name hadAlexus gotten herself into this time?

Had Alexus informed on the cartel?

"You know," Neal whispered, un-muting the TV, "we found well over eight hundred thousand dollars in cash in the condo your nephew shared with Tasia Olsen, and about an hour ago, our dogs found three kilos of cokestuffed down in their couch. And guess what was so remarkable about thosedrugs?"

Rita dropped her hands and sat up. "What?"

"They were wrapped exactly like the drugs recovered from the semi- trailer on I-94: green blue cellophane, football shaped. I've never believedin coincidence."

"Neal, I think…maybe you should leave. I feel like we might do better without each other," Rita said, her eyelids glued shut, hands tremblingnoticeably on her thighs.

She didn't really want him to go; Neal was the nicest man she had ever met. But lately he'd become the proverbial bearer of bad news, which is never an inviting title. His investigations were hitting too close to home.

The thought of possibly losing Alexus to the penal system weighedheavily on Rita's conscience.

"You don't believe that," Neal intoned.

"Yes, I do, Neal. This relationship is too complicated. I'll be starting my job as president of MTN come Monday, moving to Maywood, Illinois, to becloser to MTN's headquarters in Chicago...I won't have any time for you."

She got out of bed and went to her dresser, picked up a comb andpurposefully ran it through her hair. She looked in the mirror: Neal was regarding her with an unsettling sternness that made her look downward as she pulled out her pants drawer.

"I'm not going nowhere, Rita."

"You're absolutely correct. Going nowhere would be staying here. *Not* going nowhere..."

"I don't give a damn about grammatical errors. Bottom line, I'm staying here. And so are you. The Costilla's are as crooked as the letter s, and you know it. You see what they just tried to do to your daughter! What do you think they'll do to you?"

Changing out of her negligee and into a t-shirt and jeans, Rita wondered why Alexus had not called her after the shooting.

"Stop acting like you don't hear me, Rita Mae." Suddenly, Neal was behind her. At six-three, he loomed over her. "I know how it may seem, butI am not out to hurt your family. Your nephew rented a minivan from one ofour informants, and the next morning the van was discovered with a dead man stretched out in the backseat. I mean, no one cares about them shooting the daylights out of Blake King; we just want them to testify that King isthe gunman who shot Kevin Goldman and Johnny Lay. Then we'll pile all the other murders on King and let your nephew go."

Rita turned around, hands on her hips, nose flared. Her hostile demeanor told Neal to back up. He took a step back but kept his eyes on hers.

"You've never given me the silent treatment before," he comminuted."Mmm," she assented.

"Why are you getting dressed? Alexus will be boarding a

private jet to Miami when the feds get done with her." He commented.

"I'm not…I'm not getting dressed to race to my daughter's side. It's the cartel that has me worried. I don't think staying here is safe."

Neal shook his head despondently and collapsed onto the foot of the bed. "Rita, are you listening to yourself speak? You're afraid of the Costilla cartel…but Monday you're to start working for Vida Costilla? Explain to me how that makes sense."

"It doesn't have to make sense to you. I have an MBA, which means I'ma master of business administration. Trust me, I know what I'm doing." Ritaselected a pair of sneakers from her closet and put them on. "And noteveryone gets the opportunity to work with a billionaire. I'll be able to openso many doors, help so many people around the world. This is my dreamI'm fulfilling, Neal… and I'm not going to let anyone or anything stop me."She headed out into the living room, and Neal followed. He lounged on the sofa and gazed at her as she pulled on a Saints sweater, seemingly

oblivious to her edginess.

A sudden thump outside the front door froze both of them. "You hear that," Rita whispered, her eyes dark with fear. She was standing with her back to the door. Her right arm was in the sleeve of her coat. The other sleeve hung loosely to the carpet.

Neal moved to the window, motioning for Rita to walk to the kitchen; sheobeyed him in a hurry.

"A woman in a black dress," Neal whispered. "Long black hair. She's walking toward a white…*Pathfinder!*" He spun around, hurled over the sofa, and lifted Rita off her feet as he rushed to the rear door.

The C-4 explosive went off just as his hand reached the doorknob,decimating the yellow house completely.

FBI special agent Josh Sneed's monotonous, droning tone of questioning was really beginning to annoy Alexus.

She was pacing to and fro in front of the hotel room's minibar where Sneed and Cereniti were seated.

"So you have no idea whatsoever why the cartel previously headed by your father just made an attempt on your life?" Sneed was saying.

"No, I don't, "Alexus grumbled irritably.

"And you didn't see anything? Not even a fleeting glimpse of the shooter?"

"Nope. I put the petal to the metal and hauled ass. You've asked me the same questions a hundred times already, and I've given you the same answer every time. It's about time you stopped pestering me."

"Let the church say Amen," said Cereniti. She turned her nose up at the Federal agent.

Alexus went to one of the wide floor to ceiling windows and gazed down upon the bustling traffic. Then she looked further down the street at the 86 story MTN International Tower, a lavish multi- billion dollar building now owned by Vida Costilla.

Aunt Jenny? Alexus thought. Trying to shoot me? What did I do to her? *Dammit, I need to talk to Papi!*

She turned to Sneed and asked, "Where are you holding my father? Ineed to see him."

A conniving grin burgeoned on Sneed's pallid white face as he stood, unzipping his navy FBI jacket. "I actually visited Juan Costilla yesterday. He's quite an impressive character. The guy refused to talk to anyone. Hasn't mumbled a word since his arrest."

"You visited my…" Alexus expression was quizzical. "Why'd you go and see *my* Papi? Where is he?"

"Florence, Colorado, with all the other high risk inmates," Sneed said flatly. "I was sent to question him about the death of Rolando Garcia. Ever heard of him?"

Reflexively, Alexus gasped. But within a half second she went back to anair of calmness. "Uh, no, I've never heard of him," she lied, turning back to the widow. "Can my dad have visits?"

"He certainly can, seven days a week."

"Is he on some type of letter writing restriction?"

"He can write all the letters he wants, call whomever he

wishes to call. He's been choosing not to call or write anybody. All he does is exercise andread."

"My grandma said he wanted us to get collect calling on our phone."

"Don't know how she heard that. Mr. Costilla hasn't talked to anyone," Sneed repeated.

Alexus glanced over her shoulder and caught the agent staring at the backof her form fitting gray and white striped mini dress. Exacerbated by her five inch heels, she knew her ass was an astounding sight to behold.

But she was more focused on Granny Costilla, wondering if and *why* Vida had lied about getting a call from Papi back in October. And where the hell was T-Walk?

Sneed's cell rang suddenly, jarring Alexus from her thoughts. He steppedaway to answer it.

"Yo," said Cereniti, "our plane is ready. We'll land in Miami at five thirtythis evening." She never took her eyes off her phone. "J rented us a carfrom Hertz, the new BMW 6E0i convertible. We have it for the weekend."

"Get on Expedia.com and get us a room." Alexus said, as she thoughtfully chewed her thumbnail. "We'll stay there until I figure out what's going on. Something big is going down I just don't know what it is."

Special agent Sneed flipped his phone shut. His face looked even paler ashe took his seat at the mini bar.

"As of now," he said in that same flat tone, "Alexus, you're being placed under federal protection."

"No, I'm not." Utilizing a cantankerous mannerism she'd inherited from her mother, Alexus put her hands on her hips and glowered at the agent.

"This isn't up for debate. Your mother's home was just bombed…"

Sneed kept talking, but Alexus was no longer listening. She dropped to her knees and probably would have injured her face if Cereniti hadn'trushed to her side and caught her.

The Citation X private jet was a sleek, compact, shiny machine withwood paneling and leather seats. Its powerful

Rolls Royce engines had the plane piercing through the clouds at tremendous speeds.

Alexus looked down at the horizon and scattered clouds from forty thousand feet above ground. A small TV monitor in front of her seatdisplayed a map of the United States, with an image of the jet tracking west,along with its speed, its altitude, and their time to destination.

"I know you're like, *mad* upset right now, Lex," Cereniti said. She was inthe seat next to Alexus. "But at least Rita survived the blast. That's pretty damn miraculous, if you ask me."

Alexus didn't say a word. She was feeling too miserable to engage in a conversation. Plus, there were four FBI agents on the plane—with themtwo in back of them, two in front of them—and Papi had always warnedher against conversing around the wrong people.

She thought back to what agent Sneed had told her during the drive to theairport. "Your mother and Detective Miller are being air lifted to a hospital here in Chicago, but it looks like they'll make it. They both have a few broken bones, some second and third degree burns from the conflagration. They'll be fine, though."

Sneed hadn't sounded too convincing either.

When he had shown her a sketch artist's rendering of the I-94 shooting suspect, it had been a near perfect depiction of Jennifer Costilla's visage.

"Never seen her before," Alexus had said, lying through her teeth and crying at the same time.

Somberly, she stuck to gazing out the oval window to her left, ignoring a palate teasing shrimp salad on the food tray in front of her.

Then a sudden, frightening thought occurred to her. She nudged Cereniti,"let's go to the restroom."

The FBI agents stared at the backsides of Alexus and Cereniti as the girlsheaded up the aisle and into the restroom. Alexus shut the door and locked it.

"Eight eyeballs," Cereniti muttered, hiking up her own LV mini dress.

She pulled down her thong underwear and squatted over the toilet to piss. "What?" Alexus said.

"Talkin' about those fed boys out there, yo. Buncha perves. Yo, you saw the way they were looking at us."

Shaking her head dismissively, Alexus set her shoulder bag on the sink, stuffed her hand deep down inside it, and took out her smartphone.

Alexus whispered, "I have ten fifty pound bales of Kush and two hundred machine guns hidden in the guest house at a mansion in Michigan City, and I'm scared."

"A mansion!"

"Will you shut up and listen?" Alexus was scrolling down the list of contacts in her phone. She stopped at Tim-Tim and hit send. "I'm scared the feds might start raiding houses owned by my family if Bookie, Craig, or Tasia turn against us. I need to get rid of the weed and guns."

"You're not supposed to use phones on airplanes," Cereniti advised.

Tim-Tim picked up. Alexus skipped the niceties and got straight to the business at hand.

"You got a license?" she asked him. "Nuh-uh. Who dis?"

"The girl you gave your number to earlier today. Listen, I need you to either rent a large van or a U-haul truck. Can you do that, right now?"

"Hell yeah. Why, you got somethin' for me?"

"Get a pen and a piece of paper," Alexus said, and when he was ready, she gave him the address to the mansion and told him where the "packages" were located: in the guest house's vacant bedroom. "The spare key is under an empty flower pot to the left of the front door. You're gonna need some help, so bring a few friends. And whatever you do, don't let them see what's inside those crates and boxes. Oh, and half of everything goes to Blake. If he... you know."

"Yeah, I know," said Tim-Tim.

There were tears threatening to burst from her eyes as Alexus dropped the phone back inside her bag.

"Happy now?" Cereniti asked.

"I don't think I'll ever be happy again," Alexus replied. "I can't believe how messed up my life is. I have all the money I wanted, but look at me.I'm nothing. I'm the lowest of the low, the exact opposite of what everyone perceives me to be."

"My ma dukes always told me *you gotta suffer through the storm tosee the rainbow.* All this is a storm, Lex, and I'm with you till the rainstops falling." Cereniti wiped herself. "We're about to hit up the beaches, and the clubs, and …"

"I'm not going anywhere until I hear momma's doing better. And I'm definitely not going clubbing with a pack of FBI agents in tow."

Cereniti shrugged. "I'm with you whatever you wanna do. I just want to drive that Beamer around town a little. And to, you know, celebrate life. Wecould have been killed today."

As Alexus took her turn over the toilet, another light bulb flickered on in her head.

"Damn. I almost forgot," she said, looking over to Cereniti, who was drying her hands with a paper towel. "I have about five million in those suitcases."

"Seriously?" Cereniti's eyelids seemed to run away from each other. "What suitcases?"

"The suitcases I have stuffed in my SUV. It's in the garage next to my house on Lincoln Avenue."

"Oh my god, Lex, have you fuckin' lost it? What if somebody breaks in that garage? Huh?"

"I have a state of the art security system set up at that house. Trust me, nobody's…"

There was a knock at the restroom door. "You ladies okay in there, just checking…"

"Of course we're okay, you fuckin' pervert!" Cereniti snapped. "You gotsome type of R. Kelly fantasy? Want a golden shower or somethin'?" She grinned at the sound of the agent walking away.

Alexus searched her inner self for a laugh, but only managed to musterup a smile. "Tee-Tee, you have got to be the craziest, most psychopathic, bipolar lunatic I've ever met."

"Why thank you," Cereniti joked.

189

They finished up in the restroom and went back to their seats. Within minutes of getting comfortable on the soothing leather, Alexus fell asleep…and dreamed.

Chapter 31

Sneed's alabaster complexion turned red as an apple after only two days beneath Florida's burning sun. Four weeks later he was tan brown from the sun's unforgiving rays, but content all the same, because he was staying in Alexus Costilla's forty million dollar beach house, while his team of agents were forced to sweat it out inside several nondescript black vans and sedans parked throughout the neighborhood.

On the evening of Monday, January Twenty Fourth, he was behind the wheel of Alexus's brand new Roll Royce Phantom, transporting the girls home from Sea World, where they had spent most of the day snapping pictures of leaping whales, performing porpoises, and barking walruseswith their phones,

Five car lengths behind the white Phantom, three black Chevy voltsfollowed Sneed's every turn.

"This is the *life*, yo," Cereniti was saying. "Seventy eight degrees in the middle of winter! It's never like this in Harlem. I could live here forever. Just imagine if Tasia was here with us."

"We'll send her all the pics we've taken," Alexus said, referring to the captured moments of their recent escapades, which included jubilant trips toDisney World, Cypress Gardens, Gatorland, the Kennedy Space Center, andthe wax museum in Orlando.

For Alexus Costilla, life was getting better every day. She was living the way she had always dreamed of living; serenely, without worries of any kind, no cumbersome troubles to stress over.

With the assistance of two personal nurses and a physical therapist Alexus hired, Rita Mae Bishop and Detective Neal Miller were quickly recovering from their injuries at the rented beach house.

Shortly after the bombing, an MSNBC viewer in Houston had contacted federal authorities identifying Jennifer Costilla as the I-94 shooting suspect.A search warrant was later executed on Jennifer's Brownsville home by a platoon of FBI, ATF, and

DEA agents, resulting in the largest drug bust in Brownsville history. 750 kilograms of heroin and 1,200 kilos of cocaine were found stuffed down inside hundreds of stacked boxes in the basement. But the tunnel was never located, neither was Jennifer, who was now *pictured* on the FBI Ten most wanted Fugitives list, right next to Osama binLaden.

Besides the letter she'd written Papi, hurling a harsh stream of complaints at him for blatantly ignoring her, Alexus was avoiding all contact with the Costillas.

Seated in the back of the Phantom next to Cereniti, who wore the same white LV sundress and red patent leather peep toe Jimmy Choo pumps as she, Alexus was busy uploading pictures of their latest trip to Twitter and Facebook.

"Gandolfini...you familiar with that name?" Sneed asked suddenly.

Alexus glanced at the rearview mirror and saw that he was looking at her."Gandolfini? No, I can't recall ever hearing that name before."

"Really? That's funny...he knows all about you. In fact, he knows your father's family very well. Every time Vida Costilla went bankrupt, Gandofini pushed billions of dollars into her accounts; when Santiago's realestate company tanked in '03, Gandolfini invested two million in the company. And now, ironically, he's *still* giving hundreds of millions to yourgrandmother, and she's worth more than him. Now does that make any sense to you?"

"Is it supposed to?" Alexus inquired. "Why am I supposed to care about the financial dealings of a man I've never even heard of?"

"Maybe because you're spending his money," Sneed replied matter of factly. "Maybe because he transferred twenty-two million dollars to your bank account on December twenty-fourth."

A brief silence ensued. Cereniti's mouth was wide open, but her eyes stayed on her phone. Alexus tried focusing on her phone, too; it proved tobe impossible.

"Oh..." said Alexus. "*That* Gandolfini. I know who you're talking about now. Yeah, he approved a business loan I needed

to expand my... you know... my house, um...to buy and reno-
vate more houses.""You sure are nosey," Cereniti murmured.

"I'm paid to be nosey, Ms. Stingley. I'm a FBI a..."

"We know what you are, yo. You're an FBI agent passing
as my girls' personal assistant. But you're acting like the exact
opposite."

Alexus smirked, feeling mildly nervous from the agents
snooping. She put a hand on Cereniti's knee and gave it an ap-
preciative squeeze.

Sneed noted the grateful gesture. He considered Alexus
a horrible liar;she had clearly lied about not recognizing the
sketch of Jennifer Costilla.He sensed that she'd also lied
about not knowing Rolando Garcia. And Blind Fury could
see that she was not being honest about the millions shehad
received from Gandolfini. But her lies did not bother Sneed. He
figured it was only a matter of timebefore she and all the other
Costillas were rotting in prison.

"Yo, driver, drop me off at Miami International," Cereniti
said, hoping toinfuriate the FBI agent with her snobbish de-
mand.

"The airport?" Alexus frowned at Cereniti. "Why do you
need to be dropped off at the airport?"

"It's a surprise."

"What kind of surprise?"

"If I tell you that, it wouldn't be a surprise, now, would it?"

Smiling at her friend's antics, Alexus shook her head and
phoned her contracting manager, Danny Brunson, to check on
the progress of herproperties in Michigan City. He had good
news. The restorations werecompleted. He wanted to know if
she would like signs hung above the convenience store and the
beauty salon.

"I don't want to name the salon...not yet, anyway. But I
want to name that store after Blake King"

"The guy who killed those policemen?" Danny sounded
flabbergasted."That's only a rumor. But yes, I want it named
after him."

"From a business standpoint, that would be a terrible

mistake. People will be boycotting your store before it even opens."

"Well…" Alexus paused, thinking…" name it Bee King's." She spelled it out for him. "Put an ad in the local newspaper for the job openings. I need hair stylists and store clerks. I'll pay you an extra thousand for the work."

"Will do," Danny assented and hung up.

When Sneed pulled up at the airport, Alexus had her American Express black card out and was using her iPad to order a set of snow white 24-inch Asanti rims for her Phantom.

Cereniti hugged Alexus before opening her door and getting out. "I should be back Wednesday at noon."

"Call me when your flight lands. And don't forget to send Tasia those pictures," Alexus said. "It seems pretty odd that you didn't pack any bags."

"I'm a pretty odd kinda girl. Love you." Cereniti closed the door and waved good-bye.

Alexus gave no further thought to Cereniti's sudden departure. Louis Vuitton.com had a 20% off sale today, and there was a new bag that she was dying to get.

TMZ cameramen bombarded the Phantom as Sneed parked it in front of a Ben and Jerry's ice cream shop a few blocks over from the beach house.

Alexus had her window down, her black curtain drawn back. Originally, she had not intended to get out of the car; Sneed was the epitome of a gentleman, and he would have gladly fetched a helping of chocolate ice cream for his pregnant passenger.

But since the cameras were on her, she stepped out, smiling gracefully, and headed for the front glass door of the shop.

"Hey, I know you," said one cameraman. "You're the model who was pictured next to Lupe Fiasco in Black Men magazine, the model with all those views on YouTube."

Another cameraman asked, "Aren't you Vida Costilla's granddaughter? There's a rumor being spread across the net that you're related to Mexican billionaire Vida Costilla. Is there any truth to that?"

A pudgy black man with a Kimbo slice beard said, "can you

tell us who the official leader of the LVT is?" Standing there in a tight black T-shirt andskinny jeans, with a big video recorder on his right shoulder, the man had a smug look on his face, as if he had just asked the million dollar question.

Sneed came up behind Alexus as she was opening the shop's door."Ignore them, Alexus," he whispered through clenched teeth.

But she didn't ignore them. She turned to the man in the skinny jeans. "The leader of LVT? What is the LVT? I've never heard of it."

"The Louis Vuitton Team, I follow you all on Twitter. My boss, Harvey, categorizes you with Paris Hilton and LaLa. He says you'll have your own reality show on MTN before year's end, and that he hopes you won't endup like a lot of other heiresses... lost in an ocean of drugs, vodka, and mug shots."

"Oh yeah?" Alexus hunched her brows. "Well, you can give Harvey Levin a message from me. Tell him I said"—she picked up the back of her sundress, revealing a Louis Vuitton thong that was mostly hidden between the meaty cheeks of her butt— "he can kiss my natural brown ass."

She giggled lightly, then preceded Sneed into the opulent ice cream shop.Once inside, she spotted Miami Heat's star player, Lebron James, standing in front of the counter with his family and a dynamic duo of towering bodyguards. *The TMZ crew was here for him*, she determined.

"You should not have talked to them, Alexus," Sneed said when they were seated. "Your aunt will know exactly where you are. You just took an unnecessary risk."

"Whatever." Alexus was snapping pictures of Lebron with her phone, smiling at the fact that Cereniti was missing the chance to meet their secondfavorite NBA player. "I'm not about to be running from her all my life. I have no clue what her issue with me was, but I'm no longer associating myself with any of them, so I should be fine."

Sneed sighed. He started to protest Alexus's warped ideology, but he wasnot quick enough; Alexus jumped to her feet and ran over to get a picture with Lebron James.

King Rio

Chapter 32

Although she wasn't fluent in English, Jennifer Costilla knew several other languages. One of them was Arabic, which came in handy when conversing with a famous terrorist.

The two of them were sitting Indian style in front of a small TV in a bedroom where he often recorded footage of himself. They were on the second floor of his three story compound in Abbottabad, a major city on N- 35 Road in northern Pakistan.

Jennifer had been staying at the safe house for the past three weeks. A religious zealot, he demanded she wear the same traditional Muslim attire that his three wives wore. She obliged without reluctance, though the fabric of the abaya irritated her skin.

"I see you're really into American TV," Jennifer observed as they sat before the television, watching CNN.

He took a moment to reply. "I watch them whenever I want to watch them… They watch me only when I let them."

"Hmm." Jenny nodded. She wondered how he'd managed to go from living like a caveman in the mountainous regions of Afghanistan to residinghere in a mansion in the middle of a densely populated city.

A few silent minutes later, she said, "you're quite an intriguing man. I've always been predisposed to believing you were the zenith of evil. Turns out you're a pretty nice man."

"I am but a servant of Allah's, and he is most gracious, most merciful. It is only right to reflect his love upon his children, his hate upon his enemies."

"Is that why you destroyed the twin towers? Because you considered the Americans enemies?"

Slowly, he turned to look at Jenny. His emotionless eyes seemed void of spirit. His thick, dark beard was as long as his silence.

Feeling intimidated, Jenny broached a different subject.

"I received an e-mail from my mother while I was out shopping yesterday. We'll be able to get the uranium into the

States whenever thefeds auction off my house."

Osama went back to watching the television. "Why must we wait?" he asked impatiently.

"Because the tunnel can't be used again until the U.S. government is through investigating my family and me. As soon as they're done, I promise, the uranium will be smuggled into the states and delivered to your al Qaeda brothers without incident."

"And you're certain of this?"

"Without a doubt," Jenny assured him. "Our cartel has already received the locations of your mosques in New York City, Chicago, and Los Angeles."

"Finally...Allah's ultimate plan has come to fruition. His enemy shall falllike the towers." Osama turned to Jenny again. This time his eyes were cheery, and the corners of his narrow lips rose. "I know your mother. I've known her for many years, and not once has she let me down."

"I'll tell her you said that.""Please do."

They engrossed themselves in CNN a while longer. Then he lifted the remote and started flipping through news channels.

A familiar face caught Jenny's attention. Urgently, she tapped her terrorist friend's shoulder.

"Go back!" she nearly shouted. "Fox! Go back to Fox1." He turned back to Fox's local channel...and Jenny gasped.There on the screen was Alexus Costilla.

Chapter 33

A wave of joy splashed through Alexus's body at the sound of Blake King's familiar voice:

"Hello? Is this Alexus?" he said.

Alexus was sitting alone in the Miami Beach house's twenty seat theater, eating popcorn and preparing to watch an early morning movie, when she got the call.

"Fat man!" she exclaimed, and her eyes lit up. "How are you feeling? OhGod, I can't believe I'm actually talking to you. Are you okay? Are you outof the hospital?"

Chuckling, Blake replied, "I'm good. My jaw's still wired shut. But I'm breathing without the machine now, and I'm off that feeding tube. They gotme eatin' baby food."

"Boy you're lucky to be alive right now...*we're* lucky to be alive right now." As the movie *Why did I get married, Too* started on the vast screen infront of her, Alexus recounted the I-94 shooting and the bombing of Rita's house to Blake.

"Daaamn! Seems like my luck rubbed off on you," he mused.

"It certainly does. I hope you're through living that street life; if you're not, I doubt you'll be living much longer. I've been here in Miami for abouta month. It's really peaceful and the climate is so warm here."

"Let me guess, you want me to come out there with you."

Alexus smiled wishfully, feeling her heart inflate like a balloon in her chest. "That would be nice, Blake."

There was a short pause.

"You still fuckin' with T-Walk?"

"I haven't talked to him since Christmas Eve."

"That nigga tried to have me killed."

"Forget about him. I'm not even thinking about him, Blake. I've been focusing on bettering myself and establishing my career. After all, I dohave a child on the way."

Another pause.

"You um...think I'm the daddy?"

"I've only been with you and T-walk."

Rita barged into the room on her crutches; she had suffered a broken leg in the blast, and the left side of her head and neck had been severely burned.

All of her lustrous hair had been scorched away. Now she wore a shoulder length black wig and her usual T-shirt, blue jeans and Manolo BlahnikFlats.

She plopped down on the black leather recliner next to Alexus.

"Well, if it turns out I'm the father," said Blake, "I'ma do my best to be there for him."

"Please don't say 'him', I want a girl. I already have a name for her and everything."

"People in hell want ice water," Blake joked.

Alexus sucked her teeth. "I'd watch my words, if I were you," shewarned. "You've already been shot ten times. One more bullet might end your life."

His husky chuckle whelmed the line again. "In that case, I might be safer stayin' here. At least the nurses like me."

Rita dug her hand in the bag of popcorn on Alexus's lap and grabbed a handful. Alexus could tell that her mother was eavesdropping on theconversation.

"Don't say that, Blake. You know I love you."

"I gotta go," Blake said abruptly.

"What? Why?"

"The nurse is here to change my bandages. I'll call you back later, okay?

Alexus sighed. "But we just…"

He was already gone. She stared with disbelief at her iPhone.

"I see you're still obsessed with O-Dog." Rita's attention remained on themovie screen. She smiled at her daughter's dilemma. "Baby, I'll tell you something I've learned over the years: a good girl is a bad boy magnet. It may be the devil trying to taint the souls of the righteous, or maybe it's inherent in us to seek the tough guys for protection…I don't know."

"I don't know, either, momma. All I know is I like Blake

way more than Iliked T-Walk."

"I actually like T-walk more. He's an approachable sort of guy, street savvy and business savvy all at once. You shouldn't rekindle any oldrelationships without at least giving T-Walk another chance. He deservesit."

Alexus chortled. "Yeah right, momma. He hasn't even tried to work out our problems. He ran from our relationship."

"Blake was the problem, Alexus, and you know it. You should not have bailed him out of jail, and you definitely shouldn't have bought him thatcar. That was below the belt."

Shrugging, Alexus stuffed some popcorn in her mouth and chewed the buttery fluffs while, in her head, she chastised herself for going behind T- Walk's back to mess with Blake. She knew she was wrong for doing it—she'd known it then. But she had felt horrible after abandoning Blake the way she had. NO real woman would have done such a thing.

I'll call T-Walk, she thought to herself, and apologize for ruining our relationship. Then I'll fly Blake out here to live with me. If Neal doesn't likeit, he can get the hell out of my house. But momma's staying.

A few seconds more of deliberation was all it took to get her apology together. She went to her phone's list of contacts, and was just about to call T-Walk when her phone started ringing.

It was a restricted number. "Hello?" She answered timidly.

"Don't say my name. Your phone is tapped," Juan Costilla said. "The family is dirty. Trust no one except the old one. The cousins are just as dirtyas the womb from which they were born. You're being closely watched."

Alexus's mouth was wide open. Her heart was using her ribs as a punching bag. She elbowed Rita, and mouthed, *"Papi! It's Papi."*

"My little angel," said Papi. "I love you."

"I love you, too…" Alexus had a cornucopia of questions stockpiled in her brain for Papi, but she knew better than to openly converse on a tapped line.

She could not have said more even if she'd wanted to. Because *call ended* was blinking on her phone's screen.

Blake grinned at his attorney as she sank down into the chair next to hishospital bed. Her vivacious aura held him spellbound.

"Who was that on the phone?" Britney asked, opening a Dell laptop. "Alexus," said Blake. "I just remembered her number. She wants me to come down there to Miami with her."

"Why did you lie and tell her a nurse was coming to change yourbandages? Why lie to her about a visit from an attorney who she paid for?"

Blake's inviting grin shrunk to a smirk. He would have dismissed Bostic's question with an able bodied shrug if his body was able.

But, sadly, it wasn't. He'd been shot three times in his right shoulder, twice in his left shoulder, once through the side of his neck, once in the stomach, once in his right forearm and twice in the face. Luckily, the two bullets that had passed through the left and out the right of his face hadn't done much damage other than shattering his mandible and causing a few teeth to fall out.

Beneath his blue hospital gown, his whole torso was gauzed and stitched.There were stitches embedded in both sides of his face, and heavy duty wires holding his teeth together.

He pressed a button on the bed controls that raised him up to a sitting position. "What's going on with my cases? Judge still tryin' to lock meup?"

Britney glared at him with a modicum of disdain. "I filed a motion to postpone any and all court proceedings until you're physically fit to stand trial. Judge Crowley granted the motion. You'll undergo a physical exam every forty-five days.

"So I can go to Mlaml?"

"Not if I call and tell Alexus about the lie you just told her." "Now, why would you do that?" Blake smirked.

"Because honesty is the best policy, and you had no reason to lie to that sweet girl. Alexus has a heart of gold, Blake. If you break her heart, that'll be the biggest mistake of your life. I guarantee it."

"Guarantee this dick in yuh mouth,' Blake mumbled, lifting his eyes to the TV.

"*Excuse me?!* What was that?"

"What was what? I ain't said nothing."

"Oh, you said *somethin'*!"

"Nah," he reiterated, "I ain't said nothin'…so what's up? Why you visitin'me in the first place?"

Coldly, the lawyer studied her client for a moment. Then she took a stackof papers from her black briefcase and tossed them onto his chest.

Blake winced as a wave of intense pain reverberated through him."Aagh, shit…you crazy bitch! Fuck you do that for?"

"I ain't did nothin'." Britney said. She was typing something on hercomputer. "Don't bother looking over those papers, I thoroughly perused them over breakfast this morning. Just sign next to the X on those last two pages."

"Yeah, right. I'm, supposed to trust you five seconds after you just tried to kill me. Fuck I look like, Boo-Boo the fool?"

Blake waited for his chest to stop throbbing before he picked up the papers. It took him less than a minute to determine that he needed Britney's help in understanding the legal jargon but, out of spite, he kept quiet and read as if he knew the meaning of every word he came across.

"I don't see why you wouldn't trust me," Britney said, still hammering away at her laptop. "I didn't turn you in when Timothy Trice told my fiancéand me that you had killed Johnny Lay."

"I ain't killed nobody. And I hope you know you fucked up my relationship with Ashley when you told her that bullshit."

"You need to wash your mouth out with soap, talking like that."

Sensing a small amount of hurt in Britney Bostic's cotton voice, Blake laid the papers on his empty food tray and turned to her. He spoke in an apologetic tone. "Ay…I'm sorry. I ain't tryin' to be disrespectful or nothin'."He glanced at the papers. "Why do I need to sign these?"

"Alexus had these faxed to my office yesterday. She's giving you that newly renovated convenience store on the corner of Ninth and Willard, and a house on Lincoln Avenue. Boogie's old place, I think. I'm sure you remember Boogie." Britney closed her laptop and stowed it in its black carrying case. "Once your signature is on those papers, I'll file them in court, and ownership of the properties will be changed to your name."

Blake borrowed a pen from the lawyer and scribbled his signature on the papers like his life depended on it. He had never in his life owned aproperty, no one in his family owned property. They were renters, perpetually struggling to scrape together the cash needed to appease their landlords on the first of the month.

His main motive for dealing drugs had been to help his mother pay bills when Streets was serving time in prison on a cocaine possession conviction and his father was without a job. He had planned to give up dealing once Dale found work, but the consistent influx of cash had afforded him all the things he'd ever wanted in life. Suddenly every 'hood chick he glanced at had wanted to fuck him. He'd started rockin' the latest in urban clothing Coogi, Girbaud, Pelle Pelle; in Jordans, Timberlands, and Mauris.

And then, as he was reaching what he at the time believed was the peakof Mt. Hustle, Ashley had become pregnant with Savaria, and the notion of stepping away from the street hustle dissipated like a fog of blown breathon a window pane. There was no way he was going to raise his daughter without giving her the very best that life had to offer.

Now he had something to leave Vari if and when he passed away: a store,and a house. This fact had him smiling irrepressibly.

"...hello? Earth to Blake," Britney was saying, waving a hand before his face.

"I'm here, I'm here." With a groan, Blake swung his legs over thebedside. "You mind helping me to the bathroom?"

Attorney Bostic was hesitant. "I, um...I'll help you to the bathroom. But..."

"Ain't that what I just said?"

"...I'm not going to hold it for you."

Blake chuckled as he heaved himself to his feet. He felt the coldness of the tiled floor through his thickly padded socks, and Britney's arm as it curled around his lower back.

"That liquid diet got me pissin like a racehorse," he said, shufflingforward. "Whenever I get to eat some solid food again, I'm smashin' a sixteen ounce steak."

The door to his hospital room was open halfway. He glimpsed a light skinned man, physique hidden beneath a long black overcoat, eyes stashed behind dark shades, standing in the hallway. Blake thought the man seemedfidgety, nervous.

Then, as a nurse approached the man and asked him if he needed help locating a patient's room, Blake realized who the man was.

Instinctively, though it ached him to move, Blake dipped into the bathroom with the speed of a sprinting cheetah. He had to hold his breath tokeep from screaming out in pain.

"You really do have to go huh?" Britney mused.

"You gotta get in here with me," he replied quickly.

"Oh no I don't! I am not about to…"

"Well, if that nigga ask, tell him I'm in surgery or some-thin'," he said,kicking the bathroom door shut.

"Yes, I do need your assistance in finding a patient. I'm here to visit a cousin of mine. Blake King. I know he's on this floor somewhere. Just can'tremember the room number."

Trepidation rose in the nurse's eyes. She was slim and di-minutive, and nice looking. A kind faced, middle aged Asian woman. Her tone faded to a whisper.

"I've been working here at St. Anthony's for a long time," she said, "Twenty-five years, to be exact. And ya know, I've never heard more dark dangerous rumors about a patient than I have about your cousin. From whatI hear, the guy's a complete lunatic. They say he's the one responsible for those murders on Michigan Boulevard, at that nightclub."

Trintino Walkson nodded grimly, "Yeah, I know. That's what I'm here totalk to him about. Everybody in the family's fed up with his erratic behavior. We're afraid it's going to get him killed one of these days…He barely made it through this last incident."

"He's right here in twenty-two twelve." She motioned toward the room next to them. "You have a swell day, sir."

The little lady nimbly disappeared down the hall.

T-Walk entered room 2212 and shut the door, not wanting to draw any more attention to himself. When he turned around, pulling a razor sharp hunting knife from his coat pocket, he was confronted by yet anotherwoman. Decked out in a black pantsuit and white blouse, she was stunning and sophisticated.

She flicked an index finger at the knife. "A Rambo knife in a hospital?" She said quizzically.

"I use it to clean my nails." He stepped around her and walked deeperinto the room, holding the knife firmly in his right hand. "Where is he? Where's Blake?"

"He's…um…he went out for lunch. He left to grab some Subway about twenty minutes ago."

"Really?"

"Yes, really. He's gone. So you'll have to stop by some other time, okay?

In a couple of hours, maybe."

T-Walk sat down on the untidy, unmade bed. "I don't believe you," he said, glancing at her. "You'd be surprised how fast word spreads in this small city. I would have heard about it if somebody who was shot ten times

just a month ago suddenly walked into Subway. It would have been all overFacebook by now."

"What's your name?"

"You're a liar. I'm here to visit my cousin, and you're lying to me about where he is."

"Who are you? I'll tell him you stopped by. Give me your name and number and I'll give the information to Blake whenever he returns, I promise."

He shook his head, placed the palm of his hand on the center of the bed and felt warmth.

This bitch must think I'm mentally handicapped, he thought, shifting his gaze to the closed bathroom door.

"You're lying to me again," T-Walk muttered, "like I'm some kind of retard? I'm not retarded."

The dark, pretty woman didn't reply. She seemed frightened.

T-Walk stood up, his eyes fluctuating from the woman to the bathroom door. His alligator Mauri shoes clacked across the floor as he walked to the bathroom. He stopped outside the door, a mere four feet from the woman. Cautiously, she took a step back.

For a fleeting moment, he considered digging the nine inch blade into thebottom of her stomach and yanking it up to her sternum.

"I could kill you right now, you lil lyin' bitch," he hissed. "Gut you like apig. The fuck is wrong with you, lying to me like that?"

The woman was shaking like dice in a Yahtzee game. Her face was a mask of fear.

"I…I don't have anything to …this is none of my, um," she stuttered, struggling to find the words.

She gasped as T-walk raised the hunting knife.He stabbed it through the bathroom door.

"Blake, I bet' not see you in the streets, nigga. It's yo' ass if I do…" T- Walk warned. "You ain't makin' it next time."

Then he left the hospital room.

King Rio

Chapter 34

Alexus was lying in bed, in her spacious boudoir, reading the finalchapter in Neil McNeil's *Through the Fire* novel— the best urban novel ever written, in her opinion, and she'd read quite a few of them—when the whir of Neal's electric wheelchair made her look up.

He rolled into the bedroom, his head and hands wrapped with gauze and ace bandages, paralyzed from the waist down. Alexus regarded him with sympathy. She knew he was depressed and deeply saddened by his paralysis. It showed in his eyes, and in his cracked voice.

"Feeling any better?" She asked, folding down a corner of the page she'dbeen reading. She closed the book and set it aside.

Neal grumbled, "Better than yesterday. Doc keeps telling me that my chances of ever walking again are slim to none."

"You will walk again. Don't ever give up hope, Neal. These doctors are clueless." Alexus didn't believe herself. She was only trying to console her momma's significant other, because she felt he needed it.

"I can move two toes on my left foot now," he said. "I know it's not much, but it's a start."

He parked his wheelchair next to the bed, positioning himself so that he faced the wall mounted 50" flat screen TV. Alexus was tuned in to a Tyra rerun: the horrors of cellulite.

"I met Lebron James yesterday, "Alexus said.

"Yeah, I know. Rita told me you were on TMZ all hugged up with him. Now there's a rumor on the internet that the two of you are dating." He shook his head in disbelief. "You are a piece of work, you know that? A *reeeal* piece of work."

Alexus sighed. "What is it this time, Neal?"

"You know what I'm getting at. That TMZ stunt. You've just alerted the Costilla cartel to our whereabouts, Great job."

"I wasn't trying to alert anybody to anything. All I did was talk to a cameraman and take a picture with…'

Alexus halted mid-sentence as the penetrating sound of an

approaching helicopter invaded her ears. She slipped out of bed and moved to a window.Pushing aside her tan and brown Louis Vuitton curtain, she looked outside and saw a jet black Bell chopper land on the vast portion of private beach behind the South Beach mansion.

By the time Neal's wheel chair made it to the window, the Costilla clan—Vida, Savio, and Santiago— were hunched over, walking through clouds ofchurning sand towards the beach house.

"Great motherfucking job," said Neal. "Bravo."

The greetings Savio and Santiago embraced Alexus with seemed coldand unaffectionate. Their expressions were blank.

Savio muttered, "Hey, little cousin," without enthusiasm.

Santiago replied, "My favorite heartbreaker," just as coldly.

They were all standing off to the side of the Olympic size swimming poolin back of the luxury estate: Rita, Alexus, and the Costillas. Neal had opted to stay inside; he and special agent Sneed were watching the impromptu poolside meeting through a set of high tech binoculars from Alexus's bedroom window.

"How'd you find us?" Alexus asked acidly.

"It was the TMZ thing, wasn't it?" Rita guessed.

"We've known where to find you all along," said Savio. "We knew whereyou were ever since you left Indiana. I hired a P.I to track your credit expenses, and it led him here. But yes, Aunt Rita, we are here because ofthe TMZ thing. We fear that the video may have exposed you all to the wrong people."

"Wrong people!" Rita scoffed. "Allow me a moment to refresh your memory: *Your mother* detonated an ounce of C-4 on my doorstep, put twenty bullets in the trunk of my daughter's car....while she was *in* it, mindyou...and killed nine innocent people on Interstate 94. I believeI'm looking at the raw definition of *wrong people*."

Savio was speechless.

Santiago opened his mouth to speak, but Vida raised a silencing hand thatended all conversation.

Momentarily, the old lady remained quiet, roving her eyes over hergrandchildren and daughter in-law. Alexus had just as many questions for Granny Costilla as she had for Papi, and she was determined to get some answers today, no matter how long the old bag kept quiet.

Finally, Vida said, "we aren't here to argue and disagree. As my grandsonstated, we're here to prevent anything else from happening."

'We aren't leaving the beach house." Alexus folded her arms over her chest. "We're perfectly safe here."

Rita nodded concurrently. "There's a team of about fifteen FBI agents surrounding the place at all times. We even have one in-house agent posing as Alexus's personal assistant. He's watching us through a pair of binoculars at this very moment. So, yes, we're pretty safe, if you ask me. The *wrong people* don't stand a chance."

Abruptly, Vida turned to walk back to her helicopter, and her grandsons trailed behind her automatically.

"Grandma, we need to talk," Alexus shouted, propping her hands on her hips.

Vida stopped, twisted her waist and neck to glance at Alexus, and then continued on her way.

"Oh no the hell you ain't," Alexus said to herself, as she marched up to her grandmother.

"In the bird," Vida said when Alexus made it to her. "We'll talk in the bird."

"How do I know Savio and Santiago aren't gonna pull an Aunt Jenny on me when I get in there?"

"Because they own and operate one of this country's leading real estate companies; your FBI friends are itching to take that away."

"They are not my friends," Alexus argued. "Well, your personal assistants," Vida fired back.

Quite childishly, Alexus stuck out her tongue behind Granny Costilla's back. She was a little afraid of joining them on the helicopter, but for some unknown reason, Aunt Jenny had tried to kill her, and she was determinedto find out why.

Two feet long, maybe seven inches wide, black in color, the electronic gadget Santiago waved over Alexus's brown silk

Louis Vuitton sundress resembled a metal detector. He scanned her hair with it, her shoes and her large bag, and even her diamond framed sunglasses.

'I'm not wired, dickhead," Alexus said.

"Better safe than sorry. Who knows with you." Santiago no longer sounded like a family member; his usually suave tone had flipped to an ominous one.

Alexus shivered as a chill raised goosebumps on her arms. She put on a pair of headphones and moved the mic close to her mouth, looking down at her mother's shrinking figure as the pilot, Enrique Aleman, suddenly pulledthe chopper up, ascending a few hundred feet, then pushed it southeast over the sparkling, clear blue waters of the Atlantic Ocean.

"I'd like to know what it is I did wrong," Alexus said into the mic. She was sandwiched between her cousins. Granny Costilla sat directly across from her.

"It's not you, Lexi," Vida said. "It's not you at all. Rita's done nothing either. Your lives were put in jeopardy because of my actions. I made a dumb mistake, a mistake that nearly cost me everything. And I do mean everything."

"A mistake that makes Aunt Jenny want to kill me?"

Vida nodded solemnly. "I'm an old woman now, Lexi, old as the moon. One of these days, I'm going to lay down and never wake up. On the day that happens, I'll need one of you to take…" she gasped, her eyes went buck, and she slapped a hand over the left side of her chest.

For a split second, Alexus thought her granny was suffering a heartattack. Maybe the old lady had jinxed herself into an early grave.

But then Alexus caught sight of the object that had Vida all worked up, and she found herself mimicking Grandma's dreadful actions.

A Boeing 737 plane was plummeting from the sky, on a collision course with the beach house….

After only seconds of viewing the poolside rendezvous through his binoculars, special agent Sneed had muttered, "Something isn't right about this. I smell a trap."

Worriedly, Neal Miller had looked up at him and whispered, "Think we should get *out* of here?"

Sneed had answered by getting behind Neal's wheelchair and expeditiously rolling him out of Alexus's bedroom, down the hall to the glass elevator, descending to the first floor, and then wheeling his disabled friend out the front door. He had signaled for backup while they were on theelevator; two black SUVs whipped into the circular drive a mere twenty seconds after they'd exited the beach house.

"Get Miller to the Epic Hotel on Biscayne," Sneed had yelled to one of the agents. "Pronto!"

"Wait!" Neal protested, as he was being loaded into the back of a Tahoe.

"I'm not leaving without Rita Mae!"

They all looked skyward, watching the helicopter lift off and roar away. "I think you might be overreacting, Sneed," said the agent who had placed Neal in the SUV.

"When it comes to Mexican drug cartels," Sneed said, already turning to run to Rita's rescue, "there's no such thing as overreacting."

He knocked over a Hispanic male groundskeeper in his race to the rear ofthe towering three story gray-stoned beach house. With no time to shout an apology, he kept running.

At the same instant he spotted Rita, who was stretched out on a lounge chair next to the pool, talking on her cell phone, he saw the nose-diving plane plunging down from the azure sky like an oversized pigeon.

He wrapped his arms around her waist and, lifting her, shouted, " Hold Your breath!"

They splashed into the pool two seconds before the airplane crashed into the mansion.

The explosion rocked the neighborhood to its core.

Not since the September 11, 2001, terrorist attacks had the U.S been in such a state of fear. The FAA ordered a country wide cancellation of all flights. Every news station in the nation was reporting on the hijacked planethat had claimed the lives of forty-one passengers, nine crew members, and eight hijackers.

The president delivered a speech from the Oval Office three hours after the crash, at 6:30 *eastern standard* time, offering his condolences to the victim's families, pledging to locate and prosecute whoever was responsiblefor this horrendous attack.

An hour later, National Security advisor Robert Lemons held a news conference at the White House. Lemons informed the American people thatAunt Jenny's terrorist friends just released a video claiming responsibility for the hijacked plane crash. Apparently, in the video, the terrorist had also named his intended target: Alexus Costilla.

The video had been posted on dozens of Arabic websites in the Middle East, and it was not long before an English translated version of it landed onYoutube.

"Alexus Costilla," Osama said gravely. "Enemy of the helper, therefore enemy to Allah. It was necessary that she die, for she stood beside evil, the crooked government of the west. The Islamic nation stands beside therighteous.

"Soon, the American world will be turned upside down. Our nuclear war will begin with the flattening of your precious nation's capital. Then your major cities will be wiped out. All survivors will either convert to the true religion of Allah or parish in the same way their fellow countrymen have perished…"

All this hit Alexus like a sack of padlocks dropped from atop of theWillis Tower. She paced back and forth in the Presidential suite that had been rented for her by the FBI, at the Epic Hotel and Tower on Biscayne Boulevard.

"I'm not comfortable staying here in Miami, Sneed," Alexus said bitterly into her smart phone's Bluetooth earpiece.

Rita Mae was reposing in bed, skimming through news websites on her iPad. She had a dark blue sweat suit with FBI stenciled in yellow over its chest. It had been given to her to replace her wet clothing by a tall, stoic, ex-marine FBI agent named Paul Meyer.

Disguised as hotel security, Meyer and another agent were posted up in the hallway outside the suite.

"You won't be staying there for long," Sneed replied. "I'm on my way tothe J. Edgar Hoover Building to brief Director

Byrd and I'm sure he'll be sending for you soon after."

"Who is Director Byrd? And why would he be sending for me?" "Director Byrd is El Jefe of the FBI. He meets with the President four

times a week, runs the entire Bureau, and has a ton of pull with the attorney general. This'll be my first time ever meeting Byrd. I hear he's quiet as stone."

"I'm guessing he'll be sending for my grandma, too huh?"

"More than likely. This isn't only about you, anymore; it's become a matter of national security. Bin Laden is threatening to nuke our nation's capital and all our major cities. We're in the process of determining howyou fit into all this, Alexus, how you ended up on al-Qaeda's hit list."

"When you find out, please, let me know." Alexus stopped pacing and saton the bed with momma. "Thanks again…for saving my mom. That was some heroic shit you did."

"Watch your mouth," Rita muttered vacantly.

"I was acting on instinct," Sneed admitted. "And you can't really give meall the credit. Neal said he wasn't going anywhere without your mother."

"So you were gonna leave her?"

"No, no, of course not. I would have ran to get her either way. I just wouldn't have made it back there in time. That plane crashed maybe three seconds after we made it into the pool. Fire blanketed the pool's surface for what must have been at least forty-five seconds. Lucky for us, most of the debris landed in front of the property. If it hadn't, we would have been crushed to death."

Alexus cringed as a ghastly image of momma lying twisted disproportionately beneath a burning chunk of steel flashed in her mind. She'd envisioned the same image in Granny Costilla's helicopter, as she hadwatched the 737 slam into the mansion.

"This whole thing has turned into a horror flick, Sneed. I didn't ask for any of this," Alexus said.

"I understand that. But like I said, this isn't about you. If al-Qaeda has somehow found a way to smuggle yellowcake into this country, we are in big trouble."

"Yellowcake?"

"It's another name for partially refined uranium ore, the key ingredient needed to produce nuclear weapons. In the wrong hands it could do unimaginable damage. About seventy-five thousand people were killed when President Truman had Hiroshima bombed back in 1945. And three days later, when Nagasaki was nuked, down went another forty thousand Japanese people."

"I don't want to hear about any more explosions. Talk to you later." Alexus mumbled, feeling mentally debilitated as she ended the call.

She turned to momma and sighed. Rita reciprocated with a sigh of her own.

"Don't look so sad, momma...the grounds crews haven't even started to search for survivors. He might be okay."

"There is absolutely no chance of surviving direct impact from a 737 jet,"Rita said, fighting back tears.

The torment in Rita's face was palpable; it radiated from her sage brown eyes like steam from a teakettle. Alexus couldn't take it. She crawled over

momma and laid beside her, consoling cheek to distraught cheek, hand in hand.

"Well, God's with him if he's gone. You pray enough to save every person you've ever talked to," Alexus said.

A single tear trickled out of Rita's left eye and cascaded down towards her ear. "The Lord doesn't work that way, child." She shook her head, closed her eyes.

"I'm here with you, momma," Alexus whispered, squeezing momma's tremulous hand.

"I know, baby."

Rita Mae cried silently for twenty minutes, and she might have kept righton bawling if not for the knock at their hotel room door.

Alexus opened the door and saw Granny Costilla standing there between two FBI agents. Vida's dark blue skirtsuit was slightly wrinkled, her thin gray hair unkempt. She was not happy. Never in her life had she been held against her will.

Not until now.

Enrique Aleman, Vida, Savio, and Santiago had been forced into FBI vehicles immediately after Enrique had landed the chopper a block down from the crash. Now they were situated in a room across the hall from Alexus and Rita's awaiting questioning.

"We never finished our conversation," Vida said, stepping past her granddaughter. She went to a vintage armchair and sat down.

Alexus shut the door on the agents, then rested her forehead against it, breathing and thinking, feeling unnerved, on edge, and vulnerable.

"Come on over here, Lexi. It's about time you learned how and why yourfather and Flako were arrested," Vida said, sounding weary and fatigued.

"I'm sick of all this crazy shit happening to me, grandma. I'm *really* sick." Alexus turned around, reluctant to get any closer to the elderly cartel leader. "I lived a perfectly normal life in Brownsville. Sure, I was a lot better off than my friends, but life was still normal. I wasn't being *shot* at! There weren't any airplanes flying into my house! And there certainlyweren't any *terrorists* trying to kill me!"

No one said a thing.

Impulsively, Alexus kicked off her heels. Then she joined momma and Granny Costilla, and finally found out why all those horrible events kept happening to her.

And surprisingly, it all made sense.

Chapter 35

"Every piece of evidence we have, from the drugs we found in Tasia Olsen's condo, to the four hundred kilograms we found in that wrecked eighteen wheeler on Interstate 94, to the nearly two thousand kilos we found in Jennifer Costilla's basement, it all points to Alexus Costilla." FBI director Charles Byrd said.

He had eleven others—including Samuel Friedman, secretary of Homeland Security; U.S. Secret service Director Michael Bowman, Jeffery Henke, director of the Bureau of Alcohol, Tobacco, Firearms and Explosives; Secretary of Defense Bradford Connor and General Ronald Rosenker, director of the Central Intelligence Agency—were seated at a long mahogany conference table on the tenth floor of FBI headquarters in Washington, DC.

The president of the United States sat at the head of the table. His almond brown fingers interlaced in front of him, his thoughtful eyes fixed on Byrd.

He said, "I'm still not getting how this eighteen year old girl from a rural city in Texas is tied into this."

"Mr. President," Byrd said, "this little woman isn't as innocent as she looks. I mean, this *is* Juan Costilla's daughter we're talking about. The drugs recovered from each scene were identically wrapped and possessed equal levels of purity. Tasia Olsen's boyfriend is Alexus's cousin. We suspect that Alexus was supplying several dealers in northwest Indiana with kilos of cocaine, and that they were...."

The president raised a hand, silencing Byrd. "Get to the point, Byrd. I'm not a federal judge."

"What I'm trying to say, Mr. President, is that al-Qaeda may be planning to smuggle yellowcake into the states with the Costilla cartel's drugs. We already know that Jennifer wants Alexus dead. It seems plausible that she would facilitate an attack on the U.S....especially with a potential death penalty looming over her head for those I-94 murders in Indiana... in exchange for the death of her niece."

"Anyone have a clue as to why Jennifer is after Alexus?" the president asked, sweeping his inquisitive gaze around the room.

General Rosenker pushed a thin stack of papers across the table to the president.

"There's your reason," said Rosenker. "Can't say I blame her, either."

The sky was pitch black, the night as cold as a Lil Wayne mixtape when the automatic glass and metal doors of St. Anthony Hospital's emergency room separated at 8:45 p.m. central time and Terrence "Streets" King guided his wheelchair bound little brother back out into a world Blake had not seen since Christmas Eve.

Blake was dressed to impress in an outfit that Streets had brought him: a black cotton skullcap, black sweater, black jeans, and black sneakers, all Coogi; and a heavy black leather Pelle Pelle jacket. He had the jacket laid over his lap to conceal the Heckler and Koch MP-5 that Streets had given him after he'd gotten dressed,

"Got that from Tim-Tim," Streets had said. "Lil nigga got choppas outthe ass.'

Afterwards the brothers had discussed the impending beef with T-Walk, and the almost too ludicrous to believe situation that was unfolding onevery news channel, the terrorist attack in Miami against Alexus Costilla.

The latter had Blake powering up his iPhone and calling Alexus asStreets pushed him out the hospital.

"You're wasting your time calling her, lil bruh," Streets said. "That bitch dead. Ain't no way in hell she lived through that shit."

"I'm callin' anyway." The frigid air numbed Blake's fingers as he put thephone to his ear and listened to it ring, ring and ring some more.

"Hi, you've reached Alexus Costilla. Sorry I couldn't answer your..." Hehit end and tried again. Same result.

He sighed, raising his eyes to deserted parking lot. There were not many vehicles. Which is why he instantly spotted the seven car motorcade of candy red 1973 Chevy Caprices, each of them squatting over chrome twenty-eight inch rims.

A small grin bloomed on Blake's wounded face.

"I see you niggas done kidnapped my swag," he said with a chuckle. "Tim-Tim bought four of 'em for him, Lil Mike, Young-D, and Blubby. I bought my own. He paid for the rims on Fly's Chevy, too. And of course you know the one in the front is yours."

"Since when Tim-Tim start ballin'?" Blake asked, brows knitted together."That lil nigga got a plug on the Kush. He been sellin' pounds for seven thousand apiece, killin' the game. Especially in Chicago. I told you we've been fuckin' with Lil Cholly and Reesie Cup and 'em out in Holy City. I think they bought like a hundred pounds already."

"Aw yeah?" Blake said, eyeing the Dub Life Goons as they all started pushing their doors open.

Like Blake and Streets, the whole clique wore Coogi from head to toe. They had gold chains with diamond clustered Dub Life medallions. Lil Mike, Young-D and Tim-Tim had gold and diamond covered teeth.

'I'll be damned, mane, my nigga back! My nigga back, you hear me, mane!" Lil Mike screeched. He ran to Blake and was just about to hug him when Streets spoke.

"Don't grab him, Lil Mike. Bruh got bullet holes everywhere."

So everybody settled for the quotidian handshake, everybody exceptTiffany Jenkins, who bent over and hugged him anyway.

"Did I not just say don't touch ho. You need me to text it to you? Need me to write it down?" Streets asked.

Tiff-Tiff sucked her teeth, flipped a middle finger at Streets, then marched back to Tim-Tim's Caprice and climbed in the passenger side.

"You still gotta drive Blake's car," Streets shouted after her.

That's what I'm talking 'bout! Thought Blake, grinning as he scanned over the sexy brown faces of four other girls who had come with the goons.

"Mane, we gon' kill dat nigga T-Walk, you hear me?" Lil

Mike swore. "Hell yeah, bruh," Young-D said, "we got every kind of chopper under

the sun now, AK-47's, AR-15's, Mac-11's, Uzis, Mac-90's, MP-5's...you name it, we got it. And all them shits is fully autos."

"Stop talkin' 'bout guns in front of these females," Blake admonished. "We'll discuss all that later. I have a house of my own on Lincoln, right down the street from my momma crib. Let's slide through there first. Then I'll go talk to Carolyn, come back, and chill with y'all for the night."

"Bu-But man, I'm ha...but man, I'm happy to see you lil nigga," Blubby stuttered.

"Me, too. You know I kept you in my prayers," Tim-Tim confided to Blake. Checking his smartphone, he added, "I'm about to go and drop off some Kush to this nigga named Gusto in Gary. I'll have a couple ounces of that shit for you when I get back."

"I need more than a couple ounces," Blake said, glancing at Tiffany's big,shaking ass as she walked to his car. He was already thinking about fucking her again, remembering how wet and warm her lubricious tunnel had been when he'd pounded it the night he was gunned down.

"I got a pound for you, bruh," Tim-Tim said with a chuckle. "Take careof my girl...my wife."

"Who, Tiff-Tiff?" Blake hoped Tim was joking.

Tim-Tim wasn't kidding. "Yeah, that's wifey my nigga. I think she's the one. Told me she wanna be with me and only me a few weeks ago."

Stifling a laugh, Blake signaled for Streets to push him to his car. He wasgetting too cold. For a millisecond, he wished he was in a warmer city, a warmer state. Somewhere like Miami, Florida.

But then, as Streets was rolling him past the guys, the plane crash cameto mind, and suddenly Blake wasn't so cold.

The rear tires of Tim-Tim's Caprice churned up slushy snow as he exited the parking lot. Fly and Blubby trailed him in their Chevys, leaving Lil Mike, and the last example of young beauty slipped into the passenger'sseat of Street's car.

"Want me to put the wheelchair in my trunk?" Streets asked.

"Nuh uh, I'm good." With a groan, Blake raised himself from the mobile chair, holding the H and K submachine gun in his left hand with his thick leather jacket draped over it. "Just open my door for me." Streets pulled the door out and helped Blake get in, then closed it, slapped the roof, and said "Tiff-Tiff, if you crash the car with my lil bruh in it, I'm crushin' you."

"Boy, you better go on somewhere!" she said, sucking her teeth as Streetsheaded for his car.

Blake closed his eyes and kept them shut until the pain in his chest subsided. When he opened them, he saw that Tiffany was staring at him.She donned a pair of fury brown boots beneath a tight, knee-length walnut dress. Her lips looked infinitely moist and overwhelmingly tempting on her pie shaped face. Her left wrist was bejeweled with four thin, white diamond tennis bracelets.

Above all, it was her sensuous perfume that captivated Blake; it seemed to occupy every particle of air in the Caprice's spacious cabin.

"What the fuck are you staring at?" Blake asked. "You can start driving any time now."

"Fuck you, nigga. I'll push you out the car while I'm driving," Tiff-Tiff said. She started the engine, shifted into drive, and applied a furry boot to the gas petal.

In a single file line, the four Caprices departed from the hospital, with Nicki Minaj's Pink Friday album rattling Blake's trunk.

"Tiff-Tiff, if you don't take that shit outta my CD player we gon' have some real problems," Blake threatened.

Tiff-Tiff turned the volume down. "Oh, so you gon' act like that? 'Cause you wasn't sayin' all this slick shit in Dawn's basement."

"I ain't fuckin' with you Tenth Street bitches no more. Your punk ass boyfriend tried to murk me."

"Craig is not my man, okay? I'm pregnant by him, but I don't fuck with him. That nigga wouldn't even help me bond out of jail. Alexus had to bondme out."

"Alexus who?"

"You know Alexus, the rich girl T-walk was with, the one who was flooding Boookie n'em with all that dope. I think she was half Puerto Ricanor Spanish, or some shit like that."

"Spanish is a language."

"Correct me again and see if I don't crash this muhfucka through one of those houses."

Blake couldn't suppress his grin.

"Anyway" she continued, "Alexus paid for my lawyer, too. Crazy thing is, I don't even know the bitch. Never seen her until that TMZ show last night. Now the bitch is being talked about on every TV channel you turn to.They're saying she's dead. Supposedly some terrorist—"

"Blah blah blah," Blake said irritably. "Turn the music back up. I'd ratherlisten to Nicki."

With a smile, Tiffany rolled her eyes. Her mannerisms, combined with her delicate voice and delectable aroma, had Blake's dick straining against his zipper.

"You know what, Blake," Tiffany said. "I can't stand you." She gave Blake a light, painful shove. He was staring out his window as Tiff- Tiff cruised up a snow flaked street. In most of the houses, a warm and welcoming yellow glow brought life to the windows. The drivers and passengers of every car they passed ogled the procession of sparkling, big rimmed Chevys.

As she gazed out the windshield, Tiffany's expression and posture were peculiar. Her eyes were narrow slits; her lips were pressed tightly together. Her shoulders were drawn up, and she was clearly tense.

"Feds have been out here *heavy* lately," Tiffany said. "I mean *really* heavy. Ever since that house was bombed on Eighth street, they've been indicting everybody."

"Streets been keepin' me updated. He told me half the dope boys left the city, and the other half got locked up."

"That's the truth. Everybody's been moving to Indianapolis, Gary, South bend, and Chicago. Tim-Tim just got me an apartment in Chicago."

"Aw yeah?" Blake asked. "Where at in Chicago?"

"About eight or nine blocks from where Reesie Cup and all the other Travelers hang out at on Trumbull. It's a big apartment building on the corner of Douglas and Albany. Whole lotta Vice Lords, a few of them knowyou."

Blake nodded. He knew that particular group of Vice Lords quite will. LilLord had introduced him to the gang's chief— "Five star Universal Elite Reesie Cup"and several of their members— shortly before Lil Lord was arrested and subsequently convicted for the brutal shooting death of a rival gang member a few years ago.

The murder had taken place in front of Blake, inside a decrepit crack house on the west side of Michigan City Lil Lord had shot the unfortunate victim a total of twelve times... and that was after he'd treated the guy's face the way Blake imagined Roy Jones Jr. might have done a speed bag. But Blake had felt no sympathy for the victim, because the man had had a mentally handicapped girlfriend who he'd been beating on like a speed bag,and karma was a bitch. Fair and square, the man had gotten what he'd deserved.

"Yeah, I know them niggas," Blake said to Tiffany. He took the iPhone off of his hip and logged onto Facebook.

"I'm bringing all this up for a reason," Tiffany said.

Blake didn't respond. He typed Alexus's name into the search box and went to her page. Her profile picture was a photo of her and Cereniti pettingan open mouthed dolphin.

"I need you to get me some dope," Tiffany said. "I heard Alexus was getting like a hundred key's at a time and sellin' em for fifteen apiece. If you know where I can buy some dope at that price, I'll get two and a half."

Oh my God! Blake thought to himself, as he stared at the voluminous mounds of derriere manifested in a backshot picture of Alexus bent over the hood of a white Rolls Royce. She had a pair of brown Louis Vuitton heels and denim short shorts that were too hot for TV.

"Are you even listening to me?" Tiffany asked. She leaned over to the right to see the picture Blake was practically drooling over. "Boy, you need to be slapped. Who is that, a video model or some slut? I bet her ass is fake.It's too big to be real. And you know that car ain't hers. See that's exactly why I can't stand them fake…"

Blake looked up at last. "That's Alexus you' talking 'bout."

"Damn, for real?"

"Yup. So, you need to be slapped." He went back to perusing Alexus's page.

There were dozens of concerned comments from friends. "Are you okay's, and Call me!'s, and from Britney Bostic, "I'm glad to hear you're fine. I'm praying for you."

Blake's eyebrows moved together. He canted his head and read attorney Bostic's comment a second time. It had been posted at 7:31 central… whichmeant it had been posted *after* the crash.

"So can you get that for me or not?" Tiffany asked. "A simple yes or no will do. I'm trying to sell some to the Breeds over in The Village. I'll have Tim-Tim sell it for me so they won't try any slick shit."

Blake scoffed. "That nigga'll fuck around and take off running if it go down. But shit," he said, dialing Alexus's number again, "I'll see what I cando."

"Ma'am, I'm an operator with Brink's home security, calling to alert you that your garage's motion detector has been set off. Is everything okay?" asked the male operator.

Alexus was seated at a circular wooden table in an interrogation room at FBI headquarters in Washington, DC. Other than her Louis Vuitton shoulder bag, there was nothing on the table in front of her. Not even an ashtray, though she didn't smoke.

A crew of Secret Service agents had arrived at the Epic hotel just secondsafter granny Costilla finished explicating the obvious reason for Aunt Jenny's betrayal.

The Secret Service agents had immediately relieved the FBI agents of their protective duties, ushered Rita and the Costillas down to a fleet of armed Cadillac limousines, and rushed them to a private airport, where a government owned Learjet was waiting; flanked by four fighter jets, it had whisked them to the District of Columbia.

Deplaning, Alexus's smartphone had rang several times with calls from Blake. But with all that had been going on, and with Papi's warning, she didn't feel safe answering the phone. What if Blake had said something incriminating? He'd have been hit like road kill. That's what. Fucked in the game like the thousands of others that have fallen victim to wiretaps.

But now he was calling again, beeping in on the other line.

"That might be my boyfriend," Alexus said to the Brinks operator. "He's calling me now. Let me click over and check and I'll get right back with you."

She switched lines, staring straight ahead at a wall length mirror and wondering if someone was on the other side of it watching her.

"Is this Bad Bitch?" Blake asked.

"Yes, it's me. Don't say it if it's not legal."

Blake took a moment to reply. "Damn...I thought you...'

"I know, you thought I was dead. I'll talk to you about all that later. Are you out of the hospital already? Because you set off the garage security system. Listen, I need you to get my clothes out of those suitcases in back of my Lincoln truck. You'll have to drive them to me whenever I—"

"Wait a minute, baby," Blake cut in. "I'm on my way *to* the house. I haven't got there *yet.*"

Alexus felt her heart drop down into her stomach. She had close to five million dollars in cash stashed in those suitcases.

"We're about to turn onto Lincoln Avenue," Blake said.

"I um...the security codes is zero-four-two-one, my birth-day. Yeah, zero-four-two-one. Check the garage as soon as you get there and send me a text if you find it's been breached."

"If I find what?"

"If you find any signs of forced entry."

'You know, you startin' to sound like the police."

"You got me fucked up, Blake."

He chuckled briefly. "That's the Bad Bitch I remember. Thanks for the house, and the store."

"Just get to the house! And make sure you take all that junk out of the bathroom," Alexus snapped. She clicked over and told the Brinks operator that everything was okay. Then she ended the call and placed the phone on the table in front of her.

Leaning back in the chair, she ruminated over her life and tried to determine precisely how she'd ended up in the predicament she was now in. All her life she'd dreamed of being a story of success, a source of inspiration. Steatopygic and buxom, beautiful and enchanting, she already possessed the striking looks it took to be categorized with women likeHallie Berry and Beyonce Knowles, but with the way her life was headed, Alexus feared that she would soon be categorized with Aaliyah, or Lisa "Left Eye" Lopes.

The door to the interrogation room opened suddenly and in walked FBI special agent Josh Sneed. A second man, short in stature, beady eyed and aggressive looking, wearing a navy executive suit and silk tie, trailed closely behind Sneed.

Neither of them spoke right away.

The short, brown skinned black man stopped in front of the wide mirror and stared at Alexus. Overhead lights refracted in his eyes, giving them an intimidating shine.

Sneed planted his palms on the table, leaned forward until his and Alexus's face were no more than six inches apart, and whispered, "If I find out that you've been in cahoots with al-Qaeda...on any other Islamic extremists, for that matter, I'll be all over you like Bush on oil."

"I've never even met a Muslim," Alexus said.

"I figured as much." Sneed sat down, produced a small tape recorderfrom his pants pocket. "Mind if I record this conversation?"

"As long as I can call my lawyer and put her on speakerphone."

Sneed assented to the stipulation and within seconds Alexus had attorney Bostic on speaker. She explained the situation to her lawyer.

Then Sneed set in.

"Can you roughly estimate the number of cocaine kilograms you have personally sold?"

"Wait a minute," Bostic interrupted.

"No, I got this," Alexus said. Papi had trained her for moments like this. "I don't sell drugs. Never have, never will."

"So you know nothing about the drugs that were seized from your friend Tasia Olsen's condo? The three kilos?"

"I have no knowledge of that. To be honest, I believe she and my cousin were set up."

"That's preposterous, and you know it. We already have an informant's statement naming you as the chief supplier of drugs to several gangs in Indiana, Illinois, Georgia, Michigan, New York, and probably a dozen otherstates."

"Informants lie all the time," Alexus quipped.

Sneed's dull expression twisted into a scowl. "Listen, Alexus… we are not out to get you. Our only concern at this point is the safety of this country. If we don't find out how the Costilla cartel has been getting their drugs across the border, we will be in deep trouble."

"…and that's an understatement," said Beady Eyes, as he stepped forward. "I'm director Charles Byrd, head of FBI."

"Hmm," Alexus said, crossing her arms, poking out her lips.

"Is my client being charged with any indictments?" Attorney Bosticasked.

"No ma'am," Byrd said. "As special agent Sneed said, we are only after al-Qaeda and all who are associated with them, and we fear they may have allies within the Costilla cartel. Eighty thousand U.S. troops are beingdeployed to the U.S. Mexican border this week. Same goes for next week, and the week after. They're preparing to invade Mexico and all the Costilla cartel's strongholds, all fourteen of them, from Juarez to Matamoras."

Although her facial expression was as undecipherable as a Botox patient's, Alexus was rapidly deteriorating on the inside as she contemplated betraying the family tunnel. Weighing her options, it was not difficult to decide which one was the more prudent.

On one hand, if she cooperated with the FBI and led them to the tunnel, she would be labeled a snitch by the cartel…

virtually signing her owndeath certificate… and billions of dollars in annual drug sales for the familywould be lost.

On the other hand, if she *didn't* cooperate, she would be giving bin Ladenand his terrorist network ample time and opportunity to follow through on their threats…and bring down the United States of America.

The garage light was on when Tiff-Tiff pulled into the driveway ofBlake's new home on Lincoln Avenue. One of the large doors to the two car garage was open.

A light skinned girl in a black jogging suit was loading suitcases into the trunk of a Chrysler 300C. She turned around and stared at Blake's car.

"I thought you said this was yo' house," Tiff-Tiff said in a questioning tone.

"It is." Blake pulled the latch on his door and used his foot to kick it out. His bullet wounds were like kerosene, and climbing out of the car sparked avolcanic fire that raged through his body so intensely he had to squeeze his eyes shut and lean against the Caprice to keep from buckling.

He finally forced his eyes open. The girl, Cereniti, was standing in front of him. Young-D was next to him.

"Why are you…what are you doing here, yo?" Cereniti asked."This *my* house. Fuck is *you* doin' here?" Blake said.

"I'm …here to pick up some stuff for Alexus."

"She just told *me* to get the clothes and bring 'em to her."

"Well, she told me the same thing," Cereniti said. She turned and went back into the garage.

"We find out you lying," Young-D warned, "I'ma slap them braids outta yo' muhfuckin head."

Cereniti threw up two middle fingers as Blake and Young-D walked up onto the front porch and, after Blake unlocked the front door, into the spacious living room, leaving their passenger behind.

Blake was surprised to see that the house… well, at least the living room… was fully furnished.

The furniture was all shades of red, and the walls were an off white stucco. A sixty-inch widescreen television graced the wall across from the sofa. Wooden shades covered the windows. Young-D flipped a switch, and Blake saw that the lighting was indirect, soft and easy on the eyes. It was a restful room.

Blake kicked off his sneakers and sank down onto the sofa with a sigh of relief. "I ain't getting' up from this couch for the rest of the night. Go out there and tell everybody to come in."

"Man, bruh out there gettin' sucked off," Young-D said.

"Well, get Tiff-Tiff and the other two bitches." Blake set his jacket and the submachine gun aside.

When he heard the door close, signaling Young-D's departure, Blake got to his feet and moved as fast as his aching body would allow him to the master's bedroom bathroom.

He counted four cardboard boxes on the tiled floor inside the glassenclosed walk-in shower, and six more in front of the tub. He took his keys out and used them to cut through the clear tape on the box closest to him.

It was filled to the top with bricks of cellophane wrapped white powder. Blake surmised it was cocaine. He thought about flipping over the box to see how many kilos were in it, but instead he brought one kilo back to the living room and shut the master bedroom door.

He was already back on the big red sofa when Young-D returned with Tiffany and two girls who introduced themselves as Tiesha and Jessica. Blake remembered seeing them on Michigan Boulevard a couple of times and once at a girl named Nae's birthday party. They were sack chasers, "powder heads", a term commonly used to describe cocaine addicts, but pretty, narrow waisted, and lithesome, nonetheless.

"Take off y'all shoes," Blake said, not wanting his hardwood floor to get streaked and marred with dirty snow.

He put the MP5 on his lap, and Tiff-Tiff sat beside him. Like the others, she seemed entranced by the slab of cocaine on the wooden coffee table.

"What you want for that, bruh?" Young-D asked, pulling out a thick, rubber banded fold of Franklins. "What's that, a whole chicken?"

Blake managed a half shrug. "I don't know. I ain't even

checked to see if it's real." He turned to Tiffany. "Bust that open and taste it for me…see if it get that pussy wet."

"Nigga, I stay wet," Tiff-Tiff declared pridefully as she quickly retrieved a razor blade from her purse. Eagerly, she sliced into the kilo and filled the underside of her pinky fingernail with a small pyramid of the powder. She snorted it up her nose. Instantly, her eyes went wide, and she started bouncing up and down on the sofa, shouting "Woooo!"

Everyone burst out laughing,

"Damn, girl," Tiesha said, "is it that good?"

"Hell yeah! It's like that shit I used to get from Craig," Tiff-Tiff replied, already dipping her fingernail back into the powder.

Blake told Tiesha—a slender; dark skinned twenty year old and Jessica reddish brown and round hipped— to help themselves, and the girls dug into the coke as if it were an AIDS vaccine and they were getting ready to make a sex tape with Ervin "Magic" Johnson. Young-D joined in on the coke snorting session, too, which surprised Blake, because he had never seen his friend do anything harder than weed. The transgression, juxtaposed with Blake's aching condition, prompted him to indulge in a bit of the drug himself.

The coke didn't dull his senses; in fact, it made them more acute. Not to mention the pain relief it offered.

But he did not want to jinx it, so he left it alone after his first few bumps and phoned Alexus again.

She didn't pick up.

He called Ashley and had her put Savaria on the phone.

"Hey Daddy!" Vari's small voice made Blake smile. "What took you so long to call me? I had something to ask you, and, and momma said wait for you to call the house, 'cause the hospital was still fixing you today, so her said I had to wait."

"Well, you can ask me now. What is it?'

"Hold on, Daddy. Her right here all up in my bizness, and I don't want her all up in my bizness."

Blake chuckled at his daughter's grown up personality. He heard light foot falls as she raced out of her mothers' earshot.

While listening for Vari's voice, he watched as Tiff-Tiff

lifted a remote control from the coffee table and turned on the television. Evidently, there were cameras all over the property. Eight squares of live video popped upon the screen. In one of them he vividly see Streets and Lil Mike walkingup the front stairs with two girls behind them; the foursome looked green due to the camera's night vision being activated. Other squares showed views of the house from all sides; a view of the driveway in front of the garage; a view inside the garage, which, except for the Lincoln MKX, was now empty.

"Hell naw!" Young-D exclaimed as he stared at the widescreen. "This nigga got us in some James Bond type shit."

Through the phone, Blake heard a door slam shut. Then Savaria's voice came through loud and clear.

"Daddy, I want to come to the hospital with, with you. Momma got a newboyfriend, and him keep on sayin' mean stuff to me and, and, and him keep on hittin' momma. And he be kissin' that boy that act like a girl next door when momma at her work and they, um, they do nasty stuff like I seen you and momma do that time when you thought me was sleep, Daddy."

"What!" Blake leaped to his feet as Streets walked in the front door. "PutAsh on the phone!"

"Nuh uh, Daddy, 'cause her goin' whoop me, 'cause her whooped me lasttime I told her and her say I lied."

Blake steamed with anger. "Daddy's on the way, okay, baby? I'm comin'to get you tonight."

"Promise?" Vari sounded like she was about to cry."Promise," Blake said.

And he meant it.

The four-car motorcade of Chevy Caprices made it to Indianapolis,Indiana in record time—two hours and twelve minutes flat.

Blake played the situation carefully for his daughter's sake, telling Ashley that he was only coming to pick up Vari for the week because hewas fresh out of the hospital and wanted to spend some quality time with her.

The house was a redbrick on Seventh and Arnolda, in one of the most crime ridden sections of the Circle City's west side neighborhoods- Haughville.

Commonly referred to as "Dub City," Nap Town was essentially a twentyfour hour car show. Candy painted whips on big rims embellished thecurbside of every street, making it easy for Blake and his crew to inconspicuously skate their Caprices up to the front of Ashley Joy's home.

"Stay in the car," Blake said to Tiff-Tiff, "and keep the car runnin'?

"Don't go in there trippin'," Tiff-Tiff advised, shifting into park. "Just keep the muh-fuckin' car runnin'.'"

A clique of about fifteen dope boys were right across the street; their eyesshot to Blake as he exited his passenger's side door, his MP-5 gripped tightly in his left hand.

"Ay, my dude," shouted a gold mouthed dope boy. "On Assassin, you can't come through here like that. What the fuck is you on?

Bit by bit, the excruciating pain was returning to Blake's body. Heignored the dope boy's inquiry and headed up the concrete walkway to Ashley's porch. His bare hands were cold. His breath, warm and dry,fogged out in front of him. As he climbed the stairs, the dope boy shouted again.

"Hoe-ass nigga, we got guns, too!"

Blake turned around to let the boy know why he was here, then changed his mind, unclipped his smartphone, and redialed Ashley's number.

"I hope you know it's one o'clock in the mornin' here," Ashley said. "If you're not here in twenty min—"

"I'm on the front porch."

"Oh, I'll be out with Vari in a minute." She paused. "Are you okay?"

No answer came from Blake. He was focused on three guys across the street who were rushing to the side of the house they'd been loitering in front of.

Thunderous gunfire erupted in flashes from the driver's window of Young-D's Chevy, fully automatic and powerful, heavy and perilous. He had a Kalashnikov AK-47 with a 100 round drum, and his unrlenting hold on the trigger meant havoc for everything and everyone in its path.

Lil Mike hung out his window with an AR-15 and followed Young-D's example, sending bullet after bullet through the scattering crowd of hustlers, a great many of whom collapsed to the snow covered sidewalk, enervated and lifeless.

Blake stood motionless on the porch. He heard Ashley screaming for everybody to get on the floor. Five expensively dressed hoodrats scampered past on the sidewalk, screaming their heads off.

"Don't go out there, Matt, are you crazy!" Ashley screamed.

Turning around, Blake expected Ashley's bisexual boyfriend to come running out the door, so he stepped to the side of it and waited.

And sure enough, a lanky young nigga with dreads ran out the door brandishing a shotgun seconds later.

Blake raised the MP-5 and shot the boy three times in back of the head and watched the boy slide face first down the concrete stairs.

Then, hurriedly, he walked into the house.

He found Ashley and Savaria on the dining room floor. Ash was stretched out on top of Vari, shielding their little princess from harm's way.

Looking up at Blake with trepidation in her eyes, Ashley screamed, "What the hell did you go do out there?"

"I don't know what's goin' on out there. C'mon, Vari, get your...nah juste'mon."

"They're still shooting!" Ashley said fearfully.

"We're still shootin'; them other niggas ain't gon' get a chance to start.

Now get up and carry my baby to the car."

Shaking as if she'd suddenly acquired Parkinson's disease, Ashley did as she was told and carried Savaria outside to Blake's car, breaking down in tears as she stepped past her dead boyfriend.

Blake and the Dub Life Goons were back on the highway ten minutes later.

They left behind fifteen dead bodies.

Chapter 36

"I still can't for the life of me understand why that ungrateful bitch stole my money. And now she's changed her phone number, *and* blocked me on Facebook. No wonder she left in such a hurry."

"Baby, you need to stop stressin' yourself out about that girl. It ain't goodfor my son," Blake said, reaching over to palm the distorted stomach of Alexus's white Emilo Pucci dress.

It was February fourteenth, Valentine's Day, and they were in the back seat of Alexus's new and improved Rolls Royce Phantom, a white on white armored vehicle capable of withstanding rounds from the most powerful of large caliber weapons. They were leaving The Magnificent Mile on North Michigan Avenue, Chicago's premier shopping area.

"I really wish you'd quit thinking of my baby as a boy. I'll go crazy if I have a boy." Alexus glanced at Savaria, who was tucked in between them, struggling to keep her tired little eyes open. "I want a beautiful little girllike her. We're gonna wait 'til we turn twenty five or twenty six to have a boy."

"Man, you can't just pick the baby's gender."

"I know that, but what I *can* do is speak it into existence."

"Yeah right," Blake dissented.

"One of these days, I'm going to talk you into wearing a suit. You'd lookgreat in Tom Ford."

"Nah, baby, I ain't goin at gunpoint. I'm good in these." Blake had on a loose fitting pair of MFG blue jeans, a pearl white sweatshirt, a white and blue Colts fitted cap. And Timberland boots of the same color. His bling consisted of a watch, a bracelet, a necklace, and a set of five point star shaped earrings that held so many white diamonds, it looked as if he'd robbed a jewelry store; the bling had cost Alexus over two million dollars.

Blake and Alexus had been staying together for the past ten days in a lavish two bedroom apartment at the Trump, venturing out only when it proved absolutely necessary. Other than a few television appearances— CNN's "Pierce Morgan tonight," and ABC's "Good Morning America"— Alexus had not left out at all. She spent her days eating, fucking andsquandering money on online shopping websites. She'd already blown three million on Blake and his daughter, which included the jewelry and a $270,790 Ferrari 458 Italia. Most of the clothes she bought were shipped either to the mansion Granny Costilla had purchased in Michigan City— where Rita was now living there— or to the house she'd given Blake,where his family was residing while their home was being remodeled by thecompany Rita had put together for her and Alexus— Urban Housing Development.

At first, it had been hard for Alexus to keep Blake inside their apartment. Especially after she'd told him that Tim-Tim was supposed to have split thefive hundred pounds of Kush and the guns with him. But she had begged and pleaded with him to stay with her, to change his phone number and dissociate himself from the criminal lifestyle, to walk forward.

Reluctantly, Blake had succumbed to her influence.

She knew that the long, knee weakening blow jobs she'd been giving himevery day had played a major role in his decision making process, and now that the wires in his mouth were gone— he'd gotten them removed this morning—she anticipated feeling his tongue between her thighs.

After all, it *was* Valentine's Day.

"I'll tell you this much," Alexus said, "You better have something specialplanned for me today."

Blake's expression became cynical.

"Don't give me that look, Blake. I'm serious. With all the attention I've been—"

"Shut that bullshit up." Blake grabbed her chin and kissed her, sucking her bottom lip into his mouth before pulling back. He gazed into her eyes."I got you, a'ight? Soon as we drop Vari off, the rest of the day is yours."

"Do you think Tim-Tim is there?"

Blake shrugged. He hated that Ashley had moved in with Tiff-Tiff, her first cousin, after the pernicious shooting in

Indianapolis. He didn't want his daughter around Timothy Trice...coward-ass, fake-ass Timothy Trice...because he'd lost all trust in Tim.

In Blake's mind, Tim-Tim had *robbed* him for two hundred fifty pounds of Kush.

And Blake was unable to let it go.

Alexus said, "I'm not letting you go in if he's... you know what? Giveme your phone. I'll call Ashley and have her meet us around the corner somewhere."

"I'm good, baby," Blake promised. "You can come in with me."

"Nuh uh. Give me the phone." She had her hand out, palm up. "I've seen how damned crazy you get when you have a gun on you. This is a day for love, not hate."

With subtle grin, Blake relinquished his phone and listened as Alexus made arrangements to meet up with Ashley at a McDonald's on the corner of Roosevelt and Kedzie.

Out of the corner of her eye, Alexus studied the infamous Blake King. Hehad lost a considerable amount of weight over the past few months. His sweatshirt bulged from the Teflon bullet proof vest he had on underneath it.He looked tense, and perpetually alert. Alexus supposed being shot tentimes would have that effect on a person.

She ended the call with Ashley and gave Blake his phone back.

"Hey driver," Alexus said, tapping the seat in front of her. "New destination: Kedzie and Roosevelt. The Mickey D's."

The chauffer, a middle aged, brawny black man who doubled as Alexus's security, locked eyes with her in the rearview mirror, nodded his thick bald head once, and then moved his eyes back to the road.

Alexus leaned toward Blake. "You should not have killed that girl's boyfriend," she whispered. "She sounds so hopeless and depressed. You might need to have her checked out, if you know what I mean. A shrink might do her some good."

"She'll be alright. That bitch ain't crazy."

"She sure *sounds* crazy. I wouldn't trust her around a kitchen knife, that'sall I'm saying."

He chuckled to himself. "I think you might be the one who needs to see ahead doctor."

"Maybe I just need some head, doctor. Ever considered that possibility?

Because I've been considering it all day."

"Quit talkin' like that in front of my daughter."

"She's *asleep* for Christ's sake. So don't even try using that lame excuse." Alexus sucked her teeth, rolled her eyes, and snatched a brand newcopy of Neil McNeil's *Through the Fire* novel out of her white leather Gucci bag.

"How many times are you gonna read that book?" Blake asked irritably. "Every time I look around, you got that damn book in your hands."

"Baby, this is really a good book. I mean, next to Sister Souljah, June Miller, and Leo Sullivan... he's my favorite urban novelist, and he hasn't

even been writing that long. I wouldn't be a bit surprised if he ended up on the New York Times best-seller list for fifty or sixty weeks straight. He's just that good."

"Mmm. Let me read it next."

"You'd better read it, too. And make sure you buy a copy or two," she said, opening the book to where she'd left off. "We need to start being moresupportive of our black authors. If you can buy a twenty dollar sack of weed, you can buy a fifteen dollar book. J.K Rowling went from being homeless to being a billionaire off of those Harry Potter books. It's about time our authors started making that kind of money. There should be a long list of black Stephen Kings, black James Patterson. I really believe this manhas what it takes to do it like Donald Goines did it."

Blake started surfing the internet on his phone.

"I've been talking with my granny about turning it into a TV miniseries on MTN," Alexus continued. "She pitched the idea to Tyler, but it doesn't include much religion, so of course he isn't interested. And you know Spikeisn't involved with anything that's not revolutionary. She's scheduled a Skype meeting with the Hughes brothers... the twins who created Menaceto Society... to discuss the possibility of directing and producing it with them. It'll be kinda like The Wire, only better."

"Hmm," Blake said.

"Are you even listening to me?""Mmm hmm. I'm listenin'."

"Well, I was thinking, since the miniseries will more than likely befilmed here in Chicago...maybe you can play the role of dirty Boy. And I'llplay Shanese, his girlfriend."

"I ain't no movie actor, baby. I'm a street nigga."

Alexus sighed with discontent. "Why would you limit yourself to being nothing but a 'street nigga'? I mean, how dumb does that sound? You canbe whatever you want to be."

"Will you please shut up and read that book? I'm tryna think."

A satisfied smile spread across her face. "I'm a nagging wife already, aren't I? And we haven't even gotten married yet. Just imagine how we'llbe ten or twenty years from now."

Blake was going through her Facebook pictures, clicking "Like" on someof them.

"We're gon' be like Ice-T and Coco," he said, smiling down at thepicture of her bent over the Phantom. "Jay-Z and Beyonce."

"Are you going to at least think about starring in the Sweet Licksminiseries?" Alexus asked hopefully.

"Ask me again and we're gon' be Chris Brown and Rihanna," Blakethreatened.

The chauffer cruised the Phantom into the parking lot behind The Visionary Lounge, a five story yellow brick building on the corner ofLaramie and Chicago Avenue. It was currently the hottest club in Chicago, commonly frequented by Kanye West, Common, and several other Windy City natives. P. Diddy and his Dirty Money duo had performed there a few days ago.

It was one o'clock in the afternoon, and the sun was blazing in the sky, melting away tall piles of snow with a vengeance.

Alexus was surprised at how many vehicles were packed

into the huge parking lot. There had to be at least fifty of them.

"Wow... I bet it's packed shoulder to shoulder in there," Alexus mused, as she pushed her arms into the sleeves of her full length white mink coat.

"This is the most popular club in Chicago," Blake informed her, slipping into his own white fur jacket, "More popular than the Funky Buddha Lounge and the House of Blues combined. Oprah's even been through here a few times."

"Is this a part of my Valentine's Day present?"

"I already told you, baby...the rest of this day is dedicated solely to us. IfI don't love you the right way, I'm not doing my job as your man."

"Awww, you're gonna make me get all teary-eyed on you," Alexus murmured amorously. She kissed his lips passionately and he reciprocated. Their tongues tangled.

"Gotta save a lil somethin' for later," he said ruefully.

The chauffer, Mark Lawhorn, a retired UFC fighter, tossed the keys to thevalet and preceded Blake and Alexus into the club via a rear door that had a red "Employees Only" placard mounted on it.

Alexus knew right away that they were in the club's VIP section; it did not take a genius to discern that.

The walls were black velvet and shimmering with flecks of gold; long eighty inch flatsceen televisions and gold framed mirrors shaped like stars and crescent moons decorated the walls. Golden buckets filled with ice and bottles of Ciroc vodka sat on the center of all twelve circular tables, each of which was draped with black and gold checkered tablecloths.

The wall across the room was made of clear glass and was covered on theoutside by a large golden curtain. Alexus could hear what must have been hundreds of people speaking in hushed tones downstairs. She moved to the glass, peered through a narrow opening in the gold curtain, and saw that the club was teeming with men and women in tidy white blazers and gorgeous white gowns. She recognized rappers and R&B singers and pop stars; actorsand actresses and industry moguls; momma, uncle Dennis and his wife, and Kenya...who was standing hand in hand with *T-Walk!* They were mingling in front of a stage.

Alexus closed her eyes and gathered her thoughts before she turned to face Blake.

He was smiling happily, and he had a dozen of white roses in his hand.

His face was easy and his posture was relaxed.

"I see why you were so adamant in wanting me to wear all white today," she said with a nervous smile.

"Happy Valentine's Day, baby. I love you," he murmured gently.

His words brought tears to her eyes. She crossed the room to him,accepted the roses, picked one out of the bunch, and put it under her nose toinhale its heavenly scent, setting the other roses on the table next to her. They placed their coats on a chair.

Blake wrapped his arms around her waist, filled his palms with her ass, and squeezed.

"How did you set all this up?" She asked.

"I hijacked your…damn…bad choice of words. I had your phone while you were in the tub the other day and called that old rich lady. Told her Ihad something special planned for you, that I needed her help."

"I really wish you'd stop calling her that."

"Then I got on your Facebook page and let everybody know what I hadin mind," Blake continued, leading her to a table in front of the glass. They sat down on a comfortable set of white leather chairs. "Kenya got at me andpromised to get your family to attend the event and, of course, the old rich lady paid for everything. She got MTN cameras all over the place."

Alexus sniffed the rose again. "Did Kenya say something else?"

Quizzically, Blake's eyebrows came together. "Anything like what? Was she s'posed to tell me somethin' else?"

"I figured she might have mentioned something about T-Walk.""T-Walk? Why would she…"

"Because that whore is down there holding hands with him!" She workedto modulate the volume of her voice so Blake wouldn't get too riled up, but her anger was irrepressible.

Blake was standing to look through the glass when the door behind them opened.

Reflexively, they both turned to the door.

Alexus gasped. "What are you two doing here?" She inquired. Tyrese "Reesie Cup" Nell was tall and very light skinned, with green eyes and short, curly hair.

He had on a custom white Tory Burch suit that fit him perfectly,

Next to him stood Charles "Lil Cholly" Bultrum, a brown-skinned man witha muscular frame that completely filled out his white Givenchy suit.

They were the Traveling Vice Lords to whom Alexus had sold fivehundred kilos of cocaine and two hundred kilos of heroin, the Vice Lords who'd promised to spend at least twenty five million with the Costilla cartelevery three months.

"I own this club," Reesie Cup said. "Nice to meet you again, Miss...um,I forgot your name...Mercedes?"

"Alexus," Blake said, walking over to shake Reesie Cup's hand. "I didn'tknow ya'll knew each other."

"Yeah, we met a few months back at a business meeting." Momentarily, Blake studied Reesie Cup through squinted eyes.

"It was only business," Alexus said quickly.

Blake turned and went back to the handle of his gold plated .45 caliber Smith and Wesson handgun, the gun Alexus had given him after she'd retrieved it from her shot up Bentley.

"Man. Cup, I'm about to blow this niggas head off," Blake said through clenched teeth.

Alexus rushed to his side, balancing herself on five inch Louis Vuitton boots. In the reflection of the glass, she saw Reesie Cup nudge Lil Cholly and point at her ass. The two men shook their heads incredulously.

"It's not worth it Blake," she said. "Let me call Kenya and see what's going on first."

Reesie Cup said, "Vida Costilla has fifteen cameras set up down there, and every one of them is being broadcast live in seven countries; shoot somebody at this event and Johnnie

Cochran's law firm won't even be able to save you."

As Lil Cholly stepped forward and assisted Reesie Cup in trying to coax Blake out of a life sentence, Alexus flitted to the side of the room, took her smartphone out of her bag, and called Kenya.

"You two-faced bitch," Alexus snapped as soon as Kenya answered. "What the fuck are you doing holding hands with my ex? Have you lost your mind?"

"How'd you know we were holding hands?" Kenya asked.

"Does it really matter?" Alexus said slowly, emphasizing each word. "You're *with* him. Why are you with him?"

"Because …we're dating now."

"You're what!"

"You heard me right. I said we're dating. And you're calling me two faced? What about you and Cereniti? I didn't say a thing when you were sleeping with her!"

Alexus gritted her teeth. "What does that have to do with anything?"

"Cereniti was my girlfriend first!" Kenya said acidly. "And not even two days after we broke *up*, you were in bed with her. How do you think that made me feel?"

A frustrated sigh escaped Alexus's lips. She hadn't been aware of Kenya and Cereniti's romance. How could she have known? Cereniti surely hadnot mentioned it.

"And now look at her", Kenya went on. "Now she's somewhere in Japan with some Japanese bitch named Akemi Matsuoka, spending all that moneyyou gave her. She doesn't even want to come back to the states. What if I never see her again? What if they get married or something crazy like that? My best friend is gone because of *you*!"

"I didn't *give* her that money! She *stole* that money! And why didn't you tell me you two had been together?"

"Maybe because you didn't give me enough time to tell you. Or maybe it was because I had no idea that *let me show you my shoe collection* wasactually code for let's go upstairs and have sex."

"Whatever." Alexus terminated the call and turned to face.

Blake and the Vice Lords. The security guards were in the hall-way.

They had talked Blake back into his chair.

"If you want that nigga dead," Lil Cholly was saying, "drop a hundred thousand on me, and he'll disappear tonight. But getting yo'self personally involved would be the dumbest mistake you've ever made."

Alexus was brimming with anger. She wanted to punch Kenya in the facea few times.

"We need some alone time." She sat next to Blake.

Reesie Cup looked at his watch. "The show starts in ten minutes, which means those curtains will be opening in approx-imately nine minutes. There'll be two cameras on you. Don't make it X-rated."

The Vice Lords left the room, leaving Alexus and Blake alone.

She closed her eyes, and pinched the bridge of her nose be-tween the fingers of her left hand.

"I'm sorry, baby." Blake mumbled. "Gotta get control of my anger.Seeing that hoe-ass nigga get me so heated...I almost started shooting right then and there."

Alexus opened her eyes. She looked at him. "It's not your fault. T-walk shouldn't be here. My cousin brought him here to upset me. We can't let them fuck up our day."

'Yeah...I got too much to lose, anyway. Fuck that nigga." He movedback in his chair, stretched his legs out in front of him. "I'm about ready to pack up our bags and put us on a flight to Jamaica. Tiff-Tiff said Craig tookher to Kingston last year, and it was nice out there."

"We can go after I have the baby. I don't have much faith in airplanes. And you know, speaking of Craig, I think he got me for three hundredgrand a few months ago. The day you and your guys shot him and Bookie."

"Damn. Three hun'ed thou'?"

Alexus nodded. "They were supposedly bringing it to me when you shot his Suburban up. He claims the police got all the money out of there when they repo'd it. I think he lied to me."

"Pro'bly did. Shit, ain't no tellin'. I don't trust none of 'em. Tiff's been tryna buy some dope from me since the night I checked myself out the hospital."

"I told you not to sell that stuff. Let Young-D or Lil Mike sell it.

Honestly, I think you should just give it to them."

"Nigga, please!" Blake scoffed. "Fuck I look like givin' away a hundred fifty key's?"

"Believe it or not, you'd actually look smart," Alexus said. She deeply regretted giving all those bricks of cocaine to him. It was a stupid mistake, something she would never do again.

They launched into a conversation about the terrorist attack in Miami andfor the umpteenth time she explained to him how she had remedied the intense situation.

"I figured, as long as I didn't betray the cartel and our tunnel I could cooperate with the FBI…to a certain extent…and we all could go home happy. Plus, they guaranteed Papi, my uncle Flako, and Tasia would be released from their federal prisons if the information I gave them led to the arrest of any top echelon al-Qaeda militants. And with the info my granny had given me shortly before we were taken to FBI headquarters, I knew I had the big fish they needed."

"So you snitched on Osama," Blake said with a smile.

She glowered at him. "Don't ever call me a snitch. That is the most derogatory name you can call me."

"But you *snitched* on him. You told the Feds where to find him? You wouldn't have told…"

"Shut up!" She slapped his knee, and he laughed.Then the door behind them opened again.

This time it was Blake's parents, his brother Streets, Momma, Uncle Dennis, and his wife, Evon; and Granny Costilla with Enrique Aleman in front of her. Like seraphim, their suits and gowns were a heavenly white.

Rita Mae strode over and hugged Alexus.

"Kenya's down there with T-Walk," Rita whispered. "I know, momma. I saw them."

"Can you believe she actually wanted to bring him up here

with us! I toldher off. Who does she think she is? If I wasn't a Christian woman, I'd have knocked her upside her foolish little head, coming in here with my grandbaby's daddy."

Alexus sighed, thinking, Momma's acting as if she's already had the baby's DNA tested.

"Your lawyer wanted to come," Rita said. "But, you know, with all the publicity she's been getting since appearing beside you on Piers Morgan,her phone's been ringing off the hook."

"It's okay. I'll call her later on." Stepping aside to hug Uncle Dennis and Aunt Evon, then Granny Costilla, Alexus wondered what exactly was goingon here at The Visionary Lounge.

Was all this simply a Valentine's Day get together?

When all the hugging was over and everyone was seated, she learned thatthat was not the case at all.

Because, as the golden curtains before her separated, and R&B singer Dondria, who was onstage, started singing "You're The One For Me,"Blake stood suddenly, got down on one knee in front of her, and produced asmall white jewelry box from his pants pocket,

She was already sobbing joyfully when he murmured those five cherished words.

"Alexus, will you marry me?"

Too speechless to utter a "yes," she nodded rapidly, vehemently, and extended her shaky left hand.

Blake slid a sparkling fifteen carat diamond ring onto her ring finger.

Then he leaned forward and kissed her lips.

A round of applause and cheers followed Blake's proposal, and for a longwhile afterward, between twenty star-studded performances, the MTN cameras constantly panned in on Alexus's unwavering smile.

She was glad when the show ended, and was eager to get back to her apartment with Blake.

But Vida Costilla insisted on a private family dinner at the Calypso restaurant, so that's where everyone ended up.

Alexus was seated at a table with Momma, Blake, and Vida. She had just ingested a delicious piece of jerk chicken when

Granny Costilla easedforward in her seat and spoke.

"Loose lips have sunken a thousand ships," Vida whispered. She was staring at Blake. "Know what that means?"

He didn't seem to hear the question; his eyes were attentively focused on T-Walk, who was situated a few tables away, chatting with Kenya and her parents.

"Blake, my granny's talking to you," Alexus said, touching his elbow.

Hesitantly, he turned to Vida. "I heard you. You ain't never got to worry 'bout me snitchin'."

"I didn't say anything about snitching. Regular conversation can be justas detrimental", Vida said.

"He's not gonna say anything, grandma," Alexus vouched. "Trust me; he's more ruthless than Enrique."

With a solemn nod, Vida eased forward another few inches. "I sat and talked with Director Byrd yesterday. An elite team of Navy S.E.A.L.s are gathering information on the compound in Abbottabad, Pakistan as wespeak; however, they were told not to raid the compound until the Illumi... until the President gives the okay."

"You're that close with the director of the FBI?" Alexus asked.

"Wait a minute." It was Rita's turn to lean forward. "Were you about to say what I think?"

"I said what I meant to say," Vida replied quickly.

"No...no, you almost said the Illuminati! I heard it clear as day. The Illuminati's involved with this?"

Vida sighed, became quiet, pushed herself back on the chair, and flicked her eyes nervously around the restaurant.

For the first time in all her eighteen years, Alexus discerned fear in her grandmother's eyes. Alexus had no clue as to what or who the Illuminati were, but she knew right then that it was an entity not to be messed with.

"Come on," Rita Mae probed. "You forgot, I went to Harvard. I'mfamiliar with the Skull and Bones, the Scroll and Key, the Black Nobility. I've read *Behold a Pale Horse.*"

"Well, you're one of the few Americans who know that the

President of this great nation is nothing more than a pawn to the Bilderberg Group,"Vida whispered, "which is merely another branch of the Illuminati. The Illuminati runs the world, Rita. They are an esoteric organization of brilliantminds, and they control literally everything."

"And they're after Osama?"

"They're after *every* leader who refuses to conform to the New World Order. Pretty soon they're going to create wars in Egypt, Syria, Libya, and the Ivory Coast in a strategic effort to overthrow those governments and usher in new leaders who will help bring all the world leaders together to form a one world government."

"Aint that in Revelations?" Blake asked, his curiosity piqued.

"Yes," Vida said. "I'll get to the point. Papi and Flako will be released onthe first of May as long as bin Laden is inside that safe house as wepromised."

"I'm not certain what they're planning to do with Jenny," Vida said and hastily changed the subject. "So, when's the big day?"

"Probably next year on my birthday," Alexus said. "April twenty first. I want to make sure Papi's there to give me away.'

"Oh, he'll be there, alright," Rita Mae intoned with a smirk, "I can't wait to see the expression on his face when you finally say "I do." I'm bringing acamera to capture that moment."

"How did he get locked up in the first place?" Blake asked.

"My aunt Jenny and her two boys, Savio and Santiago, set him up by stashing a bunch of cash and drugs in a condo he owned in Houston Texas,"Alexus told him. She had learned of the betrayal from Granny Costilla that night at the Epic Hotel in Miami. "They then tipped off the Feds, resultingin the raid that put Papi and Uncle Flako away."

"Damn, baby that's fucked.... I mean, that's messed up. What did they dothat for? I mean, what was the reason?"

"Same reason they came after me.""And why is that?" Blake asked.

"Don't say it." Rita grabbed Alexus's hand and held it

tightly. "Tell him later on down the road. That isn't the kind of thing you go around justtelling people."

"I know, momma," Alexus said.

She finished off her jerk chicken, switched plates with Blake, and started in on his. All along she mentally planned her wedding. Where would it be? Here in Chicago? Back home in Brownsville? She wasn't certain, but she knew it would be lavish, posh and clandestine. No MTN cameras. Nopaparazzi. Just family and friends of hers and Blake's, with his daughter as the ring bearer.

A waitress stopped at their table and swooped up Alexus and Vida's half empty glasses of Evian water. The Mexican waitress returned a minute laterwith their refills.

At that same instant, a black couple approached Alexus and gazed at her as if she were an unidentified sitting object.

"Alexus and Vida Costilla!" the woman said, "I'm *obsessed* with *Hood Affairs* and *Mariah's Salon*." She was referring to two of MTN's critically acclaimed reality shows.

As Alexus was getting to her feet she bumped her butt against the table, and Vida's glass of water toppled.

Blake cleaned up the spill while Alexus and Vida posed for a picture withthe overzealous couple.

When they were again seated, Alexus pushed her glass of water to her grandmother and confiscated Blake's. She stared at her engagement ring, wondering how much it had cost her fiancé.

"I didn't pay for it," Blake said, reading her mind. He motioned towards Vida, "Gotta ask her about that."

Eyebrows raised, Alexus turned to Granny Costilla.

"Your grandfather gave me that ring fifty-two years ago, when we made our first billion dollars. I remember that day like it was yesterday. It was on this day in nineteen fifty nine. I was twenty one, and Papi was six, I think…yeah, he was six." Vida sipped some water through a straw. "You know, my grandmother actually helped Niermann discover cocaine back in eighteen sixty, and the family's been selling it ever since. There's nothing like good old cocaine money."

"That isn't the kind of advice my daughter needs," Rita complained."Wasn't advice I was giving her. 'Twas the truth"

Blake suddenly snapped to his feet, and Alexus saw why; T-Walk was walking toward their table.

"Ay, Blake," T-Walk said casually, "let me talk to you outside real quick.

It won't be but a minute."

Fearing the worst, Alexus intervened. "Only way I'm going to allow him to talk to you is if I go out there and stand between you two. No one's goingto ruin the best day of my life."

"It's okay, baby," Blake assured her. He put on his fur jacket. "I got this.'Cautiously, Blake trailed T-Walk out of the restaurant and into the cold of Michigan Avenue. He had an urge to blow T-Walk's brain all over thesidewalk. He glanced back; saw that Streets was watching him. Big bruh was always on point.

T-Walk fired up a Newport. "Chicago's a nice city, ain't it? Colder than Eskimo pussy, but it's still nice." He had his back to Blake. Puffing his cigarette, he nodded to himself. "I think I like it out here, my nigga. Real Talk."

I'll blow your whole head off, Blake thought to himself. Real talk.

"Met some Italian mobsters out here a couple of weeks ago. They gave me a player deal on keys of heroin. I mean the low low."

"Man I don't give a fuck about that shit," Blake said coldly. "That was some hoe ass shit you pulled sendin' them niggas to kill me over a bitch. That ain't no shit real niggas do."

T-Walk turned to face Blake. His expression was serious. "I… man, Ifucked up, bruh. I let my emotions get the best of me. Love is a muhfucka.""Nigga, I used to look up to you," Blake said. "Remember when we used to fuck with Meel and Marcus, stealin bikes and cars and everything else? Nigga, we go *way* back, and you gon' send some niggas to *kill* me?"

Shaking his head despondently, T-Walk put the glowing cigarette back tohis lips and took a deep drag from it. His posture was that of a broken man's. He had betrayed the code of the streets, and it was eating him up likean untreated cancer.

"I lied to them niggas," T-Walk admitted. "Told em you was threatenin' to kill em." He lowered his head, shook his head, and blew out a stream of smoke. "Shit backfired on me…Karma."

"That's what happens when you go against the grain. We only get one lifeto live on this fucked up planet. If you gon' waste it being fake, you might as well hang yo'self."

T-Walk lifted his head, "Bookie and Craig…they, umm…need you to give their lawyers a recorded statement saying they weren't the ones who shot you. They're facing twenty to fifty on that attempted murder charge alone, and the prosecutor got everything he needs to convict em."

Before Blake could respond to that, T-Walk said "Man, I lost my niggas, my bitch, got one of my niggas killed, and lost my friendship with you. All'cause I was sprung off some pussy. On Larry Hoover, I wish ya'll the best.She deserves a nigga like you." He flicked his cigarette into the busy street and watched as a passing motorist flattened it. "I hope you can forgive me, my nigga. For real."

After a moment of thought, Blake reached out and shook his old friend's hand.

"It's good, bruh," he said, locking eyes with T-Walk. "But I'ma let you know now, as soon as I heal up all the way, I'm *fuckin' you up!*" They chuckled in unison.

But their laughter was immediately cut short by a sudden commotion inside the restaurant.

Blake spun around and was shocked to see a crowd of people…Streets and their parents; Alexus's family; and some other curious georges gathered next to the table he'd been seated at minutes ago.

He burst into the restaurant at full speed, pushing aside chairs and nosy spectators as he went. When he made it to the crowded circle, he had to physically move a few onlookers out of the way in order for him to get through. His mouth fell open at what he found.

The elderly Vida Costilla was lying face up on the floor; her head cradledin Alexus's arms, her face tinted a nasty shade of purplish blue. Foam bubbled from her mouth. Her eyes were rolled back in their sockets, and shewas shaking weakly.

Vida's driver wasted no time in picking her up and rushing her outside toher black Rolls Royce. Blake helped load the old lady into the back of the Phantom.

Then he and Alexus climbed into the rear of their own Phantom and Blake instructed Big Mark to follow Vida's car.

Alexus cried silently on Blake's shoulder all the way to the hospital.

Chapter 37

Gucci, Prada, Dolce and Gabbana, Louis Vuitton…Ashley Joy could not believe all the designer clothes Alexus had brought for Savaria this morning.

"Girl, I didn't even know they made designer outfits for kids," Tiff-Tiff said, as she sat on her living room sofa next to Ashley. They were going through Vari's shopping bags for the fifth time. "That bitch spent forty grand on your baby for the hell of it. Hope she treats my baby like that."

"When's your due date?" Ashley asked.

"Sometime in the middle of September, which means I get the whole summer before I lose my social life."

"That's exactly what's gon' happen too." Ashley continued sifting through the bags." I can't really say I miss it, though. Most people are so fake. Smile in your face, laugh behind your back when you leave. Truth never comes out until y'all fall out."

"Who you tellin'? Bitch, tell me why I met this nigga named Jazzy at thatChristmas Eve party I told you about. I gave him my number, and the nigga started callin' me every day, talkin' 'bout he had a BMW 745, a Charger, a mansion, and sixteen houses."

Ashley laughed. "And let me guess, he was lying."

"Through his goddamn teeth! Turned out the nigga was a straight up snitch. Told on a nigga Tim-Tim be sellin' Kush to. Nigga named Gusto. And he was lyin' about all that shit he claimed he had. He even got Lil Lordwantin' to get at his fake-ass now."

"Mmm." Out of the corner of her eye, Ashley glowered at her cousin.She wanted badly to confront Tiff-Tiff about having had fucked Blake at that Christmas Eve party.

But she left it alone because Tiffany was family. Blood was thicker than water. And besides, Blake was a grown ass man. Whatever he chose to do with his dick was his business.

Savaria was sitting in her miniature white leather recliner in front of the television, her eyes glued to its screen. She had an ear to ear smile on her face as she watched her father put a ring on Alexus's finger, An MTN celebrity news correspondent was standing off to the left of the screen, enthusiastically reporting on the breaking mews of the "Billionaire heiress's" surprise engagement.

"Does that mean she's a billionaire?" Tiff-Tiff asked.

"I'm not sure. This is the first I've heard of it." Grabbing the remote, Ashley upped the volume. "I know she's rich. But I try to stay out of their business. As long as he keeps taking care of Vari, I'm fine. I could care lesshow much she's worth."

Someone knocked on the back door of the third floor apartment. "Go getthe door, Vari," Ashley said, figuring the visitor was probably one of theother little girls who lived in the building, coming over to play with Savaria."Well," said Tiff, "if I were you, I'd be askin' for a big ass house somewhere out in the boondocks. I sure in hell wouldn't be stayin' here in Chicago."

"Chanel!" Ashley shouted. She only used Vari's middle name in the instances when Savaria feigned deaf. "Did you not just hear me tell you to go and answer that door?"

Sucking her teeth indignantly, Vari hopped out of her chair and ran to thekitchen to get the door, no doubt anxious to get back to her personal little throne so she could finish watching her daddy.

As soon as the little girl opened the door, Reesie Cup, who had exchanged his elegant Tory Burch ensemble for a black Brooks Brothers suit, bent down and planted his hands on his knees. "Your daddy here?" He asked in a whisper.

"Nuh uh, him not...him on TV."

"What about your mom? Is Tiff-Tiff here?"

"She is *not* my momma, boy." The little girl put her hands on her hips, rolled her eyes at Cup, and then looked past him.

There were four masked men behind Reesie Cup. Lil Cholly and three other Vice Lords. They stepped around Cup and the child with ninja-like silence, holding AR-15 assault rifles in their black leather gloved hands.

"Chanel! Who is that at the door?" A woman shouted from somewhere inthe apartment.

"That's a pretty name you got," Reesie Cup whispered, as tears grew in the child's eyes, giving them a watery sheen. She opened her mouth to scream, but Reesie Cup's hand was on her mouth before any sound came out. He turned her back to him and lifted her into the air. She flailed and kicked and clawed at the back of his hand until he secured her arms to her

side. Lil Cholly peeled a six inch strip of duct tape from the bottom of his boot; he pressed it firmly against Vari's lips.

Minutes later they had the two young women they'd found in the living room, Tiffany and Ashley, sitting on the clean, white tiled kitchen floor with their mouths taped shut, their wrists handcuffed behind them, and their ankles taped together. Their backs rested against the stove.

"Ya'll know what I'm here for," Reesie Cup murmured as he stepped in front of the girls. He stared at Tiff-Tiff. "Your man has been selling hundreds of pounds of Kush in my city, charging me full price, and he hasn't put a single dime of it back into my community. Now, how am I, a five star universal elite, supposed to take that? Am I supposed to accept that?"

Tiffany was sobbing uncontrollably. Beside her, Ashley had tears falling profusely from her eyes, too.

"Tell me where the money is," Reesie Cup said, "and I promise we'll be out of here in no time." He squatted down in front of Tiff-Tiff, and delivered a vicious back hand slap to the right of her face. "You gon' tellme where the cash is hidden? If not, I'll be forced to have my brothers tear up this nice little apartment of yours, while I demonstrate the many ways I've learned to torture people over the years. It's really up to you." He ripped the tape off her mouth.

"I don't know where he keeps his money," Tiff-Tiff cried.

Reesie Cup quickly retaped her mouth and stood. He signaled for his "brothers" to start searching the apartment, and told Lil Cholly, who was holding the child, to take her to another room.

Then Cup took off his suit jacket and tie. He unbuttoned his white long sleeve shirt and opened it. "You see that?" He touched a large, rectangular scar on his stomach, "Niggas put steel spatula on my stove, left it on the fireuntil it was glowing red hot, and then pressed it against my stomach. Either one of you ever smelled burning flesh? Hmm?" He closed his shirt. "Because you're about to."

"MMMMM! MMMMM!" Ashley screamed from behind the tape, shaking her head from side to side.

To her, Reesie Cup said, "You know where that money is?" He was putting his black silk tie back on.

Ashley nodded in the affirmative, so he bent at the waist and removed thetape from her quivering lips.

"Listen," she said quickly, "Blake King is my baby's daddy. He'll give you all the money you want, okay? Just don't hurt our baby."

At that very moment, if Reesie Cup had been a cartoon character, radiant green dollars signs would have been blinking in his eyes. Was he actually staring at the mother of Blake's child, the same Blake who had just gotten engaged to the granddaughter of a billionaire?

"Let's ride, joe. We got that dust," Lil Cholly said as he and the others entered the kitchen with large duffel bags in their hands. "This has gotta be at least two million in these muhfuckas, and 'bout thirty pounds of that kush." Reesie Cup only nodded. He continued to study Ashley through squinted eyelids, thinking, thinking, thinking. He had several ideas, but none of them seemed to be the right one. They were rotating in his head likenumbered balls in a lottery machine. Finally an idea fell into place, and he smiled.

He turned to one of his men. "Go and get the kid."

"You have what you came for," Ashley pleaded. "Just leave us…" ReesieCup silenced her with the strip of duct tape, while, mentally, he chastised himself for not wearing a mask.

When his masked "brother" returned with the child, Reesie Cup picked Ashley up, draped her struggling body over his shoulder, and walked outthe back door ahead of his men.

***

It just so happened that Timothy Trice was sticking his key into the front door of his and Tiffany's apartment at the very same moment that the Vice Lords were exiting the back door.

After unlocking the door, he stepped inside, locked the door behind him, and tossed his keys on the seat of Savaria's little chair, then becamefrozen in shock as he took in the chaotic scene.

All the furniture was sliced open and overturned. His 65 inch HDTV wassplit in half. Hats, jackets, and shoes that had previously been stowed in the closet next to the door were now strewn all over the place. With trembling hands, Tim-Tim drew two nickel-plated .38 Specials from his white leather Gucci jacket. Fearfully, he moved through the apartment, his heart beating abnormally, his eyes rapidly ticking to and fro, absorbing everything at once. He found Tiffany stretched out on the kitchen floor, prone, whimpering, with her hands tied behind her back.

"Shit. Tiff…" he checked the pantry to see if anyone was hiding in there. "What the hell happened?" He whispered. He picked her up sat her in a chair at the table, and took the tape off her mouth.

"They took all our money," Tiff-Tiff cried. "And they took Ashley and Savaria. They just left out the door!"

"Who!"

"Only one of them didn't have a ski mask. It was that man with the black Range Rover off of Fifteenth and Trumbull, the one who was throwin' money at Clint's club on St. Louis Street the other day. Remember him?" Tiff sniffed.

"Who Reesie Cup?" "Yeah, that his's…"

Tim-Tim took off running to the front of the apartment, scared out of his mind.

"Nigga, you bet not leave me in here like this!" Tiff-Tiff screamedangrily.

But Tim was already scrambling out the front door with his

keys in hand.He descended the stairs three at a time, taking off his jewelry and pocketingit as if D-Bo was outside waiting on him to exit the building.

He breezed past a small group of preteen boys and girls who weregiggling about something in front of the brownstone building. One of them asked him for fifty cents, but he kept right on running until he was at the drivers' door of his '73 Caprice. He climbed in, started the engine, and spedback in reverse. Since Albany is a one-way street, he veered onto it with thecar still in reverse and kept the gas pedal to the floor. His intention was to shift into drive on Roosevelt Road, and get out of Chicago as quickly as possible.

However, his plan was crushed when a CPD squad car that had been parked on Thirteenth and Albany came alive with lights and sirens and chased him down before he ever even made it to Roosevelt.

"Man this some bullshit," Tim grumbled as he pulled over on the squalid west side street. With him facing the police officers...there were two of them, white and meaty faced and Hitler looking...he had no opportunity to hide the revolvers that were in his jacket pockets, or the seven ounces of heroin in the glove compartment.

A depressing vision of himself in the infamous Cook County Jail, being beaten and stabbed by a crazed pack of gang bangers and murderers, passed

through his mid, and he broke down in tears, slamming his forehead repeatedly against the steering wheel until one of the police officers snatched him out the car and cuffed him. He cried with his cheek on thecold steel of his Chevy's hood.

"Got any knives, needles, or other sharp objects in your pockets that I need to be warned about?" asked the officer who was behind him.

"Nah man. Why y'all fuckin' with me?" Tim-Tim whined.

"Ha! Was that a serious question? You come through here like a fucking stunt driver and you're asking...whoa!" The officer emptied Tim-Tim's jacket pockets and laid everything on the hood of the squad car. The two revolvers, a necklace, a watch, forty grand in hundred dollar bills. The other officer found the heroin ten seconds later.

"We've got ourselves a baller," said the officer who'd searched Tim-Tim. "Guy thinks he's still in Indiana."

"Man, please don't take me to jail," Tim-Tim pleaded. "I can tell you some shit. I can tell you about some murders, man. A whole lot of 'em."

King Rio

Chapter 38

"It was that darn waitress," Alexus said sullenly. "Can't twist my nipples and tell me different." They were in the back seat of the Phantom again, andBig Mark was driving them aimlessly through the city, because Alexus didn't feel safe going home to her and Blake's apartment.

"What did the doctor say the name of that poison was?" Blake asked her. He had one hand on her lower back, massaging it, while with his other handhe manipulated the touch screen on his tablet.

"Polonium 210. Apparently its two hundred fifty thousand times more lethal than cyanide." Alexus shuddered at the thought. She lifted Blake's right arm and tucked her head beneath it, reveling in the warmth of him.

"It was the water. And I know it was meant for me. If I hadn't slid her mywater after I'd knocked hers over, it would be me lying in that hospitalbed."

"Baby you gotta tell me what's going on," Blake insisted.

"I...I can't. Not now anyway. But what I can tell you is that I'm ready to take that trip to Jamaica. As a matter of fact, I'm ready to move there. Staying here any longer might result in me being committed to an insane asylum. Either that or they'll have me killed within the week."

"Don't say that, Alexus. I ain't gon' let nobody..."

A valley of machine gun bullets abruptly pounded the driver's side of the Phantom. Instinctively, Blake covered Alexus with his body, and Big Mark floored it.

Seconds later the gunfire ceased. Alexus moved from beneath Blake and looked out the back window.

A black Mercedes van was slicing through traffic behind them, speeding and swerving up Pulaski like an inebriated NAS-CAR driver was behind the wheel. Alexus recognized the driver.

It was Savio Costilla, her very own cousin.

"I've had enough of this," she hissed, snatching Blake's .45 from his hip, while at the same time rolling down her window.

Before Blake could stop her, she had her upper body outside her window,blasting away at the van. She'd accompanied Papi to the shooting range on numerous occasions. Her aim was pretty good. She took out one of thevan's headlights with her first shot, and all the rest of her trigger squeezes punched holes in the van's windshield. She wasn't sure if she had wounded

anyone, but at least her shooting back had achieved the desired effect... the van slowed, made a left turn, and vamoosed down a side street.

Alexus dropped down onto her seat as Big Mark turned right, getting them away from their attackers. She stared down at the gun in her lap, the goldness of it backgrounded by the whiteness of her Gucci dress. In her periphery, she saw that Blake was watching her with an awestruck expression on his face.

"I'm not running from them anymore," she said with a note of finality tingeing her cotton, resolute tone. "I'd rather die fighting."

"That's exactly why you're my fiancé," Blake announced proudly. He kissed her on the cheek, and took the gun from her lap.

They studied the windows on the drivers' side of the Phantom for a moment. Nine bullets were embedded in Blake's window, seven in Big Mark's.

"That was a desperate move," Alexus murmured knowingly. "They knowthey're running out of time."

"Just give me an address, and I'll whack all of em."

"It's not that easy. There are over thirty different factions of the Costilla cartel operating in Mexico, and every under boss takes orders directly from my cousins. Even if Savio and Santiago were eliminated, the cartel would more than likely keep up their attacks at least for the next few weeks."

"The next few weeks?" Blake was gazing blearily out the back window.

Alexus's eyes became watery. "That's how long the doctor said mygranny has to..." She could not complete the sentence. She pressed her thumb knuckles against her eyes, wiping away the tears before they spilled.

Then Blake's phone rang from a private number. He put it on speaker, held it near his mouth.

"Daddy!" Savaria shrieked.

"What's wrong, Vari?" Blake's expression turned panicky. A black man's voice, low and menacing, replaced Savaria's.

"We got your daughter. We got your baby mama. Fifty million dollars in unmarked bills will guarantee their safe return. A dollar less and they die. You have twenty one days."

Call Ended.

King Rio

Chapter 39

MEXICAN BILLIONAIRE VIDA COSTILLA DEAD AT 75
FEDSSUSPECT FOUL PLAY...

The Chicago Sun Times headline brought fresh tears to Alexus Costilla's eyes. Her grandmother had passed away yesterday, on March the sixth, at around 9:50 a.m. Per Vida's request, hospital officials had immediately phoned ADX federal prison to inform Juan and Flako of her death. Then Alexus had been called, and ever since then, on and off, she'd been a disheartened, gloomy faced, weeping woman.

And Blake wasn't looking much better.

They were sitting next to each other on their bath towels at a beach in Riode Janeiro, Brazil, both of them attempting to relax and imbibe the warmness of the sun above them, the sand beneath them. The veridical ecstatic smiles of the bikini clad, beautiful Brazilian woman. The clear blue waters.

Alexus had been perusing newspaper headlines on her computer tablet. Wiping her eyes, she put down the tablet and turned to Blake; he was just ending a phone conversation with Young-D.

"Is everything okay?" She asked worried.

He didn't look at her. His melancholic eyes remained on the iPhone in hishand. "U.S. Marshall's picked up Lil Mike and Streets about two hours ago,charged both of em with fifteen murders. They're lookin for me now. Me and Young-D. I told him stay low 'til we find out what's goin' on."

"What about Vari and Ashley?" Alexus asked, burying her face in her palms.

The kidnappers had phoned Blake shortly after daybreak and instructed him to either wire the fifty million dollars to an off shore bank account in Panama, or to have it delivered in cash to the Navy Pier in Chicago by noontime. Blake hadn't bothered asking Alexus where she had gotten the money from. All that mattered to him was the safety of his daughter. Alexushad paid the ransom. She had wired the money to the off shore account.

Thekidnappers had immediately called and told Blake where to find Ashley andSavaria. "They'll be in a blue Ford Bronco in front of Harold's Chicken Shack on Eighty eighth and Stony Island," the kidnapper had said, and Blake had told Young-D to go and get them.

"He's on his way now," Blake said tightly.

"Do you think we should call Britney see what the cops are after you for?"

"I don't give a fuck what they're after me for. If my daughter ain't alright,they gon' have a thousand more reasons to lock me up."

Alexus looked up at him. "I don't want to lose you, Blake. We're due to be married in a few months."

Blake didn't have anything else to say. A silence grew between them. After a while, Alexus sighed, and decided to fill the silence with the secret she'd been holding in.

"Aunt Jenny was never supposed to see those papers. She had beensnooping around in my granny's office at the Costilla Resorts in Cancun, being nosey, when she found them."

"What papers?"

"My granny's will. Well, the first one. Aunt Jenny found the first one lastSeptember. It left everything to Papi and uncle Flako. When she confronted Vida about her being left out of the will, Vida told her it was for the best, that Papi would see to it that the family business continued to grow and expand."

"So she set up Papi and Flako?" Blake asked.

Alexus nodded, adjusting her Louis Vuitton bikini top. "Which is when my granny made a new will, naming me as the sole recipient of the business. We think Aunt Jenny might have paid off my granny's attorneyfor a copy of the second will, and she's wanted me dead ever since. I guess she figured that, with me out of the way, Vida would have no choice but to leave the money and businesses to her. And whoever gets the money gets the cartel."

Blake smiled lightly. He opened his mouth to say something, but then hisphone rang.

"I got Savaria, bruh," Young-D said drably. "She's good.

They had her blindfolded and tied up in the back."

"What about Ash? She a'ight too?"

Young-D's pause spoke volumes. "Man, bruh...they fucked her over. Slither throat. She's gone my nigga."

Vida Costilla's funeral was to be held on Friday, March eleventh, at theCatholic Church she'd been a member of for over fifty years. It was located about a mile up the road from her fifty six acre ranch in Matamoras,Mexico.

Alexus and Blake arrived the night before the funeral in the new Honda Jet that Alexus had purchased in Brazil for $4.5 million. She had always wanted a private plane. Now she was capable of buying a thousand of them,if she wanted to. She was worth forty-eight billion dollars.

As the plane landed on a private runway behind Vida's...well, now it wasAlexus's...ranch, Blake commented on the fifteen black on black Rolls Royce Phantoms that were lined up perfectly alongside the smoothly paved landing strip.

"These are the top Costilla cartel members," Alexus said, staring out her window. "Lieutenants. They're responsible for basically all the drugs flowing into Texas, Arizona, New Mexico, southern California, Nevada,and Louisiana. If it weren't for them, the cartel wouldn't be anywhere near the seven billion dollars a year operation it is. They're the core of the Costilla cartel."

"You sure they ain't gonna start bussin'?" The lieutenants had AK-47's intheir hands.

"I'm sure," Alexus said knowingly. She turned to Blake. "You do know that the cops are going to be on you as soon as you step foot back into the States, right?"

Blake nodded his head. He had on a wife beater, baggy tan Louis Vuittoncargo shorts, and matching loafers. His diamonds were refulgent.

Alexus laughed, shaking her head. She felt her smartphone vibrating in her bag. Taking it out, she saw that the call was coming from a 517 area code, and figured it was Kenya calling from East Lansing, Michigan.

But it was not Kenya.

It was Cereniti Stingley.

"I know you're pissed off at me, Alexus. I swear I'm so sorry. But five million dollars was too tempting, yo. I'm dumb as hell, I know. You don't have to tell me that. I'm only calling 'cause I heard about your grams' passing, and my girlfriend Akemi wouldn't let me run around partying here in Fukushima while..."

Alexus was just about to set it on Cereniti when a sudden, loud rumbling sound came through the phone. She heard Cereniti scream out in terror, the distinctive shattering of glass, then the line went dead. She tried callingback a couple of times and got no answer.

A few hours later, after Blake had thoroughly pounded her pussy from every angle he could imagine, Alexus turned on a fifty inch HDTV in front of her seat and watched CNN.

Fukushima, Japan had just been wiped out by an earthquake and a Tsunami.

To Be Continued...
The Cocaine Princess 2
Coming Soon

About the Author

Rio was born in Chicago, Illinois and was raised back and forth between there and Michigan City, Indiana. Currently incarcerated,he began writing during a one-year stint in disciplinary segregationin 2008, and has been writing ever since. After realizing the flawsof his old way of thinking, he's now realized the importance of a quality education, and his mission is to get the "gangster" urban community to overstand the detrimental effects of the gangster mentality. "Killing is not cool," he says. "If you want to be cool, do something GOOD for the human civilization! Put a smile on somebody's face. Be "real" (honest), and stay loyal to your team."

Lock Down Publications and Ca$h Presents assisted publishing packages.

BASIC PACKAGE $499
Editing
Cover Design
Formatting

UPGRADED PACKAGE $800
Typing
Editing
Cover Design
Formatting

ADVANCE PACKAGE $1,200
Typing
Editing
Cover Design
Formatting
Copyright registration
Proofreading
Upload book to Amazon

LDP SUPREME PACKAGE $1,500
Typing
Editing
Cover Design
Formatting
Copyright registration
Proofreading
Set up Amazon account
Upload book to Amazon
Advertise on LDP Amazon and Facebook page

***Other services available upon request. Additional charges may apply

The Cocaine Princess

Lock Down Publications
P.O. Box 944
Stockbridge, GA 30281-9998
Phone # 470 303-9761

Submission Guideline

Submit the first three chapters of your completed manuscript to ldpsubmissions@gmail.com, subject line: Your book's title. The manuscript must be in a .doc file and sent as an attachment. Document should be in Times New Roman, double spaced and in size 12 font. Also, provide your synopsis and full contact information. If sending multiple submissions, they must each be in a separate email.

Have a story but no way to send it electronically? You can still submit to LDP/Ca$h Presents. Send in the first three chapters, written or typed, of your completed manuscript to:

LDP: Submissions Dept
Po Box 944
Stockbridge, Ga 30281

DO NOT send original manuscript. Must be a duplicate.

Provide your synopsis and a cover letter containing your full contact information.

Thanks for considering LDP and Ca$h Presents.

NEW RELEASES

MOB TIES 5 by SAYNOMORE
KING KILLA by VINCENT "VITTO" HOLLOWAY
JACK BOYS VS DOPE BOYS by ROMELL TUKES
KILLA KOUNTY 2 by KHUFU
IN A HUSTLER I TRUST by MONET DRAGUN
THE COCAINE PRINCESS by KING RIO

Coming Soon from Lock Down Publications/Ca$h Presents

BLOOD OF A BOSS **VI**

SHADOWS OF THE GAME II

TRAP BASTARD II

By **Askari**

LOYAL TO THE GAME **IV**

By **T.J. & Jelissa**

IF TRUE SAVAGE **VIII**

MIDNIGHT CARTEL IV

DOPE BOY MAGIC IV

CITY OF KINGZ III

NIGHTMARE ON SILENT AVE II

THE PLUG OF LIL MEXICO II

By **Chris Green**

BLAST FOR ME **III**

A SAVAGE DOPEBOY III

CUTTHROAT MAFIA III

DUFFLE BAG CARTEL VII

HEARTLESS GOON VI

By **Ghost**

A HUSTLER'S DECEIT III

KILL ZONE II

BAE BELONGS TO ME III

By **Aryanna**

KING OF THE TRAP III

By **T.J. Edwards**

GORILLAZ IN THE BAY V

3X KRAZY III

STRAIGHT BEAST MODE II

De'Kari

KINGPIN KILLAZ IV

STREET KINGS III

PAID IN BLOOD III

CARTEL KILLAZ IV

DOPE GODS III

Hood Rich

SINS OF A HUSTLA II

ASAD

RICH $AVAGE II

MONEY IN THE GRAVE II

By Martell Troublesome Bolden

YAYO V

Bred In The Game 2

S. Allen

CREAM III

By Yolanda Moore

SON OF A DOPE FIEND III

HEAVEN GOT A GHETTO II

By Renta

LOYALTY AIN'T PROMISED III

By Keith Williams

I'M NOTHING WITHOUT HIS LOVE II

SINS OF A THUG II

TO THE THUG I LOVED BEFORE II

IN A HUSTLER I TRUST II

By Monet Dragun

QUIET MONEY IV

EXTENDED CLIP III

THUG LIFE IV

By **Trai'Quan**

THE STREETS MADE ME IV

By **Larry D. Wright**

IF YOU CROSS ME ONCE II

By **Anthony Fields**

THE STREETS WILL NEVER CLOSE II

By K'ajji

HARD AND RUTHLESS III

THE BILLIONAIRE BENTLEYS II

Von Diesel

KILLA KOUNTY III

By Khufu

MONEY GAME III

By Smoove Dolla

JACK BOYS VS DOPE BOYS II

By Romell Tukes

MURDA WAS THE CASE II

Elijah R. Freeman

THE STREETS NEVER LET GO II

By Robert Baptiste

AN UNFORESEEN LOVE III

By **Meesha**

KING OF THE TRENCHES III
by **GHOST & TRANAY ADAMS**

MONEY MAFIA II

LOYAL TO THE SOIL II

By **Jibril Williams**

QUEEN OF THE ZOO II

By **Black Migo**

THE BRICK MAN IV

THE COCAINE PRINCESS II

278

By King Rio

VICIOUS LOYALTY II

By Kingpen

A GANGSTA'S PAIN II

By J-Blunt

CONFESSIONS OF A JACKBOY III

By Nicholas Lock

GRIMEY WAYS II

By Ray Vinci

KING KILLA II

By Vincent "Vitto" Holloway

<u>Available Now</u>

RESTRAINING ORDER **I & II**

By **CA$H & Coffee**

LOVE KNOWS NO BOUNDARIES **I II & III**

By **Coffee**

RAISED AS A GOON I, II, III & IV

BRED BY THE SLUMS I, II, III

BLAST FOR ME I & II

ROTTEN TO THE CORE I II III

A BRONX TALE I, II, III

DUFFLE BAG CARTEL I II III IV V VI

King Rio

HEARTLESS GOON I II III IV V

A SAVAGE DOPEBOY I II

DRUG LORDS I II III

CUTTHROAT MAFIA I II

KING OF THE TRENCHES

By **Ghost**

LAY IT DOWN **I & II**

LAST OF A DYING BREED I II

BLOOD STAINS OF A SHOTTA I & II III

By **Jamaica**

LOYAL TO THE GAME I II III

LIFE OF SIN I, II III

By **TJ & Jelissa**

BLOODY COMMAS I & II

SKI MASK CARTEL I II & III

KING OF NEW YORK I II,III IV V

RISE TO POWER I II III

COKE KINGS I II III IV V

BORN HEARTLESS I II III IV

KING OF THE TRAP I II

By **T.J. Edwards**

IF LOVING HIM IS WRONG…I & II

LOVE ME EVEN WHEN IT HURTS I II III

By **Jelissa**

WHEN THE STREETS CLAP BACK I & II III

THE HEART OF A SAVAGE I II III

MONEY MAFIA

LOYAL TO THE SOIL

By **Jibril Williams**

A DISTINGUISHED THUG STOLE MY HEART I II & III

280

LOVE SHOULDN'T HURT I II III IV

RENEGADE BOYS I II III IV

PAID IN KARMA I II III

SAVAGE STORMS I II

AN UNFORESEEN LOVE I II

By **Meesha**

A GANGSTER'S CODE I &, II III

A GANGSTER'S SYN I II III

THE SAVAGE LIFE I II III

CHAINED TO THE STREETS I II III

BLOOD ON THE MONEY I II III

A GANGSTA'S PAIN

By J-Blunt

PUSH IT TO THE LIMIT

By **Bre' Hayes**

BLOOD OF A BOSS **I, II, III, IV, V**

SHADOWS OF THE GAME

TRAP BASTARD

By **Askari**

THE STREETS BLEED MURDER **I, II & III**

THE HEART OF A GANGSTA I II& III

By **Jerry Jackson**

CUM FOR ME I II III IV V VI VII VIII

An **LDP Erotica Collaboration**

BRIDE OF A HUSTLA **I II & II**

THE FETTI GIRLS **I, II& III**

CORRUPTED BY A GANGSTA I, II III, IV

BLINDED BY HIS LOVE

THE PRICE YOU PAY FOR LOVE I, II ,III

DOPE GIRL MAGIC I II III

King Rio

By **Destiny Skai**
WHEN A GOOD GIRL GOES BAD
By **Adrienne**
THE COST OF LOYALTY I II III
By Kweli
A GANGSTER'S REVENGE **I II III & IV**
THE BOSS MAN'S DAUGHTERS I II III IV V
A SAVAGE LOVE **I & II**
BAE BELONGS TO ME I II
A HUSTLER'S DECEIT I, II, III
WHAT BAD BITCHES DO I, II, III
SOUL OF A MONSTER I II III
KILL ZONE
A DOPE BOY'S QUEEN I II III
By **Aryanna**
A KINGPIN'S AMBITON
A KINGPIN'S AMBITION **II**
I MURDER FOR THE DOUGH
By **Ambitious**
TRUE SAVAGE I II III IV V VI VII
DOPE BOY MAGIC I, II, III
MIDNIGHT CARTEL I II III
CITY OF KINGZ I II
NIGHTMARE ON SILENT AVE
THE PLUG OF LIL MEXICO II

By **Chris Green**
A DOPEBOY'S PRAYER
By **Eddie "Wolf" Lee**
THE KING CARTEL **I, II & III**

The Cocaine Princess

By **Frank Gresham**

THESE NIGGAS AIN'T LOYAL **I, II & III**

By **Nikki Tee**

GANGSTA SHYT **I II &III**

By **CATO**

THE ULTIMATE BETRAYAL

By **Phoenix**

BOSS'N UP **I , II & III**

By **Royal Nicole**

I LOVE YOU TO DEATH

By **Destiny J**

I RIDE FOR MY HITTA

I STILL RIDE FOR MY HITTA

By **Misty Holt**

LOVE & CHASIN' PAPER

By **Qay Crockett**

TO DIE IN VAIN

SINS OF A HUSTLA

By **ASAD**

BROOKLYN HUSTLAZ

By **Boogsy Morina**

BROOKLYN ON LOCK I & II

By **Sonovia**

GANGSTA CITY

By **Teddy Duke**

A DRUG KING AND HIS DIAMOND I & II III

A DOPEMAN'S RICHES

HER MAN, MINE'S TOO I, II

CASH MONEY HO'S

THE WIFEY I USED TO BE I II

By Nicole Goosby

TRAPHOUSE KING **I II & III**

KINGPIN KILLAZ I II III

STREET KINGS I II

PAID IN BLOOD **I II**

CARTEL KILLAZ I II III

DOPE GODS I II

By **Hood Rich**

LIPSTICK KILLAH **I, II, III**

CRIME OF PASSION I II & III

FRIEND OR FOE I II III

By **Mimi**

STEADY MOBBN' **I, II, III**

THE STREETS STAINED MY SOUL I II III

By **Marcellus Allen**

WHO SHOT YA **I, II, III**

SON OF A DOPE FIEND I II

HEAVEN GOT A GHETTO

Renta

GORILLAZ IN THE BAY **I II III IV**

TEARS OF A GANGSTA I II

3X KRAZY I II

STRAIGHT BEAST MODE

DE'KARI

TRIGGADALE I II III

MURDAROBER WAS THE CASE

Elijah R. Freeman

GOD BLESS THE TRAPPERS I, II, III

THESE SCANDALOUS STREETS I, II, III

FEAR MY GANGSTA I, II, III IV, V

THESE STREETS DON'T LOVE NOBODY I, II

BURY ME A G I, II, III, IV, V

A GANGSTA'S EMPIRE I, II, III, IV

THE DOPEMAN'S BODYGAURD I II

THE REALEST KILLAZ I II III

THE LAST OF THE OGS I II III

Tranay Adams

THE STREETS ARE CALLING

Duquie Wilson

MARRIED TO A BOSS I II III

By Destiny Skai & Chris Green

KINGZ OF THE GAME I II III IV V VI

Playa Ray

SLAUGHTER GANG I II III

RUTHLESS HEART I II III

By Willie Slaughter

FUK SHYT

By Blakk Diamond

DON'T F#CK WITH MY HEART I II

By Linnea

ADDICTED TO THE DRAMA I II III

IN THE ARM OF HIS BOSS II

By Jamila

YAYO I II III IV

A SHOOTER'S AMBITION I II

BRED IN THE GAME

By S. Allen

TRAP GOD I II III

RICH $AVAGE

MONEY IN THE GRAVE I II

King Rio

By Martell Troublesome Bolden
FOREVER GANGSTA
GLOCKS ON SATIN SHEETS I II
By Adrian Dulan
TOE TAGZ I II III
LEVELS TO THIS SHYT I II
By Ah'Million
KINGPIN DREAMS I II III
By Paper Boi Rari
CONFESSIONS OF A GANGSTA I II III IV
CONFESSIONS OF A JACKBOY I II
By Nicholas Lock
I'M NOTHING WITHOUT HIS LOVE
SINS OF A THUG
TO THE THUG I LOVED BEFORE
A GANGSTA SAVED XMAS
IN A HUSTLER I TRUST
By Monet Dragun
CAUGHT UP IN THE LIFE I II III
THE STREETS NEVER LET GO
By Robert Baptiste
NEW TO THE GAME I II III
MONEY, MURDER & MEMORIES I II III
By **Malik D. Rice**
LIFE OF A SAVAGE I II III
A GANGSTA'S QUR'AN I II III
MURDA SEASON I II III
GANGLAND CARTEL I II III
CHI'RAQ GANGSTAS I II III
KILLERS ON ELM STREET I II III

JACK BOYZ N DA BRONX I II III

A DOPEBOY'S DREAM I II III

JACK BOYS VS DOPE BOYS

By **Romell Tukes**

LOYALTY AIN'T PROMISED I II

By Keith Williams

QUIET MONEY I II III

THUG LIFE I II III

EXTENDED CLIP I II

By **Trai'Quan**

THE STREETS MADE ME I II III

By **Larry D. Wright**

THE ULTIMATE SACRIFICE I, II, III, IV, V, VI

KHADIFI

IF YOU CROSS ME ONCE

ANGEL I II

IN THE BLINK OF AN EYE

By **Anthony Fields**

THE LIFE OF A HOOD STAR

By Ca$h & Rashia Wilson

THE STREETS WILL NEVER CLOSE

By K'ajji

CREAM I II

By Yolanda Moore

NIGHTMARES OF A HUSTLA I II III

By King Dream

CONCRETE KILLA I II

VICIOUS LOYALTY

By Kingpen

HARD AND RUTHLESS I II

MOB TOWN 251

THE BILLIONAIRE BENTLEYS

By Von Diesel

GHOST MOB

Stilloan Robinson

MOB TIES I II III IV V

By SayNoMore

BODYMORE MURDERLAND I II III

By Delmont Player

FOR THE LOVE OF A BOSS

By C. D. Blue

MOBBED UP I II III IV

THE BRICK MAN I II III

THE COCAINE PRINCESS

By King Rio

KILLA KOUNTY I II

By Khufu

MONEY GAME I II

By Smoove Dolla

A GANGSTA'S KARMA I II

By FLAME

KING OF THE TRENCHES I II

by **GHOST & TRANAY ADAMS**

QUEEN OF THE ZOO

By **Black Migo**

GRIMEY WAYS

By Ray Vinci

XMAS WITH AN ATL SHOOTER

By Ca$h & Destiny Skai

KING KILLA

The Cocaine Princess

By Vincent "Vitto" Holloway

BOOKS BY LDP'S CEO, CA$H

TRUST IN NO MAN

TRUST IN NO MAN 2

TRUST IN NO MAN 3

BONDED BY BLOOD

SHORTY GOT A THUG

THUGS CRY

THUGS CRY 2

THUGS CRY 3

TRUST NO BITCH

TRUST NO BITCH 2

TRUST NO BITCH 3

TIL MY CASKET DROPS

RESTRAINING ORDER

RESTRAINING ORDER 2

IN LOVE WITH A CONVICT

LIFE OF A HOOD STAR

XMAS WITH AN ATL SHOOTER